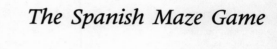

The Spanish Maze Game

NOAH WEBSTER

The Spanish Maze Game

A CRIME CLUB BOOK
DOUBLEDAY
New York   London   Toronto   Sydney   Auckland

A CRIME CLUB BOOK
PUBLISHED BY DOUBLEDAY
a division of Bantam Doubleday Dell Publishing Group, Inc.
666 Fifth Avenue, New York, New York 10103

DOUBLEDAY and the portrayal of a man
with a gun are trademarks of Doubleday,
a division of Bantam Doubleday Dell
Publishing Group, Inc.

Library of Congress Cataloging-in-Publication Data
Webster, Noah, 1928–
    The Spanish maze game / Noah Webster.
        p.   cm.
    "A Crime Club book."
    I. Title.
PR6061.N6S6   1991
823'.914—dc20   90-19584
                                                      CIP

F
WEB

ISBN 0-385-41738-1
Copyright © 1990 by Bill Knox
All Rights Reserved
Printed in the United States of America
June 1991
First Edition in the United States of America

For Julian and Lisa

The Spanish Maze Game

H.M. Exchequer Office, Edinburgh, Scotland.

"The Barons of the Exchequer and their principal officers, the Queen's Remembrancer and the Lord Treasurer's Remembrancer, later combined in function, were created by The Exchequer Court (Scotland) Act, 1707, (6 Anne, c. 53), which was passed in pursuance of a clause in the Treaty of Union between Scotland and England."

Today's real-life Queen's and Lord Treasurer's Remembrancer is a senior and highly experienced civil servant. I am grateful for his tolerant help.

Noah Webster, Edinburgh

CHAPTER 1

Jonathan Gaunt leaned on the balcony rail of the *Gasthaus*'s open verandah, enjoyed the warmth of the sun working on his back, and felt like a tourist. Early May was a good time to visit Bavaria. It was a Wednesday morning, the sky was a cloudless blue, and there was the scent of woodsmoke in the air. He could hear bees humming among the flowers which edged the verandah and filled the gardens below.

Yet it was only a few hours since his British Airways scheduled flight from Scotland had touched down in a rainstorm at Munich airport. It had been past midnight, and the big Airbus had been three hours behind schedule, one of those delays that began with an earlier flight by the same aircraft from Athens to Edinburgh being caught up in a work-to-rule involving French air traffic controllers. Then the delay had meant another wait before the newly arrived passengers could recover their luggage at the Munich terminal—and Gaunt had discovered that no one knew anything about the rented car that should have been waiting for him.

The rainstorm had become worse by the time he used his rusty German and found a nighthawk taxi driver willing to take him the sixty-kilometre trip south to a village called Rottach beside a lake called the Tegernsee. Gaunt only knew these as marks on a map, and his unshaven driver lost the way twice as they travelled through the pitch-black night and over flooded, rain-lashed roads.

But he was in Bavaria and they were on the foothills of the visitor-conscious Bavarian Alps. Even at 2:30 A.M. there had still been someone on duty at the reception desk of the Gasthaus Rotwild, and Gaunt's room had been ready.

"The world is beginning to dry out again," said the man who joined him at the railing. His voice was slightly wary and he spoke in English, without any trace of accent. "Not like last night, Herr Gaunt."

"No way like last night," agreed Gaunt, glancing round. The other

man, tall and lanky, was the reason Gaunt had travelled over a thousand miles. His name was Florian Beck, he had hair the colour of
corn straw, a short, neatly clipped beard and blue eyes. Beck was in
his late thirties, with a narrow face and prominent ears, wore a red
roll-neck shirt with blue jeans, black leather ankle-length lace-up
driving shoes, and a dark blue corduroy jacket. Gaunt smiled at him.
"Do they often get rain like that?"

"The Bavarian Tourist Board would say you imagined it." Florian
Beck moistened his lips. He was a man who seemed still shaken by
what he had just been told, a man still trying to believe it, trying to
keep a tight grip on his feelings. "This is your first visit?"

"Here, yes." Gaunt went back to leaning on the rail again. It was
exactly twenty minutes since he met Florian Beck, joining him at one
of the *Gasthaus*'s verandah breakfast tables. Beck had been expecting
him since the previous evening. They had shaken hands, Gaunt had
talked—and Florian Beck had lost all interest in the rest of his breakfast. Gaunt took another deep breath of the lakeside air. "But I know
Munich."

"There's a difference," said Beck.

Gaunt nodded. The Gasthaus Rotwild was on the edge of Rottach, a
thin scatter of houses and hotels and shops among the trees beside
this part of the long, blue water of the Tegernsee. The sun had already
burned away the last traces of mist from the thickly forested hills
which fringed the lake. In the distance, the outlines of the first alpine
peaks were sharp and clear. But near to the balcony there were ducks
and swans gliding along in the placid water. Further out, a large
motor launch was cutting a white wake, heading towards the north
end of the Tegernsee. Across on the opposite shore, a cable-car was
climbing a steep hillside towards a church and some chalets.

"Herr Gaunt, you showed me identification." Beck made an almost
apologetic gesture. "I know you were sent by this strange Queen's
Remembrancer in Scotland. Does that make you some kind of civil
servant?"

"So they tell me," said Gaunt.

His eyes had been drawn back to those brooding, distant Alps. One
great rising ridge stood out from all the rest in the clear air. Its lower
slopes were green, blanketed by forests, but up above, where the trees
ended, broad banks of naked rock glinted in the sun. The whole crest
of the ridge was still dappled in snow.

Gaunt pointed. "Is that the Zugspitze?"

"Ja." Florian Beck nodded and gave a brief glance towards the distant giant. "She is big—very big, almost three thousand metres."

The map translated that as 9,700 feet, crowned by an observatory. On the border between Bavaria and Austria, the Zugspitze was the highest point of land in the Federal German Republic. Anyone collecting mountains would have to travel some way south, to the Grossglockner in Austria, to find bigger.

"Herr Gaunt." Beck stuck his hands in his jacket pockets, his uncertainty still plain. "This Queen's Remembrancer—what does he do?"

"He heads a department of people like me," said Gaunt easily. "We do a lot of things, depending on what comes along. Things that don't fit in anywhere else. Sometimes we have to locate people like you."

A car passed outside the *Gasthaus.* Beck stood silent until the engine note had faded. Someone was singing in the restaurant kitchen and a dog was barking somewhere among the trees.

"The first time I ever heard of the Queen's Remembrancer was when I received his letter," said Florian Beck quietly. "The letter came to my apartment in Stuttgart. It said there might be 'something to my advantage' if I answered questions about my family." He shrugged. "I did. Next there was another letter, more questions—still nothing to tell exactly what it was about. But again I answered."

"Most people do," said Gaunt.

Then Florian Beck had received a telephone call, saying the Remembrancer was sending someone over from Scotland to meet him. When Beck had explained he had to go south to Bavaria because of his work, he'd been told that the meeting could be there.

Jonathan Gaunt had brought out the kind of news most people like to hear.

Florian Beck had almost choked on his breakfast when told that he was the owner of a British investment worth approximately four hundred thousand pounds sterling. All because a Scottish great-grandfather had once invested ten pounds in an ailing little company, then had written it off as lost money, a bad investment.

Except that the ailing company had recovered. Translate four hundred thousand pounds into any kind of currency and it was still a magic figure. There might even be more to come.

"Accept," suggested Gaunt. "Accept it all, man."

"Ja. I—I—" Beck gave up and glanced at his black plastic-bodied wristwatch. He drew a deep breath. "I should be on my way to work. Other people—several people—will be waiting for me." He made up his mind. "This once, they can wait. I want to hear this story again."

"Then you'll maybe believe me?"

Beck nodded. "And you can tell me what I have to do."

Gaunt laughed. He let Florian Beck lead the way back to the breakfast table. It had already been cleared, and only one other table in the verandah restaurant was still occupied. A middle-aged couple sat at it as if they'd grown roots, reading English newspapers.

"Kaffee, bitte." Beck signalled the plump, brown-eyed waitress as he and Gaunt settled again. He was still watching his visitor.

Jonathan Gaunt didn't look like anyone's usual notion of a civil servant. It was part of his natural stock in trade. Still in his early thirties, tall, with a compact build, he had a likeable, raw-boned face which had a slight dusting of freckles, and the kind of grey-green eyes which could easily become moody. His fair hair was untidy and overdue a visit to a barber.

In the same way, the average civil servant wasn't supposed to dress for work in a much-used leather jacket over a light blue shirt and dark blue tie with lightweight grey trousers and scuffed leather moccasins.

"All I need is to see the documentation you were told we'd need. Then I've some papers in here for you to sign." Gaunt indicated the thin manilla folder he'd left lying on the table, then took a moment to settle more comfortably in his chair. His back had the kind of low-grade ache it always did after any journey. He had taken a painkiller tablet when he had wakened, he should have taken another. But that could wait. He looked across at Beck. "We can leave the paperwork for later, if you want it that way."

"I do." Beck paused as the waitress brought them a tray with a fresh pot of coffee and cups. She poured for them both, smiled at Beck, gave Gaunt a glance of mild curiosity, then left them. As soon as she was out of earshot, Beck leaned forward. "This story, Herr Gaunt—please."

"All right—from the start," Gaunt said. "Your full name is Hans Florian Beck, you are single, and you live in Stuttgart. You're an engineering graduate, you work as a research engineer—"

"With SPO Motoren of Stuttgart. We develop power transmission systems for the automobile industry. Sometimes for German firms, sometimes Far East, sometimes multi-national—we work for anyone who needs our kind of engineering research." He took a sip from his own cup. The coffee was hot enough to surprise him. "Your people know why we have a team down here."

"Vaguely," said Gaunt. He knew precisely. It had been in the file prepared on Florian Beck back in Edinburgh.

Beck shrugged. "We've to test drive a new car for one of the multinational markets. It's fitted with a new SPO transmission system that should be able to cope with more power." He swirled the coffee in his cup. "I do some of the test driving. We use the Federal-owned test track at Scheckheim, in the next valley. Any time we're using Scheckheim, I stay at the Gasthaus Rotwild. There are nearer places, maybe better places, but I like it here." His impatience took over. "Does any of this matter?"

"Sorry," said Gaunt soothingly. "You're a German national, you were born in Frankfurt, your father was a German engineer named Hans Beck. But your mother was Scottish—and that's why we've chased you, what this is all about." He didn't need to check, but he flipped open the file and took a glance at the top sheet inside. "Her maiden name was Ann Church, she was a farmer's daughter from Stonehaven in north-east Scotland. You were an only child, your father died five years ago, your mother died two years ago."

Beck gave a nod, frowning, concentrating on every word.

"That's the part we asked you to prove." Gaunt paused. "How much do you know about your mother's family?"

"Not a lot." Beck shook his head. "She talked about them sometimes."

"Any photographs?"

"Photographs of her family?" Beck frowned, hesitated, then shrugged. "I threw them out after she died. All except one—it was taken when my mother was a girl and I've always liked it. She's standing outside the family farmhouse with my grandmother. Will you need it?"

"Later, maybe." Gaunt doubted it, couldn't see any particular problems ahead. "Like I said, this goes back another couple of generations before your mother—back to her grandfather, your great-grandfather." A small winged insect hovered in front of his face and he waved it away. "His name was Peter Church, in the year 1921 he was working as a distillery manager in Aberdeen—Aberdeen, not Stonehaven. Remember that."

"Aberdeen." Beck looked puzzled but nodded.

"Then here's how it goes from there." The insect was back. This time, Gaunt caught it with a flick. "Maybe he was helping out a friend. But for no apparent reason, Peter Church invested exactly ten pounds in a little local animal feedstuffs company called Hartondee

Products. Soon after that, this Hartondee company suddenly had a rough time. They didn't close down, but their shares weren't worth anything. Probably your great-grandfather just wrote off his ten-pound investment."

"But he kept the shares?" asked Florian Beck, suddenly beginning to understand all the rest.

"He certainly couldn't sell," said Gaunt dryly. "Who'd buy? We'll presume he forgot about them. Eventually, he moved house but forgot to tell Hartondee he'd changed his address for their shareholders' list." He paused. "Do you ever play the stock market, Florian?"

Beck raised a surprised eyebrow. *"Nein."*

"I do, sometimes." At pocket-money prices, usually when he'd been paid at the end of the month. As far as Jonathan Gaunt was concerned, it gave the rest of the story an extra sadness. "Well, the years pass. Your great-grandfather dies, then your grandfather dies. Suddenly, big things begin to happen to Hartondee Products. They're taken over, they get new capital, they start paying miraculous dividends, there are rights issues one on top of another. Then, only about three months ago, Hartondee's accountant decides to do some house cleaning—like sorting out one block of voting shares that have been lying asleep since 1921, doing nothing but grow and grow—"

Florian Beck forgot his immaculate English. He muttered under his breath in German for a few moments. Then he sat back and gave a baying bellow of sheer delight. Their waitress, working further along the verandah, swung round, startled. Then she raised an amused eyebrow and shook her head. The middle-aged English couple who were still lingering lowered their newspapers, stared, then hid behind them again.

"Great-grandfather Peter, I never knew you—but *danke.*" Gradually, Florian Beck subsided again, grinning. "It's all true?"

"The way I've told you," said Gaunt. "You're the only direct blood relative—we've checked, every way there is."

"This Hartondee firm—"

"Had to come to us for help. That's the law."

It was a legal right that the Queen's and Lord Treasurer's Remembrancer used every now and again. His department had the duty of investigating when unclaimed shares or dividends in a limited company were reported, and shareholders couldn't be traced. They could also step in and seize property held by a dissolved company.

"When do I get the money?" asked Florian Beck.

"Soon." Gaunt had been waiting on the question. "All we have to do is complete a few formalities. Part of the money is lying in dividends—immediate cash. The rest is in shares, but Hartondee want to buy them in. I'd talk to a stockbroker first—but even so, it should take no more than a few weeks."

"I think I can wait that long." The man scratched at his straw-fair hair, then at his neatly clipped beard. "Right now I suppose I should do the sensible thing and get on with my regular work."

"Test driving?" Gaunt almost blinked. "Today?"

"It concentrates the mind," said Beck. He patted his pockets, rose to his feet, and produced car keys. "Don't worry, Herr Gaunt. I want to live to spend my money. Anyway, the Scheckheim track is a good, safe place to drive. Your average road with its average traffic is a dam' sight more dangerous." He paused. "If you want to see for yourself I'll leave a permit at the security gate. If not, I'll be back here before dusk."

"I'll come out," promised Gaunt.

"Then tonight we talk formalities." The man gave a pleased nod. "But suppose you hadn't found me, suppose you hadn't found anyone? What would have happened to the money?"

"Our Queen would have taken it." Gaunt saw Florian Beck's startled blink. "That's Scottish law. If it doesn't belong to anyone else, it belongs to the Queen."

"Not this time," said Beck. "No way, your Queen—no offence meant to her."

"None taken," said Gaunt. "She's not exactly short on housekeeping money."

Grinning again, Beck walked away.

Moments later, a car started up outside the *Gasthaus* and Gaunt went over to the balcony rail. He was in time to see the man drive away at the wheel of an elderly Porsche. The Porsche accelerated as it reached the road then raced off with a smooth, snarling exhaust note.

Florian Beck was in a hurry to get to work.

After another cup of coffee, Jonathan Gaunt picked up the slim folder headed "Hartondee—Peter Church and Heirs" and started back to his room. It was on the top floor of the four-storey building, and he took the tiny elevator up. His door was the third on the left beside a fire escape exit. When he used his room key, the door swung open.

He stepped inside, sensed as much as saw a movement, then heard a sharp, short hiss. Something that was ice cold one moment then burning the next sprayed his face and eyes. Blinded, shocked by the sudden, searing pain, animal instinct brought his hands up to shield his eyes as another short hissing sprayed him.

Then it stopped. Someone shoved past him out into the corridor. He heard the fire escape door crash open, followed by the sound of feet hurrying down a concrete stairway.

His eyes still burned, he couldn't see. For long seconds Gaunt was blundering around the unfamiliar bedroom, falling against furniture, knocking over something that went down with a crash. A gasp came from somewhere behind him, from the direction of the room door, then a girl's voice cried out in German. He heard more footsteps, quick and light this time, then a strong young arm was round his waist.

"Water," he managed. "Get me to some water—"

"Okay," soothed the girl. "Okay, *kommen Sie*—"

He was half dragged, half piloted in a different direction. Then water was running into a basin, cold, soothing water that he dowsed over his eyes while the pain gradually subsided and he began to see again. Hazily at first, but seeing was what mattered.

A soft towel was thrust into his hands. He held it against his face, his eyes still smarting, his mouth and nostrils raw as if burned. When he put down the towel, he was looking at a thin slip of a wide-eyed teenage girl who had short dark hair and who looked very pale but resolute. She wore a room maid's work overall.

"Danke, Fräulein." He managed to twist a brief, reassuring grin and saw her relax a little. Steadying himself with a hand on her shoulder, he looked out of the little bathroom area into his bedroom and swore under his breath.

His uninvited visitor had made a thorough job of ransacking the room. Every drawer had been opened and emptied, the few clothes he'd hung in the wardrobe had been dragged out and tossed aside, and his travel bag and briefcase had been searched then tossed into a corner. Even the little waterproof pouch in which he kept his razor had been ripped open, examined, and discarded. Leaving the girl, he went out into the hall. As he'd expected, the fire escape door was lying open. The concrete stair led down to the *Gasthaus* car park.

When he went back into his room, the maid was already using the telephone and talking with the switchboard. By the time Gaunt had given his eyes another soaking in cold water and dried his face, the manager had appeared. A small, plump, grey-haired man, neatly dressed and with thick spectacles, he muttered with the room maid for a moment. She left and he turned to Gaunt.

"Herr Gaunt, I have sent for our Doktor Huber and the police are on their way." The man peered anxiously at Gaunt through his spectacles. "How do your eyes feel now?"

"Like someone rubbed them with sandpaper."

"Ich weiss nicht"—the man shook his head unhappily—"you found this thief in your room?"

"Behind a door I'd left locked," said Gaunt.

"Can you say what is missing?"

"I'm making sure I can see first," said Gaunt, and saw the manager wince. He could almost read the worries behind the plump face, from insurance claims onward. "But I'm sure there was nothing of real value."

Making a noise that was as much relief as sympathy, the manager backed out. The summoned Doktor Huber was next to arrive. She was a thin, angular woman with a no-nonsense smile, trousers, and a wedding ring, and her hair pinned back. She dumped her black medical bag on the dressing table, gestured Gaunt into a chair, sniffed hard around his face and shirt for a moment, then produced a tiny pen-torch and examined his eyes under its light.

"Danke." She lowered the pen-torch and surprised him with a smile. "You can relax, Herr Gaunt. I will leave you some eyedrops. You have some temporary irritation, but there will be no permanent damage."

"I'm glad," said Gaunt. "What was it?"

"Very carefully diluted ammonia." She went over to her bag and brought out a small bottle which she laid on the dressing table. "This will soothe—two or three drops in each eye, as needed."

Gaunt nodded, frowning at her. "You've seen this before?"

"Ja." She closed the bag again. "Not here, but once in another hotel robbery last year. There had been other cases in Munich—someone who probably steals for a living and who seems to carry something like a perfume spray filled with a weak ammonia solution."

"To frighten, not to injure?"

"That way," she agreed. "A thief who doesn't want to be caught—but who doesn't want to risk a long prison sentence because someone's eyes are damaged. But this thief could make a mistake, and ammonia can blind. Be glad, Herr Gaunt. You were lucky—my worry is what happens to the next victim."

He thanked her and she took her medical bag and left. A lot easier in his mind, he made a first proper check around the room.

Very little had been taken. Some British money had gone from a drawer, with a half bottle of duty-free malt whisky he'd bought during the flight out. His briefcase had been opened by cutting across the leather with a razor or a very sharp knife. The thief had taken everything that had been in the briefcase—a road map he'd bought at Munich airport, two American paperbacks about some of the old-time jazz greats, his return air ticket, and some typewritten notes which had nothing to do with Florian Beck's inheritance. They covered other cases which Gaunt was handling, and he had shoved them in as get-them-done-and-finished reading while he was away. His credit-card wallet was safe in his inside jacket pocket, nestling beside his passport. The Peter Church–Hartondee file had been with him, and was still lying on the bed where he had dropped it. For a moment he thought his bottle of painkiller pills had been taken, then he rescued it from the floor, where it had almost rolled under the dressing table.

Gaunt left the rest of the room untouched and was trying out the eyedrops when the police arrived. There were two of them, the younger in a grey casual suit, the other in sergeant's uniform. They glanced around with mild curiosity.

"Welcome to Bavaria," said the younger man sadly. He showed his identification. "Kriminalinspektor Vogt"—he gave a fractional pause, considering Gaunt, as if looking for a reaction—"Dieter Vogt." He paused again, in that same odd way, then sighed. He had a chubby face, dark hair, and a cut on his jaw from shaving. His sergeant stayed in the background. "Herr Gaunt, I have talked with the manager and I met Doktor Huber. She says you will have no lasting injuries. But you didn't really see this attacker?"

Gaunt shook his head.

"A man was seen leaving the building. We've no real description, but we don't particularly need one." Vogt glanced at his sergeant. "We think we may know him, eh, Franz?"

His sergeant gave a slight nod.

"So far, the *Gasthaus* staff have found three other bedrooms which seem to have been robbed—guests who are still out. You came back at the wrong moment." The young police inspector paused again, watching Gaunt, as if trying to make up his mind about something. "The trick with the ammonia spray tells us everything. He is one of our better hotel thieves—every police station anywhere around Munich has heard of him." He gestured at the room. "He doesn't leave fingerprints, I won't waste time searching. What did he get?"

"Nothing that matters very much."

"We will need to ask you for a statement. But that can wait." Vogt wandered across the room and frowned at Gaunt's briefcase. The cut through the leather ran across the stamped royal crest which marked it as government issue. "The *Gasthaus* register says you are a British civil servant. The receptionist says that you are here to meet one of the SPO people, Florian Beck. Official business?"

Gaunt nodded.

"Herr Beck from Stuttgart. I know him—I know most of the SPO people. The Scheckheim test track comes into my territory." Vogt nodded then looked round at his sergeant. "Franz, here we have a real live British civil servant. Have you seen one before?"

The sergeant shrugged. But his face showed that degree of companionship any state employee keeps for anyone else in the same kind of trap. At the same time, a slight grin began building on Vogt's lips and Gaunt had a sudden suspicion he should know what was amusing the young *Kriminalinspektor.*

"Herr Gaunt." Vogt's voice was mild. "I am a reserve officer in the Federal German Army. About four years ago I was with a light infantry battalion taking part in a NATO war games exercise in North Germany. My unit had a British paratroop unit as neighbours." His grin widened. *"Ja,* I remember a night when we were drinking together—"

"Go on." Suddenly, it was Gaunt's turn to remember and grin.

"There was a British paratroop lieutenant, young like me. He insisted that he was not an Englishman, that he was *ein Schotte*—a Scotsman."

The night was one Gaunt wasn't likely to forget. Faces, he wasn't so sure about.

"This other lieutenant drank me under the table," complained Vogt. "Or somebody did." He scowled round. "Franz, that part you didn't hear."

His sergeant's mouth twitched.

"You were regular army." Vogt raised an eyebrow.

"I got a medical discharge." Gaunt left it at that. Dieter Vogt was stirring a memory which belonged to what had become another time, another life.

"Bad luck." The German gave a sympathetic nod. "How long will you be in Rottach?"

"Long enough to buy you a drink before I go," said Gaunt.

"Just one?" Vogt winked. Then his official face slipped into place. "We will be in touch then, Herr Gaunt." But as he turned to leave, the grin was back again. "That last time, I remember I asked if *ein Schotte* who was a paratrooper had to jump wearing a kilt."

"It was that kind of a night," agreed Gaunt.

"But now we're older and wiser," said Vogt sadly.

He was gone and his sergeant had followed him before Gaunt could answer.

The maid who had helped him earlier appeared again and spent a few minutes sorting out his room. When she had gone, Gaunt flopped down on the newly made bed then used the telephone beside it. The reception desk had sorted out the problem of the hire car that should have been waiting at Munich. Another car would be delivered to him by noon. He thanked the girl, replaced the receiver, and lay with his hands clasped behind his head.

His eyes had stopped feeling like they had been sandpapered. The ache was still there in his back, but was no worse. He thought of those NATO war games, looked up at the painted ceiling above him, and wasn't sure whether to laugh or curse.

The military career of Lieutenant Jonathan Gaunt, the Parachute Regiment, had come to a sudden end when he'd been the victim of a partial chute failure on a training jump.

He'd spent six months in hospital with a broken back. Then he'd been discharged with a token disability pension, a prescription for painkillers, and a broken marriage. Patti had been young, she had been blonde, she had married a pair of paratroop wings, and she carefully waited until he was out of hospital before telling him it was over. They had a quiet almost amicable divorce. They still stayed in touch because she wanted it that way.

But then had come the bad time, when he was a civilian again without knowing what to do about it. His only asset had been a few terms he'd spent at university studying law and accountancy before the army had beckoned him. After the gap, he didn't relish trying to finish a degree course.

Out of nowhere, the Queen's and Lord Treasurer's Remembrancer had been the answer to it all. There was a job for an external auditor, and with it the very quick discovery that being a civil servant didn't have to be dull routine.

Not when you worked for the Remembrancer.

Which was what he was supposed to be doing. Rolling over on the bed, Gaunt took the telephone again and tapped the international trunk code for the United Kingdom, Edinburgh, and then the Remembrancer's Office. In twenty seconds he heard the bright voice of the red-haired female who was new on the Remembrancer's switch-board. Her name was Jean. He'd dated her twice, she liked Sunday-night jazz concerts and Italian cooking. But he had stopped it about there.

He wasn't ready for anything more permanent, not until he was very sure.

She asked about the weather where he was, the way everyone always did, then he had his call put through to Henry Falconer. Falconer was the Remembrancer's senior administrative assistant and the focus of most things. He wasn't at his desk and it took about a minute to find him.

Gaunt was patient. Henry Falconer was the man who had first guided him through the maze of power that lay behind the strange, archaic organization which dated back so very many centuries that people were not totally sure when it had really begun.

The first Queen's and Lord Treasurer's Remembrancer had been exactly that—a royal courtier who went around remembering things for his King or Queen at a time when the fact you were a royal didn't necessarily mean you were any good at joined-up writing.

Remembering, or, as Falconer had pointed out, sometimes being sensible enough to forget. It had never been easy being a mix of walking notebook and official conscience. Then the role had adapted to one of doing strange jobs that didn't seem to fit anywhere else.

Until now, as the Western world began to look ahead towards the not so distant next century, the Remembrancer was a senior government service professional—even if most people didn't even know he existed.

He was government paymaster for Scotland. He could act as his own court of law, he regulated company registrations, and when anyone died intestate and without heirs—whether a few pounds in a pensioner's bank account or what had been a financial empire—the Remembrancer brought it in for Queen and Crown. Or, to be more exact, the government's general account.

That, and a whole lot more at home and abroad, from safeguarding the Scottish Crown Jewels to what was casually called "state intelli-gence."

There were times when, unbelievably, it even didn't feel all that much different from the Parachute Regiment—except that the coffee wasn't as good.

"I wondered when we'd hear from you." Brusquely, Henry Falconer's voice was on the line. "How do you say 'wine women and song' in German?"

"Hello, Henry," said Gaunt easily. Falconer was a broad, heavy-faced man, middle-aged and overweight, occasionally pompous, yet at times unexpectedly human. "My flight was three hours late getting in, I met up with a thief, the only woman I've had look into my eyes was a doctor."

"Don't come to me for sympathy," said Falconer. "I got a parking ticket this morning. Have you made contact with friend Beck?"

"Made contact and told him the good news," confirmed Gaunt.

"Suitably pleased?"

"Once he believed me." Gaunt could still smile at Beck's initial reaction. "Everything seems straight enough."

"Make sure," urged Falconer. "The Remembrancer worries about us handing bags of gold to the wrong person." It was an understatement. The Queen's and Lord Treasurer's Remembrancer was always at his happiest when clawing in assets and almost screamed in pain on the few occasions when he had to pay some of it out again. "Get everything in writing, Jonny—signed and witnessed." His mood changed. "Why the hell did a doctor have to look at your eyes?"

"My thief had an ammonia spray."

"You should try to avoid that kind of thing," said Falconer, unimpressed. "How long will you need out there?"

"Another day." Gaunt decided to give himself some elbow room. "Two days at the most, then home."

"It's a long time since I visited Bavaria." Falconer gave an audible sigh. "There was a wine, a riesling type and dry. I—ah—remember the name. Franken Thungersheim. If you could find it—"

"You'd like a bottle," said Gaunt resignedly. "I'll try, Henry. But cash on delivery."

"I didn't think you took credit cards." Falconer was indignant. "While we're talking, it might be good advice to tell Florian Beck to beware of friendly strangers—the kind who might offer a fancy cash deal for his Hartondee Products before the ink dries on his signature."

"Why, Henry?" Gaunt knew the Remembrancer's senior administrative assistant didn't hand out casual warnings. "What's going on?"

"The word seems to have leaked out about them—a few people have had to know what we're doing. We've had an approach from a merchant bank, wanting to buy. I've had telephone calls from two men claiming to be long-lost friends of Beck and wanting to get in touch." Falconer grunted. "One of them said he'd heard we had sent someone out to the Munich area. So remember the magic words. Beck shouldn't do anything without getting professional advice—that keeps us clear of any responsibility."

"I'll tell him." Gaunt frowned at the telephone. "But what's it all about?"

"I don't know," said Falconer shortly. "Neither do Hartondee—I asked. But warn him. And if—ah—you can also remember that wine—"

"I'll try," promised Gaunt.

He replaced the receiver and stayed on the bed. The ache in his back had almost gone, the way it usually did when another day got going. He thought about what Falconer had said, then considered a small crack in the ceiling and grimaced. Whatever was going on, he could warn Beck to be careful. But there wasn't much else he could do until he returned to Edinburgh. There, Gaunt knew people who made a highly professional living by knowing the answers to strange questions. It might be interesting to see what they could stir.

Gaunt tried the bedside radio and roamed his way from AFN Munich through the local music stations. Then he switched off, got up, grimaced at the sight of his red-rimmed eyes in the bathroom mirror, used the eyedrops again, pulled on his leather jacket, and went out. A path led from the Gasthaus Rotwild down to the Tegernsee then along the shore and through the trees towards the village. Some of Rottach's chalets had large alpine murals painted on their gable walls. Some also had large dogs to make it plain they didn't take kindly to strangers.

Two women who were feeding ducks beside the lake directed him along another path which took him up into the village at a small supermarket. It was the kind of supermarket where any food for sale was almost lost under the display of wines and it stocked Falconer's treasured memory. Gaunt bought two bottles of Franken Thungersheim, had them packed in a brown paper sack, then started back to the Gasthaus Rotwild.

He was about halfway there when he heard footsteps and an occasional snapping twig and realized someone was walking behind him. Curious, he slowed and heard the other footsteps slow. When he glanced round, he couldn't see anyone. His instincts beginning a warning, he quickened his pace again and heard the footsteps resume. He came to a deliberate halt in a clearing, turned, and waited. A moment later, he made a silent apology as a copper-haired woman appeared from the trees and walked straight past him. She was wearing a long nylon waterproof coat with an imitation fur collar and was carrying a shopping basket. She spared him the briefest of glances and went on.

So now he was getting jumpy. Grinning at himself, Gaunt went on into the *Gasthaus*. When he went over to the reception desk, the manager made a fast retreat into a back office, but the girl on duty gave him a friendly enough smile.

"I saw you out walking, Herr Gaunt." She leaned across the reception counter in a way that put a strain on her thin white blouse and displayed a tantalizing outline of firm young breasts. "How do your eyes feel now?"

"They're doing fine," he solemnly assured her. "Taking in the local scenery—all of it."

"Ich freue mich." She gave him a teasing grin and eased back just enough to reduce the pressure on her blouse. Reaching under the counter, she placed a set of keys in front of him. "Your car has arrived."

Gaunt signed a receipt for the car, took the keys, and asked for the wine to be sent up to his room.

"It's for a friend back home." The manager was still in hiding, but he decided that the girl would probably be friendlier. "The police told me some other guests had their rooms robbed. Did they have much stolen?"

"We don't know." She shook her head. "They are all people we don't expect to see back before evening."

"Do you think they left their rooms locked, the same way I did?"

"Warum . . . why?" She looked around and lowered her voice. "With our locks, it wouldn't matter. If a maid forgets to take a passkey, she opens the doors with a hairpin. We all know the trick."

Gaunt asked her for directions to the Scheckheim track and she sketched them on the back of a postcard. They were simple and it would take him less than half an hour. As he went out again he had a glimpse of the manager sneaking back into view.

The car was a metallic-blue German-built Ford hatchback. The rental firm had supplied a few tapes for the radio-cassette but hadn't heard of jazz. He settled for a Burt Bacharach as background, but kept the volume down.

The car handled without fuss, and Gaunt followed the directions he'd been given for Scheckheim. That took him on the main road towards the west, one of the local Austria–Germany routes, busy in both directions with traffic that included strings of trucks, tankers and tourist cars.

Almost immediately the road began climbing into wooded hill country. He passed over a bridge which spanned a torrent of milky-white snow water finishing its long rush down from the high country, then the Ford dived into a deep, wide tunnel carved through the solid rock, a tunnel with overhead lights and an emergency break-down telephone. Out in the open again, he had to turn right at a junction and take another right. Then the car topped a ridge and the long, broad valley of the Scheckheim track lay ahead. The ground was a barren stretch of poor soil, broken rock and stunted trees, but that hardly mattered.

Down the middle of it all, running for several kilometres, a high fence of corrugated metal sheeting topped with barbed wire created what amounted to a long sausage-shaped compound shut off from the outside world. Here and there a rooftop showed behind the fence. There were radio masts and he could spot a couple of satellite dishes.

Outside the corrugated iron boundary, the valley was empty. When he came to a large gate and stopped beside a glass-fronted booth, a grey-uniformed security man popped out.

"Herr Gaunt?"

Gaunt nodded. "To see Florian Beck."

"Danke." He wrote the Ford's licence number on a clipboard, then pointed. "Through the gate."

The man ambled back into his glass box without explaining more. The gate swung open, Gaunt drove through, and another grey-uniformed security man was waiting for him on a motorcycle. The new man signalled, the motorcycle began moving, and Gaunt followed.

They were on a service road which ran along the inside of the security fence, a track which skirted strange, anonymous buildings and stranger structures with vehicles parked around them. He saw an expensive open sports car suspended on the end of a crane, hanging nose down. Suddenly, as the Ford was passing, the sports car fell and smashed into a concrete pad. Some men in overalls had been watching. On ahead, the motorcyclist didn't as much as turn his head.

He saw lengths of track laid in cobblestone, others with opposing curves of camber, and one studded with what looked like concrete molehills. Further out, a small car that looked familiar yet was strangely different came howling into a screaming, swinging skid which lasted two complete turns before the vehicle halted. A tripod-mounted video camera had been taping it all from the top of a parked van.

Then the motorcyclist was signalling again and Gaunt stopped beside a line of cars outside a large office trailer and a canvas marquee which had signs for SPO Motoren. The rider nodded, pointed, and the motorcycle turned away. Getting out, Gaunt saw some people standing talking beside the marquee. He could hear vehicle engines and another sound, an odd, rhythmic cross between a whirr and a thrashing that he couldn't place.

"Over here, Mr. Gaunt," hailed a voice, and one of the group came towards him. A pleasantly plump woman aged around forty, she had short, greying hair and wide smile. Her teeth were strong and white, with a small gap at the front. "I'm Bessie King. Florian asked me to watch out for you."

They shook hands. Her grip was firm and friendly. Bessie King was wearing a faded denim jacket and trousers with a dark blue blouse and sandals. She also spoke in English, with a Northern Irish accent, and saw Gaunt's surprise.

"Belfast born and bred," she agreed. "I'm just a poor Irish girl who knows about computer mathematics and who ends up in Germany, working for SPO." Pausing, she considered him with care. "Florian told me why you're here—the money, I mean. Is it all true?"

"Depending on what he told you—yes." Gaunt gave a quick glance towards the group. "Has he told everyone?"

"No." She shook her head. "But he had to tell someone, or he said he'd burst. You could call me a friend."

"A close friend?"

"Yes. Close enough." Her eyes challenged him, then her smile was back again. "Mr. Gaunt, what do people usually call you—friendly people?"

"Jonathan." He winced as a small white car went past on the track with an ear-torturing engine howl. "Make it Jonny."

"Jonny." She nodded approval then gestured towards the little car, now shrinking in the distance. "And that was Florian. He won't be too long. Come and meet the rest while you're waiting."

Gaunt followed her over to the group, then was plunged into a round of names and faces and handshakes, knowing he wasn't expected to remember anyone. The SPO team included Germans and Italians, two English mechanics, an Austrian time-keeper, and a Swedish woman who was Beck's co-driver. Bessie King was the only other woman. Someone made apologies that beer wasn't allowed when they were working. Someone else presented him with a mug of coffee. Bessie King shoved a thick slab of sausage sandwich into his free hand.

The prototype project that involved them all was a joint Nissan-Fiat design study, Italian styling combined with Japanese technology. The motor industry was multi-national. There was nothing unusual about having a specialist research and development concern like SPO develop a high-performance power transmission layout—and if the car ever got beyond being a study project it could end up being manufactured in a couple of Brazilian car plants.

Everyone tried to tell Gaunt what could happen, what might happen, what should happen—without revealing any real details about the basic project. They had six prototypes with them, all fitted with the new transmission. Beck, the Swedish woman and two Italians were the test drivers, the others had a variety of jobs. Two cars were out on the track, two more were in a small, roped-off area, and two still waited as spares aboard a big transporter parked nearby.

All the time, people talked and shoved more sandwiches at him while the screaming rasp of an exhaust came round again as one of the test cars completed yet another timed circuit.

"Had enough?" asked Bessie King, appearing beside him.

He nodded and she beckoned. They left the marquee and went to the king-sized trailer unit. Two small and intent Japanese technicians were watching dials on a row of racked monitor units, a third Japanese man was using a telephone in a compact, well-equipped office. They looked at Bessie King, then at Gaunt, murmured a greeting, but otherwise ignored them.

The rear of the trailer was a small workshop with a ladder at one side. He followed Bessie King up the ladder and through a hatch to a railed observation platform. The view was out across the whole Scheckheim test track.

There was no real wind. The warm air held the blended scents of smoked rubber and burned fuel, and Bessie King countered them with a Parisian perfume. Gaunt became aware of the perfume as she gestured at the expanse of interwoven tracks and the scatter of small buildings.

"That's where Florian earns most of his living." She looked deliberately at Gaunt. "Some people might call it glamorous—I don't. When he's out there, he's ruled by a stopwatch. He says it can be dull monotony. I say that if he gets bored, if he makes just one small mistake at the wrong moment, then that mistake could kill him." One of the white cars was snarling towards them and she let it pass on its way to another lap, then shook her head. "Whether he goes fast or slow, someone else makes the decisions."

"But now he could give it up? Because of the money?"

"He could, he might," she said pensively. "Wheels do strange things to a man, stranger things than any of the old Irish witches in the stories my mother used to frighten me near to death with." She paused. "You saw that car, the prototype?"

He nodded.

"Prototypes are made from dreams. They drive around with disguised bodywork, with fake badges—that's if they ever get outside a track like this one. Mostly, we know they'll never reach the real world. Instead, the dream will be scrapped—"

"And they'll build another?"

"Yes." Bessie King frowned at the distance. "The locals have a word for those cars. They're the *Erlkönige*—imaginary figures in a fog. Our damned *Erlkönige* matter most because they don't totally exist, or it's how Florian feels about them. Does that make sense?"

"I'd need time to catch up with it," admitted Gaunt.

She shrugged. "But that's how it is."

"You can do him a favour," said Gaunt. "Don't let him rush into anything with his money. Make him take time."

"I can try." She shook her head. "Florian told me how much there is—and why. It's strange, unbelievable!"

"So let him get used to the idea."

Gaunt had spotted the source of that strange, throbbing, whirring background noise. Over to their right, four giant fans were spinning on frames beside one of the test stretches. Another four fans, their blades motionless, were mounted on the other side of the area. Each fan was about the size of a single-storey housefront. They were electrically driven. Even as he watched, the four working fans began to increase their speed and the noise grew.

"Wind machines," explained Bessie King. "For sidewind stimulation. They can be scary—like you're in a sixty-mile-an-hour gale. Or they've a nice set of water nozzles waiting if you'd like instant rain as an extra." Her mind went back to Florian Beck. "The kind of money involved explains the telephone calls."

"What calls?" asked Gaunt, mystified.

"Some taxman," said Bessie King. "Florian told me yesterday. The Bundesamt Finanzen has started chasing him. They'd been told Florian was getting some kind of legacy money, they wanted details

—so Florian had to say he was waiting to find out, that it could amount to nothing."

"When did he get the calls?" There was no way any German tax official could know about the Hartondee shares and what had happened. But suddenly Gaunt was hearing Henry Falconer's voice and remembering the warning about strange approaches made to the Remembrancer's office.

He found himself thinking about the way his own hotel room had been raided that morning—even if other rooms had been hit. He gripped Bessie King's arm. "I asked when, Bessie."

"Sorry." Her interest had been far out on the circuit. "I think he said the first call was late on Monday. The other was yesterday—but check with him." She pointed. One of the white cars was snarling towards them. Waiting, she waved as the little vehicle swept past. "That's Florian into his last lap. He'll come in next time round."

The big wind-fans at the other test area seemed to have reached operating speed and their noise was settling into a steady whine. Someone's technicians were fussing beside them and a light truck had appeared and was being positioned for its sidewind ordeal. But Bessie King beckoned and Gaunt followed her down the ladder and back out into the open. Then they waited until the white car finally came round, to coast in and halt. In a moment, it was surrounded by SPO people and Florian Beck was getting out. The fair-haired test driver removed his safety helmet, looked around, saw Gaunt and Bessie, and came straight over.

"I'm glad you came, Herr Gaunt." He nodded, then smiled at Bessie King. "Did you guard him the way I asked?"

"Like he was your bank," she said cheerfully.

Gaunt smiled. He saw all he wanted to know in the easy intimacy that existed between the couple. There was no need for it to be spelled out in words or physical contact. Beck and Bessie King had their own understanding.

The car Beck had brought in was being pushed away. Another was nosing out, the Swedish woman behind the wheel. Beck raised a hand in greeting as she went past, then turned to Gaunt again.

"Did your car turn up?"

"That's how I came."

"Then suppose you give me a couple of minutes, and I can give you the guided tour." Beck walked off towards the marquee, whistling to himself.

The fresh SPO car headed out on the circuit, the technicians drifted back, and Gaunt saw Bessie King glance at her wristwatch. She frowned, then gave him an apologetic grimace.

"I'm due back at work," she apologized. "But I'll see you again— and I'll do what you said. I won't let Florian rush into anything. That's a promise."

She left Gaunt, and he waited in the sunlight. The other SPO car on the circuit, the car with the Italian crew, had begun throwing out a cloud of thick blue-grey exhaust and he heard two mechanics standing near him begin cursing as it went past. Then Florian Beck returned. He had left his helmet in the marquee and was chewing on a sandwich.

"Someone has troubles—but they're not my worry." He took another bite. "You said you had wheels, Herr Gaunt. Let's go."

They walked together to Gaunt's Ford, where Beck was content to settle in the passenger seat. Gaunt started the car but let the engine idle for a moment.

"Bessie King says you've had a couple of calls from someone in the Federal Tax Office." He leaned on the steering wheel and looked at Beck. "They'd heard something about a legacy."

"Sometimes that woman talks too much." Beck grinned, still enjoying his sandwich. "*Ja*, some idiot called. It was late on Monday, when I got back to the *Gasthaus*. Then out here, to the track yesterday —about this time."

"What did he want?"

"What do taxmen always want?" grumbled Beck. "Everything they can get. They'd heard a story. Could I confirm it? What was going on?" He winked. "I told the vulture I didn't know anything—which was near enough true. When he tried again, I said I still didn't know, and hung up on him."

"It's a stupid question," said Gaunt softly. "But are you sure he was German?"

"From the accent, I'd put money on him being a woodentop from around Düsseldorf—" Beck stopped, the question sinking home. "Why?"

"Did you get a name?"

Puzzled, Beck shook his head. "Who wants to know a taxman's name?"

"You do, if he calls again," warned Gaunt.

Beck frowned, then gave a slow nod. He looked at what was left of the sandwich, wound down the passenger window, threw out the sandwich, and fished a thin black cheroot from his top pocket. He lit the cheroot, then swung his feet up on the dashboard.

"Guided tour, starting now," he suggested. "You drive where I tell you, nowhere else—not unless you want to risk being killed, understood?"

"Understood," agreed Gaunt.

They started.

Florian Beck knew what he was talking about and knew how to talk about it. While Gaunt kept the Ford moving, his passenger kept up a commentary on each site they visited.

Scheckheim wasn't just a test track—it was several layers of proving grounds for engineering and safety.

There was the windfan area, and the main acceleration and handling track. But then came the special tracks, the surfaces which were potholes and troughs or cobblestones, or the specially crafted tarmac made to create sinus waves and vibration. Each had its trackside monitoring units. It was the same at the giant skidpad and its extension with a running water surface for aquaplaning.

Along from there, they came to the water ditch—except that it was more like a stretch of shallow canal, to test braking and electrical systems. There were test stands for exhaust emission analysis, there were dynamometer units where a vehicle could travel on rollers at high-performance speeds without moving. A special test hill like a slalom course was meant for just that—a range of different gradients, to check everything from starting and gears to chassis stresses.

"And that one?" Gaunt gestured towards yet another track. It looked newer than the rest, broad, a long stretch made up of separately coloured, separately textured sections.

"That's where we do collision and rollover work—usually by remote control, but every now and again they want somebody inside for real." Beck chuckled. *"Ja,* that's what we call real-time stuff." His attention moved on. "Take a left here and you'll see where they've built in railway level crossings and half a genuine river bed! We're driving on an investment that cost over sixty million Deutschmarks to build, and they're still not finished—yet it makes a profit. How many different test teams have you seen around?"

Gaunt shrugged. Starting with the sports car he'd seen dropped from a crane, going on through the SPO team and the light van outfit and others, there had to be at least ten separate activities under way.

"Fourteen," said Beck. "We're sprats, all of us. We rent space by the hour. When the major projects move in, they take exclusive hire by the day, sometimes the week. People like Seat from Spain, or Volvo down from Sweden—*ach*, we even had Lada arrive from the USSR. We've had Japanese, we've had Koreans. We had a British Rolls-Royce team over, with something disguised like it was a dump truck." He suddenly froze. "Stop! Now!"

Gaunt slammed the brake pedal. The Ford bucked and squealed to a halt as something large and black and more than a little out of control wobbled and skidded on a nearby track. Three complete circles later, an anonymous station wagon thumped a row of photoelectric beam sensors and stopped. The driver got out, throwing up his hands in despair as a back-up car came screaming to the rescue.

"We'll stay clear for a moment," decided Florian Beck. He scratched at his short, neat beard. "That's my motto. When there's trouble, don't get involved if you can avoid it." He indicated the other driver. "And that one shouldn't be allowed to drive outside of a fairground." Pausing, he lit another of his thin black cheroots and gave Gaunt an almost apologetic sideways glance. *"Bitte . . .* could we talk about my money again?"

Gaunt nodded. "Any time."

"I just want to be sure, absolutely sure." Beck drew hard on his cheroot then let the smoke out slowly. "I have all the documents I was told you needed. I brought them with me from Stuttgart—my parents' wedding certificate, proof of my birth and of my mother's death."

"Where are they right now?"

"In the *Gasthaus* safe."

"Keep them there." Gaunt nodded approval. "A thief got into my room this morning. You don't want to lose them."

"I should be all right. Thieves prefer foreigners—richer pickings." Florian Beck grinned a little, his mind otherwise occupied. "Your people are sure no one else has a claim?"

"No one. Not the way you have."

Beck gave a sigh. "When I was very small, my mother and father took me to visit this Stonehaven once or twice. I can remember a small, grey town by the sea—and the farmhouse. I always felt very cold there. After that"—he shrugged—"maybe there was a quarrel. I don't know."

Gaunt shook his head.

"The only other thing I remember is the strange way the people celebrated New Year. They"—he frowned—"yes, they swung balls of some kind of fire round their heads. My mother used to say it was to frighten evil spirits."

"It's a good way of having a party," said Gaunt dryly. He was watching the fuss around the damaged car on the track. The back-up team had given up trying to push-start it and now seemed to be waiting on a tow truck. The air inside the Ford was becoming thick with cheroot smoke, and he opened a window a little. "What time do we meet tonight to get the paperwork finished?"

"There's no problem?" persisted Beck.

"None," repeated Gaunt patiently.

"Then could we do it tomorrow?" asked Beck unexpectedly. He smiled in a strangely earnest way and avoided Gaunt's eyes, his voice quiet. "You haven't just brought me money, Herr Gaunt. You've brought me freedom, a chance to start a few things over again. I have promised someone that we will have our own meeting tonight, have our own celebration, and then maybe we can make some plans—just the two of us."

"You mean Bessie King?"

Beck nodded. "I've never married. She's a widow, she has never had children. We—well, we're good for each other."

"She'd like you to stop test driving," said Gaunt. "Is that what you mean about 'freedom'? Getting away from it?"

"*Nein.*" Beck gave that strange smile again. "Something else." His mood lightened. "This test-driving thing is no big deal, Herr Gaunt. You just pretend you're a stopwatch"—he looked over to where a tow truck was drawing up—"at least, most of us do. When you are home in Scotland, what do you drive?"

"A very rebuilt BMW." It had been put together, budget style, from two old accident-damaged cars. Gaunt decided not to add that the man who had done the rebuild, who maintained it, was a deaf-and-dumb giant whom he'd first met in military hospital. Gaunt's broken back had been mending, Dan Cafflin had been a Royal Tank Regiment NCO until he'd been blown up by a landmine during one of those Arab Trucial States skirmishes where there were always some British military around. It had left Cafflin without speech or hearing, but he could tune any engine to perfect pitch by fingertip feel as it vibrated.

"You like driving? Real driving?"

"I haven't exactly tried." Real driving cost money. Gaunt had helped out as a substitute navigator in an occasional forest roads rally. He'd tried a few small club events in a borrowed car. Even that wasn't cheap. "But when I get the chance, yes."

"Then you understand." Beck was satisfied. "This paperwork— would tomorrow afternoon be all right?"

"Tomorrow afternoon will be fine." Gaunt looked around. Apart from the fuss around the tow truck, the track was deserted. He stroked the rented Ford's steering wheel. "Florian, what would happen if I was caught doing a lap round this track?"

"Right now?" Beck considered, then laughed. "First, you have to be caught. Suppose we find out?"

Jonathan Gaunt grinned like a schoolboy, revved the Ford, slapped it into gear, and the car took off with a howl of engine and a blast of exhaust.

He did his lap. One of the motorcycle security men was waiting at the SPO marquee when the Ford pulled in. The man glared at Gaunt, said nothing, but waited until Beck had got out of the car. Then, pointedly, the security rider fell in beside the Ford as it moved again, and stayed as an escort as Gaunt drove towards the exit gate.

CHAPTER 2

It seemed inevitable that a few hours later he was eating dinner with
Dieter Vogt and that Vogt was anxious to make it clear that he was off
duty and willing to match his guest drink for drink again, as long as it
took.

"Not this time." Jonathan Gaunt had to make it almost an apology
as Vogt beckoned their waitress to bring over two more giant steins of
beer. "I'm *kaputt*, out of training, Dieter." He had also taken another
of the painkiller tablets for his back, and the things didn't totally mix
with alcohol. He threw up his hands in mock surrender. *"Kamerad."*

"Lieutenant Gaunt, you sound like one of your football teams."
Vogt grinned without malice. He held up a single finger to the waitress, who nodded and went to fetch his order. "Do you remember
what our Bayern München did to your Edinburgh Hearts in the European Cup?"

"I'd rather forget," said Gaunt. Hearts Football Club had gone to
Munich in high hopes after managing a home win against the West
German side. But Bayern München hadn't merely won the second,
away leg. It had been an unhappy thrashing. "I saw it on TV."

"I was there." Vogt's plump face shaped a grin which included the
waitress as she brought his beer. He raised his mug in a magnani-
mous toast. "To your Scottish footballers—they foul and they play
dirty, almost as well as we can!"

Gaunt didn't rise to the bait. It was safer to study the menu.

When he'd driven back from Scheckheim, he'd looked in at Rottach's small police station. Vogt's sergeant had emerged from a back
office and had made a laborious job of taking Gaunt's statement about
the attack in his *Gasthaus* room. Gaunt had signed it once it was typed
up. Then he had asked about Dieter Vogt. Vogt was sorting out a
problem in a village a few kilometres away, but within two minutes
they had Gaunt connected to him by a radio link. Two minutes after

that, Vogt had arranged to collect him from the Gasthaus Rotwild at 8
P.M.

That gave Gaunt enough time to scribble out the start of the report
to add to the file which was now going to have to be renamed Florian
Beck–Hartondee, put the paperwork away, shower, change into a
clean white shirt and—because it was Vogt—put on a faded but well-
pressed maroon and blue Parachute Regiment tie. He swopped his
leather jacket for a plain dark blue blazer, and was in the front lobby
of the *Gasthaus* when the police inspector arrived. Vogt was in the
same grey casual suit as that morning, but had teamed it with an
alarming striped blue and white shirt and a string bow tie.

He also emerged from an Opel Coupé driven by a copper-haired
young woman—the same woman Gaunt had seen that morning,
walking the lakeside path with a shopping basket. She gave him a
friendly smile.

"Krissa is one of my sergeants," said Vogt casually. "You—ah—
remember her?"

Gaunt nodded. "You were keeping an eye on me?"

"Enough to discover we weren't the only people doing it," said
Vogt. "You were also followed from here to Scheckheim—there were
two of them, a man and a woman, maybe late twenties or early
thirties, no real descriptions. They had a grey Mercedes, and they
kept very much in the background." He frowned. "Krissa is good. But
that was all she could get—and even that was partly luck."

"Any idea why I'd interest them?"

"You? *Nein.*" Vogt shook his head. "But some people might be curious about why you are interested in Herr Beck."

"The same kind of people who break into hotel rooms?" asked
Gaunt.

"Maybe." Vogt shrugged the possibility aside. He signalled the copper-haired woman and she smiled at Gaunt again, nodded, and set
the Opel moving. As the car drew away, Dieter Vogt beckoned Gaunt.
"Forget about it for now. You are, as of this moment, in the care of
one of the *Kriminalamt*'s finest." He winked. "That's a bad start to any
evening. First, we take a little walk."

They did, along a path beside the Tegernsee to a concrete jetty and
a small water-bus. There were a few other passengers already aboard
and soon after Gaunt and Vogt joined them and a last scurrying pair
of teenagers with backpacks had arrived, the water-bus was under
way.

They crossed the Tegernsee, heading north-west, the lake's surface lightly broken by an occasional breeze coming down from the mountains, the evening cool, the first lights beginning to show here and there along the lake. There was another concrete jetty where they came in at the opposite shore, close under a great green rise of hill, and a waiting cable-car. Five minutes later they were being shown to their table in the restaurant which had been hidden among the trees at the very top of the hill.

There were full-length windows to give a panoramic view across the sweep of the Tegernsee at dusk. There was a log fire smouldering under a central copper canopy. The first steins of beer arrived as they settled.

But the prices on the menu made Gaunt's eyebrows rise.

Vogt seemed to read his mind. He laid down his own menu. "The evening is on me. I spoke to my boss and he says this goes on expenses."

"Because he wants something?" asked Gaunt.

"*Ja.*"

Gaunt watched a tiny moth flirt round the flame of the butane-powered candle on their table. He sighed. All the way across the lake, then on the cable-car, they had stuck to personal things. He knew that Dieter Vogt was to marry in two months' time, and that his fiancée was twenty-five, blonde, and a qualified lawyer who worked for the Bavarian state prosecutor. In turn, Gaunt had told the dark-haired policeman just enough to explain why he now worked for the Remembrancer.

But it had stopped there, until now.

"Maybe we should order," Vogt said. "They do a pan-fried pork, thinly sliced, with a cream and herb sauce." He paused. "Who told you about Franken Thungersheim?"

"My boss." It seemed inevitable that Vogt should even have known about the wine for Henry Falconer.

"Here, we'll go for a carafe of the house wine. Maybe it comes out of a storage tank, but it comes like an angel's breath." Vogt signalled the waitress back, ordered for them both, then took another swallow at his beer. He took a casual glance around, checking the people at the nearest tables, and was satisfied. "Jonny, I'm *Bayers Landes Kriminalamt*—Bavarian State Police. We work with the *Bundeskriminalamt,* our BKA Federal Police. The BKA have no proof but a lot of suspicion that when Florian Beck makes test trips out of the country he uses them as a cover for smuggling."

"Drugs?"

"We think so. Two months ago, when he came back from a trip to North Africa, he was strip-searched at the airport—being strip-searched is very thorough, very unpleasant. We found nothing, we had to make some very apologetic noises. But we had been told by a good source."

"And that could be why people are interested in me?"

"Because you're interested in him." Vogt nodded.

The moth was still playing around the butane flame. Gaunt's thoughts went to the fair-haired test driver and the way they'd talked in the Ford, the way Beck had gone on about having been offered a new chance in life. Maybe that new chance included leaving some of the present behind him.

"What I told you about your hotel thief was true," said Vogt slowly. "We know how he works—including how he uses the ammonia spray." He looked at Gaunt. "Do you believe in coincidences?"

"Not often." Gaunt drew on the tablecloth with the tip of his fork. "These people in the drugs trade—do you know who they are?"

"Maybe. We're not positive." Vogt was frank about it.

"I came to Bavaria to tell Florian Beck he had inherited money from a Scottish great-grandfather," said Gaunt.

"Bitte?" Vogt stared. "How much?"

"Four hundred thousand pounds—give or take a few."

The police inspector swore softly. "You mean it?"

"That's what Beck keeps asking," said Gaunt.

He told Dieter Vogt the rest of the story, and finished it exactly as their meal arrived.

It was cooked in the lavish sturdy Bavarian style, with servings that made nonsense of portion control. Soup almost thick enough to stand a spoon upright was followed by the delicately crisp pan-fried pork. It came with the kind of sauce which had Vogt cheerfully mopping around his plate with a chunk of bread. The house wine was a dry white, clear as mountain water and as local. To follow, Gaunt settled for cheese and watched Vogt shovel his way through a plate of chocolate-covered pastries topped with cream. He was glad the coffee came in bowl-sized cups.

"Good, *nicht wahr?"* Vogt said. "Better than when we played at war games."

"Away ahead of them." Gaunt still had memories of lukewarm field-kitchen food prepared in a sea of tank-churned mud and what it had done to his digestion. "Did anyone ever hear who won?"

"Did anyone ever care? Ask the Russians," suggested Vogt cynically. "They usually know that kind of thing." His interest had strayed across the restaurant. "There's something that could be more exciting—"

The woman was an attractive, quietly dressed brunette whose age was probably around thirty. Her hair was held back by an antique silver and pearl clasp and she was eating alone. For a moment, as if sensing she was being watched, her head turned and she glanced across at them. Her expression was empty of interest and she looked away again.

"Exciting, but chilly." Vogt gave a mock shiver. "Anyway, I only window-shop since I got engaged." He rested his elbows on the table. "So—back to your Florian Beck, who says he remembers his mother taking him to visit her family at Stonehaven?"

"We knew about that." Gaunt nodded. "We sent someone up there to ask around, and he found a few people who still remembered Beck's mother. Florian was about seven years old on that last visit."

"Then the family row," mused Vogt. "That happens. I have an uncle the rest of the family pretend doesn't exist." He shrugged. "And Stonehaven —do they really have this strange fire-waving custom the way Beck says?"

"Every New Year, scores of fireballs being swung on chains down the high street." Gaunt tried to explain. "It goes back to Viking times, maybe earlier. They've got to burn out all the old evil."

"Mad. Except it would be good if it worked," said Vogt. "What came first? His family tree?"

Gaunt nodded. In Scotland, that meant only one thing—sessions at New Register House in Edinburgh.

It was a unique facility. One massive neo-Georgian building held under its domed roof what many people claimed was still the most comprehensive single collection of genealogical source information to be found in the modern world. It amounted to the complete gathered records of births, marriages and deaths in every part of Scotland since the year 1885 and thousands of parish records which went back centuries before that date. There were people on the Remembrancer's staff who knew their way around New Register House as if it was home. Give them any kind of a start point, and the rest was easy.

Before he realized it, his glance strayed across the restaurant again. She was still there, still on her own, a waiter hovering almost paternally in the background. She had hazel eyes and a strong, fine-boned face. But this time she didn't look his way.

He heard Vogt make a small, patient, throat-clearing noise, realized the German expected more of an answer, and started back where it began.

"Peter Church, the man who bought those shares for ten pounds back in 1921, married a Mary White. They had three children, two died as infants. The survivor, a son named James Church, married a Martha Richards. They became tenant farmers near Stonehaven." He had read the little family tree so often that he could recite it from memory now. "James and Martha had two children. One, their son, remained a bachelor and died a few years ago. The other child, a daughter, was named Ann—"

"Who married Hans Beck of Frankfurt," murmured Vogt, finishing it for him. "Then, like you said, Florian was the Becks' only child." He sighed. "So you can prove direct descent."

"Hans Beck met Ann Church when he spent a summer working in Scotland. He took his bride back to Frankfurt. They visited Stonehaven a few times until that family row, then they weren't seen again."

"Until your people found Florian." There was a small amount of wine left in Vogt's glass. He drank it carefully. "How?"

"We knew he existed. People remembered him at the Stonehaven end." Gaunt smiled across the table. "You're *Polizei*. What's the first thing you do when you're trying to trace someone?"

"Try the telephone directory—" began the policeman. He stopped and stared.

"We do the same," said Gaunt. "We telexed the British consul in Frankfurt, he tried the telephone directory, he started phoning anyone named Beck—one in the first batch he tried was a distant relative, who knew that Florian Beck was a research engineer and lived in Stuttgart."

The rest had been simple enough. Gaunt suddenly realized that how they'd found him was something that Beck had never asked. He might later. For the moment, it probably didn't matter to him.

Something like a tiny cinder landed on the tablecloth. The moth had flirted with the candleflame once too often. People could sometimes act that way.

"If Beck is a smuggler, how would you rate him?" he asked Vogt.

"Small-time." Vogt was positive. "He's the kind that people in the smuggling fraternity call a mule. He usually doesn't know what he's carrying, he just does it when he makes a genuine business trip, so that he makes some extra cash."

"But now he probably knows he's being watched?"

"Knows, and is frightened. He may not try it again." Vogt gave a small, caustic grin. "And now he has a meal ticket, thanks to your Remembrancer."

"How will the people who've been using him feel about it?" asked Gaunt softly.

"If they're who we think they are, they won't be happy," said Kriminalinspektor Dieter Vogt. *"Nein . . .* they won't be happy."

They ordered another carafe of the house wine. As it arrived Gaunt saw that the brunette had left. There was no trace of where she had gone, and it was none of his damned business. If Vogt had noticed, he said nothing.

By the time they had finished the wine they had put the matter of Florian Beck aside and had begun talking a mix of football and sol-diering, then back to football. Jonathan Gaunt tried a mention of jazz, but Vogt's view was that people who liked jazz belonged in a zoo. Somewhere along the way, Gaunt abandoned caution and any worry about his painkiller pills and switched back to beer.

It was after midnight when they left the hilltop restaurant and took the cable-car way down to the lake. From there, they took a water-bus which followed a different route with two extra stops but finally delivered them back to Rottach. They parted outside the *Gast-haus,* where Gaunt vaguely registered the fact that Florian Beck's old Porsche wasn't in sight in the floodlit parking lot.

It was hardly a surprise. Beck had plenty to celebrate.

There were no messages waiting when he checked at the reception desk. He asked for an alarm call at 8 A.M. and made his way up to his room. It was around one-thirty when he finally yawned his way in between the sheets.

Jonathan Gaunt was asleep almost as soon as he closed his eyes.

It was also one of those nights when he didn't have the usual nightmare—that falling through space with nothing to stop him, fall-ing in a way that usually wakened him in a sweat just before he hit whatever was waiting for him.

Instead, he was dragged out of sleep by the telephone. It kept ring-ing while he found the light switch and checked his wristwatch. The time was after 4:30 A.M. Swearing, he grabbed at the telephone. Dieter Vogt was at the other end, sounding tired, sounding as grey as the pre-dawn Gaunt could see outside his window.

"I'm over at Scheckheim," said Vogt without preliminaries. "Your Herr Beck has been murdered, Jonny. I thought you should know, that you'd want to get out here."

"You're sure it's Beck?" Gaunt was still partly dazed by sleep, the question came automatically.

"He was found by a night patrolman. The patrolman knew him." Vogt anticipated Gaunt's next question. "Someone shot him. It looks like he tried to run."

"I'll come straight over," said Gaunt.

"But you're not driving," ordered Dieter Vogt. "Not after our kind of evening, not any more than I am. If you even looked at a Breathalyzer the reading would throw you in jail. I've detailed a police car to collect you in fifteen minutes."

Fifteen minutes was long enough to endure a long, ice-cold shower that brutalized him totally awake, to dress, to get down to the *Gasthaus* lobby, and to beg a cup of coffee from the flask the night reception clerk kept hidden behind his desk.

Then the car arrived, a green BMW with *Polizei* on the doors and a blue light flashing on the roof. He got in beside the driver, a grizzled constable who looked as though he had spent all of his life on night shift. The man knew very little about what had happened. Gaunt sighed, sat back, and let him get on with driving while the car's radio churned out messages.

The grey pre-dawn gradually lightened as they drove over the mountain road and down into the Scheckheim valley. Other traffic was almost non-existent, a deer darted from the trees at one point, paused, then fled again. As the sun rose, he saw it begin to touch the high distant peak of the Zugspitze, turning it into a fiery pink.

Then they were dropping down the minor road and the Scheckheim fence was a thick black line ahead of the car. When they reached it the main gate was open but with two uniformed police on duty who carried machine-pistols. Gaunt's veteran constable eased the BMW to a brief halt beside them, wound down a window, handed out a pack of sandwiches to the nearest man, then had the car moving again.

They drove to the SPO trailer and marquee. There were lights all around them, along with several cars, more police, and a number of other people. Someone shouted to his driver, pointed, and the BMW swung away, bouncing over the nearest of the test tracks. They stopped where another huddle of cars had parked and where emergency lights were glinting on the long, broad water-test feature.

Gaunt walked over to where a small group of figures were gathered. One of them was Dieter Vogt. He was wearing rubber boots, and looked fragile in the early morning light.

"Jonny." Vogt greeted him with the merest fraction of a nod, then beckoned. The rubber boots were wet almost up to his knees. "Watch how you go."

They went to the edge of the long, shallow stretch of artificially flooded road. Vogt's sergeant was standing guard and someone else Gaunt recognized and who was also wearing rubber boots rose from beside something lying at the water's edge.

"Herr Gaunt." The same angular woman doctor who had treated his eyes gave a small grimace of recognition.

"Doktor Huber also acts as our local police surgeon," said Vogt.

She nodded and took a step to one side, the water splashing ankle-deep around her feet. Some of the ripples reached the dead man beside her. Florian Beck lay on his back, with his mouth hanging open and his straw-fair hair and beard like so much dank, tangled fur. His whole body was an untidy sprawl. He had been wearing a smart dark blue suit with a shirt and tie, all now soaked with water. One of his shoes was missing.

"He was face down when he was discovered." Vogt's voice was harsh and angry at the thought. "The night patrolman turned him over to see who it was."

"When?"

"He was found at three a.m."

"But he died at least three hours earlier, around midnight," said Doktor Huber, as if she were discussing the weather. "He was shot twice in the back, probably at fairly close range, probably by a hand-gun." She took a moment to choose her words. "Even with medical attention, either wound could have caused his death. But I would still say he drowned."

Gaunt stared at Dieter Vogt. Vogt merely nodded.

"We need the autopsy to be certain." The woman moved her feet again and another swirl of water touched Beck's lifeless face. "A person can drown in a puddle of water—as long as that person falls face down, as long as that person is too weak to move again. The water here is only a few centimetres deep. But a few millimetres could be enough."

"It slopes to about half a metre in depth further out," said Vogt. The chubby-faced police inspector glared around in the gradual sunrise. His face was pale, his eyes looked tired and swollen, and he was obviously nursing a hangover. He paused and listened as his sergeant murmured a question, then glanced at the woman for approval before he nodded. *"Ja,* Franz. Move him now."

His sergeant turned and waved an arm towards the nearest group of waiting figures. Two of them detached from the rest and came over with a folding trolley. Doktor Huber had picked up her medical bag. She gave another of those same small, tight smiles and left them.

"If that woman says he drowned, then he drowned," said Vogt flatly. "She knows her job. It doesn't matter too much—one way or another, his inheritance didn't bring him any luck."

"It didn't." Jonathan Gaunt forced himself to take another, closer look at the dead man, then he glanced at Vogt. "Have you searched him?"

"Just a little more money in his wallet than I would have expected. Maybe he felt he could afford to start spending." Vogt led Gaunt away at a slow walk back towards the SPO team base. He sucked hard on his lips. "I didn't have any kind of a watch on him. I didn't anticipate anything like this."

"How much can you put together?" asked Gaunt.

"So far?" Dieter Vogt gave an acid scowl. "Not a lot. His Porsche is parked beside the SPO tent, there's blood inside and on the ground. I've spoken to the night security people here, who help a little. His woman is here"—he saw Gaunt's surprise and nodded—*"ja,* Frau King. Franz went to her hotel and brought her. She was asleep. When she was wakened and told"—he shrugged—"Franz says it was bad, so it must have been."

"It would be." Gaunt felt a strong sympathy for the grey-haired woman. "They mattered to each other."

"Ich weiss." Vogt touched Gaunt's arm and stopped him. The detective's face was grim. "Be glad we were together, Jonny. Bessie King's story is that when Beck left her last night he said that you had to see him straight away. It was urgent, it was about his money."

Gaunt stared at him.

"She says that when Beck finished work at the track, he drove back to Rottach to shower and change his clothes. Frau King is staying at a hotel on the Garmisch road, and he went over in the Porsche to collect her. Then they went out to celebrate. He'd booked a table at a restaurant near Garmisch." Vogt looked back. Florian Beck, now covered in an anonymous black plastic body-bag, had been loaded on the trolley-stretcher and was being wheeled towards a waiting mortuary van. "At the end of their meal, Beck was called to the telephone.

When he came back, he told her you'd been phoning around, trying to find him."

"But—" began Gaunt, bewildered.

Vogt stopped him. "I know. By that time, you and I were trying to decide whether to get drunk together. The rest of it is that Beck told her there was an unexpected problem, one that couldn't wait till morning."

"Was I supposed to be doing the talking?" asked Gaunt bitterly.

"No. It was a woman. She'd told Beck she'd arrived from the British consulate with new papers that caused the problem. You were busy on another phone."

"But he was to meet me here?"

Vogt surprised him. "You were to be waiting back at the *Gasthaus* in Rottach. But you had to see him alone, in a hurry. Beck dropped Bessie King off at her hotel—that would be around eleven last night. He said he'd contact her in the morning."

"So you choose between whether Beck got that kind of call and believed it or—"

"Or got another kind, from some of his friends, and was lying." Vogt stuffed his hands into his jacket pockets, then swung a kick at a small stone at his feet. The stone flew viciously and hit a metal track barrier. "He sets off for Rottach, he ends up here, and dead. All the *verdammt* night security people here know is that they saw his Porsche drive up to the gate. They knew it, they waved it through, there may have been two people aboard—there was nothing unusual about someone turning up to work late, even around midnight. They only need special clearance if there's to be any night driving on the test tracks. Nobody left that they know about—though it would be easy enough. The way that night patrol spotted him lying in the water was sheer chance."

"Nobody heard shots?"

"These people wouldn't notice World War Three if it went past," Vogt said resignedly.

"Can I talk to Bessie King?"

"*Ja.* I've told her that you were with me last night." Vogt pointed towards the SPO trailer. "Over there. I'll be in touch."

They parted, and Gaunt walked across to the trailer. It was going to be another fine day, without a cloud in the sky. The sun was up, and a big black and white magpie was perched on top of one of the wind-fans, looking down at him. He heard a vehicle start up, then the mortuary van whispered past him, heading away.

Bessie King wasn't at the trailer. He found her standing out in the open, near where Beck's old Porsche lay under guard. She heard him coming, turned, and he saw she had been crying. New tears weren't far away. Without make-up, her grey hair barely combed, she seemed to have aged overnight.

"I'm sorry," he said quietly. "Really sorry, Bessie."

She bit her lip and forced what was meant to be a very small smile.

"Is there any way I can help?" asked Gaunt.

She shook her head, looking again towards the Porsche. A heavy sheet of police plastic had been draped protectively over the opened driver's door and covered some of the ground below.

"We made plans," she said in a slow, almost disbelieving voice. "What we'd do when he got the money. We'd do this, we'd do that—" She stopped it there. "The *Kriminalinspektor* told me how you couldn't have been involved."

"Can we talk about it?" he asked.

She hesitated then nodded. "If it can help find who did this."

"Think back to before last night. Did Florian tell anyone else about the money—anyone at all?"

"Nobody I knew about." A fresh tear ran down her cheek.

"We know he was in some kind of trouble," said Gaunt. "Maybe bad trouble, Bessie. Did he talk about it?"

"He wouldn't." Bessie shook her head. "I knew something had been worrying Florian—he even admitted it. But he wouldn't tell me anything more, except that he didn't want me dragged into it. He'd find a way out." She looked at Gaunt and was almost defiant. "That was the first thing he was going to do with the money from his inheritance—get out, right out. I was going with him to Australia."

"For a new start?"

"We'd be married." She paused, the stunned disbelief hoarse in her voice. "You know the worst part? I don't even know why he was killed. Do you—does anyone?"

"No, not yet." He needed to try one last question. He hoped she could take it. "Florian told you that a woman made that telephone call. Could there have been another woman—someone he knew, someone he knew well?"

Bessie King didn't answer for a moment.

"Not the way you mean, Jonny," she said with a total certainty. "Not with Florian. Are you finished?"

Jonathan Gaunt nodded, touched her gently on the shoulder, and turned away.

Bessie King was crying again.

About all he could do after that was hang around. The Scheckheim test facility had been closed for the rest of the morning, and only a few staff and a handful of the SPO team had been admitted within the barrier fence. Gaunt drifted among them, talked with some, heard nothing new that could matter, and watched a squad of uniformed and plain-clothes police carry out the kind of thorough, methodical search round an area which police do when they've nothing better to try.

Dieter Vogt had gone. Bessie King was driven back to her hotel by Vogt's copper-haired woman officer, and soon after that Gaunt managed to get a lift of his own in another police car. The driver was taking some evidence samples all the way to the *Bundeskriminalamt* forensic laboratory in Munich, and dropped him off at Rottach.

Guests were still eating breakfast in the *Gasthaus*'s verandah restaurant. Planning what they'd do with their day. The same English couple were again rooted behind their newspapers.

But the staff knew what had happened. It showed in the startled expression on the waitress's face when he sat at an empty table, then the carefully blank-faced way in which she took his order for coffee and rolls. He saw her quick, earnest conversation with another waitress a few moments later, then how they both looked over in his direction.

The waitress brought his order. He sipped the coffee and ate one of the rolls, then decided he had no appetite, that his mind was still too occupied with that picture of Florian Beck lying dead in the shallow water at Scheckheim. Then there was Bessie King, and the trapped grief that had shown through during every minute they had talked.

Gaunt gave up, shoved back his chair, and left the restaurant. He was walking across the reception lobby, on his way to his room, when he heard his name called by the girl at the reception desk. She was mousy-haired, with an attractive face and white-framed spectacles. He hadn't seen her before. Her lapel badge said her name was Maria.

"Herr Gaunt." She gave an awkward, slightly uncertain half smile. *"Bitte,* I was sorry to hear about Herr Beck. He was pleasant to everyone."

Gaunt nodded. "He seemed that way."

"Pleasant—and friendly." She reached down to a shelf behind her desk. "There is a message for you. A lady telephoned and asked if you would call her."

Gaunt read the message slip. Someone named Joan Dennan had called him at 8:45 A.M., and gave a number to call back.

"The Hotel Wald," said the receptionist. She peered wisely at him through her white-framed spectacles. "That's on the other side of the village—I have a sister who works there."

"Did you take the call?" asked Gaunt.

"*Ja.* Around here, who else?" She smiled past him at a couple who were going out, then frowned a little. "I think she is the same lady who telephoned yesterday—"

"Asking for me?"

The girl hesitated. "The first time she telephoned was yesterday afternoon. She left no message and no name, you were out, and so was Herr Beck—"

"She asked for Florian Beck?" Gaunt froze.

"Herr Beck first, then for you." The receptionist looked worried. "You were both out, and she said she would try later. She—*ja,* she did, maybe an hour or so later. You were both still out."

Gaunt leaned his hands on the desk. "You say your sister works in the Hotel Wald?"

The girl nodded. "In reservations."

"Do something for me, Maria," suggested Gaunt. "Call your sister. Ask her if she knows this Fräulein Dennan. When did she arrive, anything else your sister knows about her." He saw the trace of doubt in the girl's eyes behind the pert spectacles. Equally important, the *Gasthaus* manager was heading in their general direction. "It stays private, Maria. It's a business thing, nothing more. Will you do it?"

The girl nodded. He turned away, and went up to his room.

The room was still the rumpled way he'd left it when Dieter Vogt's call had wakened him and had sent him rushing out. Gaunt washed, shaved, and was putting on a clean shirt when he heard a light tapping on his door. When he stuffed his shirt into his trousers and opened the door, the mousy-haired receptionist was there.

"I called my sister, like you asked." She gave a quick, almost conspiratorial glance back along the corridor to make sure it was still empty. "She says that Fräulein Dennan is British, like I thought. She arrived at the Wald yesterday, at about noon. A taxi brought her direct from Munich airport—my sister says the flight tags were still on her luggage."

"Does your sister happen to know when Fräulein Dennan made her room reservation?" asked Gaunt.

"Late the night before, by telephone." The girl was pleased with her detective work.

"Thank your sister." Gaunt found his wallet. "When Fräulein Dennan telephoned here this morning, she didn't mention Herr Beck?"

She blinked. "She just asked for you—"

"And you didn't mention Herr Beck's death?"

Maria shook her head. "The manager says anyone who talks about it will be in big trouble—that it is bad publicity."

Gaunt silenced her half-hearted protests and folded some money into her hand. Tucking the money into her skirt pocket, she gave him a pleased nod of thanks and left.

Gaunt closed his door then went over and grimaced at his reflection in the dressing table mirror. His next task was to tell the Remembrancer's Office about Beck's murder. It was the kind of news guaranteed to spoil Henry Falconer's morning, whatever the weather was like back in Edinburgh.

He decided to make it formal. There was Gasthaus Rotwild headed notepaper in one of the dressing table drawers, and the heading included telex and FAX numbers. Gaunt settled on the edge of the bed, took his pen, thought, and began writing. The Remembrancer's Office used a simple enough code for routine traffic, and he was satisfied with his wording at the second try.

As he read it through, the bedside telephone rang. Gaunt put the written report aside, rolled over, and lifted the receiver. When he answered, he gave his name.

"Mr. Gaunt, I've been trying hard to contact you," said a woman's voice in a husky accent that was Scottish mixed with vague mid-Atlantic. "I left a message while you were out—my name is Joan Dennan."

Gaunt sat upright on the bed.

"I decided I had to try again." He heard the woman take a breath. "I'm here for the same reason you're here—Florian Beck. One straight question, Mr. Gaunt. Has something happened to Beck?"

"He's dead," said Gaunt bluntly.

"Dear God," said the woman almost to herself. "So it's true." She paused, then asked, "What happened?"

"He was murdered." Gaunt kept it simple. "He was shot in the back. His body was found out at the Scheckheim track."

For a moment there was a total, stunned silence on the line. Then she spoke again. "Do the police know who killed him?"

"Not who and not why."

"I tried to contact him yesterday. I was going to try again today, straight after breakfast." Joan Dennan's husky voice sounded shaken. "Then I heard the hotel porter gossiping on the phone with someone. He talked about something that had happened to Florian Beck. So— well, I called you."

"Did you know Beck?" asked Gaunt.

"No," she said. "I didn't know him, he didn't know me."

"Then what's your interest?"

"That's why we should talk," said Joan Dennan. "Mr. Gaunt, I'm over at the Hotel Wald—you can see it from your *Gasthaus*. I'm the chartered accountant who wanted to know who owned those sleeping Hartondee shares."

Gaunt stared at the telephone mouthpiece.

"Can we talk?" asked the woman.

"I think we should," said Gaunt. "When?"

"When you can," said Joan Dennan. "I'll wait." She hung up.

Jonathan Gaunt slowly replaced his receiver. He sat where he was for a moment, his grey-green eyes narrowed and puzzled. Then he picked up the report he had written, carefully tore it into narrow shreds, and flushed it down the lavatory.

As he came back, his telephone rang again. Two steps took him over and he answered it curtly.

"I'm down in the lobby," said Dieter Vogt. "Anything wrong, Jonny? You don't sound happy."

"And you don't win a prize."

"*Ja*, it's been that kind of morning," admitted Vogt. "I'm going to look round Florian Beck's room. Second floor, number 216. I'd appreciate you being along."

"I'll be there," promised Gaunt.

Using the fire-stair down, he arrived on the second floor as the elevator unloaded Vogt, his sergeant, and the flustered manager. They followed the man along the corridor to room 216, and waited while he opened it with a pass-key.

"*Danke.*" Vogt sent the manager on his way, then nodded to his sergeant, who led the way. Then he gave a grimace of a smile to Gaunt, and they followed. Once they were inside, Dieter Vogt closed the door.

The room was larger than Gaunt's on the top floor, but the general furnishing and layout were identical. Florian Beck's work clothes were still draped over a chair near the window. A large leather suitcase lay on top of the wardrobe, Beck had left his electric razor, his aftershave, and some change on top of the dressing table. The book he had been reading was open on the shelf beside the bed.

"The usual, Franz," Vogt told his sergeant, with a vague gesture that took in all of the room. "But we don't break anything—not like last time." He winked at Gaunt as the man began his search. "Last week we were looking in a loft. Franz fell through the *verdammt* ceiling. There was a display cabinet full of china dishes underneath, wasn't there, Franz?"

Franz scowled, pulled the suitcase from the top of the wardrobe, and tossed it on a table.

"I have a few things I'd like you to look at, Jonny." Dieter Vogt was wearing a waterproof gabardine jacket. He reached into an inside pocket and brought out a small bundle of papers, tied together with household string. "These are from the *Gasthaus* safe. They were in an envelope—Florian Beck wanted them kept securely. They seem like your territory."

Gaunt took the little bundle over to the window and loosened the string. The bundle included a passport, then the documents, from his mother's Scottish marriage certificate onward, that Florian Beck had been told would have to be produced to prove his family tree. A glance through them was enough. As far as the Remembrancer was concerned there would have been no problem.

"It's the way we expected," he told Vogt. "Total proof."

"Except he's dead." The detective inspector allowed a wry grimace to cross his plump face. "Take a look at the passport."

Gaunt did, and raised an eyebrow. "He got around." Page after page was covered in official stamps of every kind. Closing it again, Gaunt considered the whole collection. "Could we have photocopies?"

"*Ja,* this afternoon." Vogt paused as his sergeant finished searching some drawers and turned to Beck's bed. The big, uniformed figure took the mattress in one large hand and threw it on the floor, underside up. But there was nothing hidden there. Turning, Vogt looked out of the window. The view was towards the glinting blue water of the Tegernsee. "Jonny, some very senior people in Munich would like to see this case finished quickly. We could have television crews and newspaper teams flooding in if that doesn't happen—and that's even before they hear anything about why you came here."

"My people feel the same about publicity," said Gaunt. "Usually, they find a hole and hide." He returned the passport and documents to Vogt. "What about yesterday's hotel thief?"

"This room wasn't touched—as far as we know." Vogt rubbed a finger along the window glass, doing it hard enough to make a squeaking noise. "We're still trying to trace the Federal tax official that Beck told you about. Just like we're still trying to trace the couple in the car who followed you yesterday." He snorted to himself. "Add Frau King's story about the woman who telephoned Beck at the restaurant last night, giving him this phony message. He was to come here, yet he turns up at the Scheckheim track, where he gets killed. But why? Why to any of this? Is it the legacy that you brought him? Or is it something in his own background?"

"You said drugs," reminded Gaunt.

"He was small-time." Vogt scowled. "I told you. When he was going on a trip, he just looked around for a way to make some extra cash. He'd have smuggled horse-droppings if there was the price of a couple of beers in doing it."

"Only for the money?"

"I asked Frau King about that. She said he also liked the excitement —except that he was getting older. He was starting to worry."

"If he talked enough, could he be trouble for anyone?"

"In the drugs rackets? He might." Vogt scratched his chin and turned in from the window, watching his sergeant still at work. "Doktor Huber recovered both bullets from the body, and I've got her preliminary autopsy report. Our people found two ejected cartridge cases out at the track. Time of death is now firm at around midnight."

"What else?" asked Gaunt.

"So far?" Vogt shrugged. "With what we've got, including some bloodstains and where we found the cartridge cases, I can guess some of it. The first time he was shot, he was standing beside the Porsche. But he still tried to run for it."

"And he was shot again."

"It was a dark night," reminded Dieter Vogt. "I'm not totally sure, Jonny. But maybe the person who shot him couldn't find him afterwards. Because he was lying face down drowning in that test pond thing." He frowned. "One bullet clipped a lung, the other hit a rib at an angle and did messy things. But it's still possible that he could have kept going."

"*Ja,* volitional movement," said his sergeant unexpectedly.

"Franz knows all about it." Vogt gave him a grateful nod. "He used to be a pork butcher—it comes in handy. Go on, Franz. Explain."

"Volitional movement, Herr Gaunt?" The big sergeant beamed. "Someone can be dying, next best thing to dead, yet just keeps on going, running around—like with chickens." He warmed to it. "Last year, we had a man who had cut his throat—"

"*Bitte.*" Vogt stopped him, his face pale again.

Gaunt felt the same. His stomach was still marked "fragile" from the previous night's drinking. It had been more than two years since he'd had an evening to match it—and that time, he'd been drinking to hide from misery.

Last night, Jonathan Gaunt had been enjoying life.

While someone was killing Florian Beck.

"What do ballistics say?" he asked.

"An automatic pistol. Nine millimetre, possibly a Heckler and Koch parabellum. The state of the cartridge cases makes them think it was the eight-shot model—a good weapon."

"German made," said Gaunt.

"They export a lot—and to a lot of countries." Vogt did his trick of switching topics. "The people at the reception desk reckon that Beck got back from Scheckheim at around six yesterday evening. They saw him leave, wearing a suit, about an hour later. While he was in his room, they put through a telephone call."

"There's a woman—" began Gaunt.

"Fräulein Dennan—they told me about her." Vogt shook his head again. But this was a man. He made a second call to Beck and spoke to him again within that hour. The same receptionist thinks this man called Beck at least twice more over the last couple of days or so." Vogt paused, his eyes hardened and his voice softened. Briefly, an outer layer had been removed and Gaunt knew his instincts had been accurate. Kriminalinspektor Dieter Vogt was a very shrewd policeman. The mildness hid a diamond-hard core. "I'm going to find this man's name, Jonny—and some of the truth with it. Someone has been a liar, and that liar may even have been the late, not totally lamented Florian Beck. Tell me, are you going to meet this Fräulein Dennan?"

Gaunt nodded.

"I think you know she didn't arrive until yesterday. I'll maybe see her later." The man's grin slid back into place. "I—uh—almost forgot. I have a message for you, Jonny. Your Herr Falconer says to wish you a *Guten Morgen.* He sounds an interesting man."

Gaunt sighed. "You checked on me?"

"After a murder, I would even check on Franz's mother—maybe

because she is Franz's mother." Vogt added a murmured comment to his sergeant, then faced Gaunt again with the same apologetic grin still in place. "I telephoned your Queen's and Lord Treasurer's office in Edinburgh an hour ago. This Henry Falconer said he was your boss. I told him Beck was dead and Herr Falconer confirmed why you were here."

"That helps," said Gaunt.

"In Bavaria, we don't take chances," said Vogt. "That's why we win at football. If you're still angry later, I'll buy you a beer and say sorry, okay?"

Gaunt sighed and shrugged. A klaxon sounded outside. He saw a large white private launch coming in towards one of the Rottach jetties. A corner of his mind decided that he'd put a boat like that on his shopping list if the day ever came when unexpected fortune dropped in his own lap. He'd make sure of a few other things too—

A sudden delighted sound came from Vogt's sergeant. The man was crouching just inside the bathroom, beside a large mirror fixed to the wall from waist height upward. There was a tiled unit in front of the mirror, with a washbasin central and a broad shelf on either side. He looked round at them, grinned, then reached under the tiled shelf on the left side of the washbasin. Very carefully, he peeled at something taped on that hidden underside, then eased loose a second strip of tape.

Still crouched down, he turned and held up a small cardboard cigar box wrapped in plastic film.

"Inspektor?" He gave Vogt a wolfish grin and brushed some dust from his uniform.

"Nice, Franz," said Dieter Vogt. "You just made up for that ceiling you wrecked last week!"

Vogt led the way over to the window. He used the wooden ledge as a table, removed the plastic film from the little cigar box, then opened it. He stared, and his mouth fell open.

"Hell, I don't believe it," said Jonathan Gaunt, looking over his shoulder.

The top item inside the box was his return airline ticket—the ticket stolen from his room by the thief with the ammonia spray. He watched Dieter Vogt remove it then spread the rest of the box's contents along the window ledge. They included most of the stolen Remembrancer paperwork, tightly folded into a wad.

"It looks like I wasn't the only one who wondered about you," said Vogt sourly. He tapped the British Airways ticket. "And now your little thief makes sense. While you're downstairs having breakfast on the verandah and telling Florian Beck you're really the Good Luck Fairy in disguise, little thief is busy upstairs in your room. Doing a favour for a friend? A friend who had it organized before you even got here?" He gave Gaunt a sardonic grin. "Florian Beck was the kind who could have good reason to worry about a visiting stranger— particularly your kind, so anxious to give him money."

Gaunt heard the sergeant snort in amusement. Shrugging, he examined the array along the window ledge. The stolen papers could only have underlined the fact that the Hartondee shares story was genuine. But Beck had apparently used the little cigar box to conceal some of his own things. He helped Vogt set aside a thin bundle of U.S. fifty-dollar bills, held together by an elastic band, then a small address book, an even smaller pocket diary, and one of the new European Community style British passports which had Beck's photograph but a very different name. It didn't seem to have been used.

"His Just-In-Case kit?" suggested Vogt. He picked up the address book and diary with almost loving care. "These could be good reading. You won't mention any of this part to Fräulein Dennan?"

Gaunt shook his head.

"I'd also like to hear if anyone else like her happens to arrive," mused Vogt. "Maybe you could catch up with me at Scheckheim, Jonny. I want to talk with some of the SPO people again—though they've as many nationalities as the United Nations out there, and it's as difficult to get sense." He paused, frowned, and ran a hand through his dark hair. "I'm going to have Bessie King brought out there again too. I want to try leaning on her—just a little." He did another of his mental jumps. "Who gets the Hartondee inheritance money now?"

Gaunt shook his head. He didn't know. It would be someone else's worry—he hoped.

Fifteen minutes later he walked into the Hotel Wald. It was big, a modern blend of concrete, glass and plastic, and even the log fire to one side of the lobby was a gas-flame fake. The staff were mostly dressed in tourist Bavarian lederhose style and there was a souvenir shop crammed with wood carvings and deerskin items.

He asked for Joan Dennan at the reception desk, and one of the lederhose team, a plump redhead, guided him over to a quiet coffee lounge which had a small alpine waterfall flowing down part of one wall. The redhead indicated a table beside it, the woman at the table gave a slight, welcoming smile, and Gaunt stared as she got to her feet.

"Danke." He stared again as he shook hands with Joan Dennan. She was the woman with the silver hair clasp he had seen eating alone in that hilltop restaurant. He made an awkward, throat-clearing noise. "I—uh—think we ate in the same restaurant last night, Miss Dennan."

"I noticed you." Her hazel eyes twinkled for a moment. "What do people call you?"

"Jonny." As she sat again, Gaunt took a chair opposite.

"I'm Joan." She considered him calmly. "I'll start cards-on-the-table style, Jonny. Last night wasn't some cosmic accident of fate. I saw your photograph before I came out to Bavaria. I was in that restaurant because I followed you."

He blinked. "Why?"

"I thought the man with you might be Florian Beck—I needed to talk with him. But when I caught up, you were trying to drink Bavaria dry." The restrained amusement was back in her husky voice with its faint mid-Atlantic accent. "I was told he was a policeman."

"And an old friend. His name is Dieter Vogt."

She nodded, and the smile had gone. One of the spotlamps lighting the fake waterfall was throwing a glow which framed her dark, shoulder-length hair. Joan Dennan had to be around thirty, and she had the kind of long-jawed Celtic face which went with firm features, a broad mouth, and a long, slender throat. There were the first early lines of living around her eyes and she was wearing a pale shade of lipstick but no other make-up. She was dressed in a dark green corduroy trouser suit with a white blouse and tan leather shoes. It was the kind of outfit which said quality and didn't need a price tag.

"I've heard the story—about how Florian Beck was murdered." She moved in her chair and clasped her hands round one knee. She wore a wafer-thin gold watch on a leather strap. Her only jewellery was a small gold signet ring on her right index finger. "Your policeman—?"

"He's handling it."

"And I'm going to be told that I might as well take the next flight home?"

"You know why you came out," said Gaunt wryly. "I don't."

"But you're ready to guess?" She made it a challenge.

"You wanted to do a deal on the Hartondee shares?"

She hid most of her surprise, and nodded. "A fair deal."

"Would I expect differently?" asked Gaunt mildly.

"Thank you." Joan Dennan gave a soft chuckle. She paused as one of the lederhose girls, a blue-eyed, rake-thin blonde, brought coffee and placed the tray on a table beside them. The girl poured for them both, then departed, and Joan Dennan took a first sip from her cup. "Jonny, I brought a prepared, typed agreement out with me. As soon as we had Q and LTR acceptance that Beck was the sole legal heir we'd have purchased them from him. We're authorized to offer current marketable value plus thirty per cent."

"We?"

"We meaning Hartondee—I work for the firm that audits their accounts. Hartondee has become a particularly wealthy little company—"

"That nobody knows much about," suggested Gaunt.

"They left animal feedstuffs behind a long time ago. Now it's property management and financial services. They don't like their shares traded on the market—they don't like it at all." She frowned at her hands and fingered the gold signet ring. "I'm nobody's favourite for what I did. Hartondee were quite happily letting the whole thing drift, the way it always had done. Now I've a very unhappy boss with a very unhappy client."

"Until you straighten it out?"

She nodded, her face troubled. "I'm totally sorry that this man has been murdered. But he's someone I didn't meet, someone I didn't know. I can't exactly mourn him—I'll observe the decencies, but I'll keep doing my job. Fair?"

"Fair."

"Thank you." Joan Dennan relaxed a little. She took another sip of coffee, then took a deep breath. "I'm asking the obvious. Who inherits now?"

It was like an invitation to take a stroll through a legal minefield. Gaunt frowned and shifted uncomfortably in his chair. But it was still a fair question. He eyed the artificial waterfall for a moment.

"The German connection ends with Florian Beck." That much he was certain about. "We go back to the Church bloodline and take a wider look—at least give it a try. Remember, Beck died before he could formally inherit."

"Did he have anyone—well, close?"

He nodded. "Her name is Bessie King. She's Irish, she works for SPO, and they planned to marry."

"Hasn't she any kind of claim?"

"In law? No."

"Even if there's no one else?"

"The Crown can consider a moral claim—that's if there's enough evidence to show the deceased might have been reasonably expected to make provision for someone." It was a thin-ice area. "If it happens, it's a gift from the Crown. We give something, we keep the rest."

"Does Bessie King know?" Joan Dennan stopped, flushed, and shook her head. "Sorry. That was a damned stupid question—"

"You're doing your job." Gaunt's coffee was finished. He nodded his thanks as she poured him more. "That's what I want to know about. How you turn up here, and now."

"I work for an Edinburgh-based accountancy firm." She opened a small tan leather Gucci handbag, and handed him a small, engraved visiting card. It said Ms Joan Dennan, Chartered Accountant, was an Associate with Gladstone Baxter Accountancy, offices in Edinburgh, Glasgow and London. "That could be a valuable souvenir before long—if this Hartondee affair gets worse, I'll be looking for another job."

"You said they weren't pleased." Gaunt knew that plenty of companies could be strange in their ways. There were rules, there were regulations, but there were always ways of stretching them at the edges. "That can happen."

He'd seen some of the results, heard more. It happened to be one of the Remembrancer's Office odd-job tasks to run the Scottish end of the Crown-supervised Companies Branch. Companies Branch lived in a basement, where a handful of people and a computer were responsible for receiving, filing, and maintaining the legally required records of any business company. Every now and again, Companies Branch ended up slapping someone's wrist or sending someone to jail. One of the most recent was when a highly suspect investment house suddenly changed its trading name and tried to suggest that some top royals were nonexecutive officebearers.

"It happened." Joan Dennan pursed her lips at the reminder. "My boss is Gladstone Baxter. Six months ago, when I'd only been with the firm a few weeks, he was in a car crash and ended in hospital. I thought it was my big chance—keep the show running till he got back. That was when the annual Hartondee paperwork came in—"

"Which he normally handled, his own special way?"

She gave a wry nod. "And I started howling about those damned fast-asleep shares that somebody called Church had bought umpteen years ago. Then, the moment Gladstone Baxter came out of hospital and back to his desk, I got hell from everyone—"

"And told to sort it out." That part Gaunt understood. There was a burst of noise and laughter behind him. He looked round, and saw that a coach-load of Japanese tourists had just been unloaded and were swarming around the Hotel Wald's lederhosed reception team. The first cameras were already snapping on motor-drive. "So you tailed me here."

"Wrong." She rejected that. "I found out my own way—the records at New Register House are public property, I built my own version of the Church family tree, I got up to Stonehaven and researched there just days after your people had been around."

"And you found Florian Beck too?"

"Gladstone Baxter put a West German private inquiry agent on that," she admitted. Then she frowned. "You know we're not the only people who were—" She suddenly left it there and stared at Gaunt.

"Who were chasing Beck?" Gaunt nodded. "I know."

"And somebody killed him." Joan Dennan said it very softly, ignoring a passing eddy of smiling Japanese women. "Jonny, is anyone suggesting it could have been those shares?"

"Maybe not. He had his own problems." Gaunt looked at her business card again, then tucked it in his top pocket. "Joan, you said you knew me when you saw me. How?"

"A photograph." She drew a deep breath and looked wryly apprehensive. "And my own family tree, Jonny. I'm related to John Milton —I'm his wife's cousin."

It was Gaunt's turn to stare. John Milton was a plump, easygoing Edinburgh stockbroker, the kind who was easygoing enough to tolerate Gaunt's pocket-money-sized stock market gambling. To play poker with Gaunt one night each week. He even had enough of a sense of humour to have the telegraphic address "Paradise Lost, Edinburgh."

"You leaned on John?" he asked incredulously. Milton's wife was another Joan. They had one of the strongest, most reliable—awesomely reliable—marriages he'd ever known.

"We both did," said Joan Dennan. "Joan and Joan."

Gaunt swore to himself. "All right, John Milton's wife's cousin— tell me one thing more." The question had begun as barely a wisp of a doubt in his mind a few days before. In the last few hours, that wisp had become thundercloud sized. "How much are those Hartondee shares worth—for real?"

"I don't know—"

"Try guessing." It came out like a snarl.

"I can't, Jonny." She said it wearily. "John Milton can't. Their books seem right, the four hundred thousand offer they were ready to make to Florian Beck was generous without being wild—"

"Try."

"When Gladstone Baxter found out what I'd done, I thought he was going to faint." There was no humour in her voice. "I haven't seen the Hartondee file again since." The professional accountancy front cracked. "All right, there could be something more. Even a lot more. Hartondee should be called Midas. Anything it touches turns to gold."

Jonathan Gaunt said nothing. It hadn't been that way for Florian Beck.

CHAPTER 3

It was noon when he left the hotel and walked back along the lakeside towards the *Gasthaus*. There had been a subtle change in the weather. Although the day was still warm and the sun shone down through the trees, he saw small, white-crested waves rippling across the Tegernsee and it had taken on a steel-blue colour. The wind had shifted and was coming in light gusts from the mountains to the west, making the trees stir.

There were patches of grey cloud moving overhead by the time he reached the *Gasthaus*. The manager was alone at the reception desk, and gave a dutiful, not particularly friendly nod as Gaunt came in. Guests who seemed to act like a catalyst for troubles couldn't expect much more.

Gaunt went up to his room. With the door closed, he crossed to the window and looked out. Across the water, the hills were still bright and clear. But the distant alpine peaks were beginning to mist, and the brooding, dominating, Zugspitze had lost most of its crown.

The locals seemed to know what it meant. Only one launch was still out on the Tegernsee, and it was plugging in fast towards shelter. Down below him, a man was hauling a dinghy out of the water, winching it on a trailer. The sun canopy on the verandah restaurant had been brought in.

He had a feeling he'd know why soon enough. Turning away, Gaunt took more of the hotel notepaper and drafted a new version of his FAX message for Edinburgh. The new version was longer. It included the finds in Florian Beck's room, then reported Joan Dennan's arrival.

Henry Falconer would worry over that last part like a middle-aged dog given an unexpected bone. Gaunt grinned as he added his initials below the last line of the three sheets of FAX message. The Remembrancer's senior assistant shared at least one thing in common with

Kriminalinspektor Dieter Vogt. Falconer believed in checking every-thing—usually at least twice.

He took the message down to reception and saw it transmitted while he waited. That took under a minute.

"Charged to my room account," he instructed.

"*Ja*, Herr Gaunt." Maria, the young receptionist with the spectacles, was back on duty. She beckoned him nearer with a conspiratorial finger and lowered her voice. "My sister says you saw Fräulein Dennan. Fräulein Dennan made some telephone calls as soon as you left." She paused, dropping her voice to even more of a whisper. "Are you interested in something else she did?"

"I might be." Gaunt gave an uncommitted nod.

"She rented a car. To be delivered at two o'clock—no later." The girl flashed a quick smile and the paper money Gaunt laid on the reception counter somehow vanished. "*Danke*. The car will be a white Volkswagen. Fräulein Dennan didn't say why she wanted it."

"Don't let it worry you," said Gaunt dryly.

He turned away. By now, the FAX message could already be on Henry Falconer's desk in Scotland. It was a good time not to be available.

The wind from the mountains had begun snatching at anything loose by the time Gaunt collected his car and set it moving. He had about an hour to kill before Joan Dennan's car was due to be delivered, and he found a roadside sandwich bar at the far end of the village. He felt hungry enough to eat his way through two of the inevitable sausage sandwiches, washed them down with a beer while the rising wind began rattling the windows, then fought his way back through the gusts and into the car again.

At two o'clock he was parked three hundred yards from the Hotel Wald. His swaying car was being peppered by light dirt and twigs as the wind reached gale force.

Minutes after two, a white Volkswagen pulled up at the hotel and another car stopped behind it. The Volkswagen's driver, a man in overalls, hurried into the hotel with an envelope in his hand. He emerged again, got into the second car, and was driven away.

Joan Dennan came out soon after that. She was carrying a briefcase and she clutched a white gabardine coat around her shoulders as she made for the Volkswagen. Gaunt saw the way she had to struggle to open the door as it was caught by another howl of wind.

Then she was aboard. A brief plume of exhaust showed as the car started up, then she had the vehicle moving. It headed in the direction that Gaunt had taken when he had driven to the Scheckheim test track. It pulled away, accelerating briskly, confidently handled, weaving past two lumbering, heavily laden timber trucks. Swearing mildly, Gaunt started to do the same. Then, instead, he let his foot come right off the accelerator and allowed the Ford to slow as another vehicle appeared ahead.

The grey Mercedes, driven by a man, a fair-haired figure beside him in the front seat, seemed to appear out of nowhere. It tucked into the traffic, staying separate from Joan Dennan by just a few vehicles, seeming perfectly happy to keep to that distance.

Dieter Vogt had warned about a grey Mercedes carrying a man and a woman—Gaunt's attention was hauled back to his own vehicle as another timber truck blasted an air-horn from behind. He picked up the Ford's speed again and gestured an apology to the truck driver.

On ahead, Joan Dennan's white Volkswagen maintained the same smart pace through the traffic. Still keeping its distance, the Mercedes did the same—and Gaunt attached himself, convoy-style, another few vehicles back from the Mercedes. For the moment, he couldn't think what else he could do. It mattered to find out where Joan Dennan was going, it mattered as least as much to find out anything he could about the couple in the Mercedes.

At the same spacing, still travelling into the teeth of the same gale of wind, the three vehicles kept on. Gaunt saw where a high-sided delivery van had blown off the road and was lying on its side in a ditch with the driver climbing out of his cab. He passed a house which had shingles peeled from its roof then another which had smashed chimney pots lying on the road and a broken TV aerial dish halfway through a front window.

The sun had vanished behind thick, racing cloud, and the road was a litter of debris. Every now and then a gust stronger than the rest would clutch at the Ford and send it lurching and swaying.

But Joan Dennan kept going, and the Mercedes kept going. Except that the traffic had now thinned, until it was almost non-existent— and Joan Dennan had just passed the turn-off sign for the Scheckheim valley, was still driving at the same confident pace on a road that led straight towards Austria, or towards Garmisch Partenkirchen —to the hotel where Bessie King was staying.

The Volkswagen and the Mercedes had both rounded a bend ahead. Another shriek of wind clawed at Gaunt's Ford, some spots of rain spattered across the glass in front of him as he accelerated to catch up with the other vehicles.

The Ford rounded the bend. They had been climbing, now the road dropped away, winding through trees and rocks, and he caught a glimpse of the Volkswagen far ahead. In the distance, there was a blackness where the road plunged into a tunnel.

But he couldn't see the Mercedes. What the hell had happened to it?

The answer came as a sudden flicker in his rear-view mirror as the Mercedes emerged from a narrow forestry road he had just passed. Within seconds that big, distinctive radiator grille was growing in Gaunt's mirror, coming after him in the kind of way that meant only one thing. He'd been spotted, they'd been waiting for their chance to switch places, and now they were behind him and they wanted rid of him.

He shoved his accelerator hard on the floor, but a moment later the Mercedes nudged the Ford in the rear, then Gaunt was fighting with the steering wheel to stay on the road. Briefly, the Mercedes had fallen back. But it was starting to come on . . . as Gaunt brought the Ford under control again and avoided a postal bus travelling in the opposite direction. The bus went past as a blur.

For another few seconds he even had time to see the white Volkswagen still in the distance. Then the Mercedes hit the Ford again, a crunch of an angled impact which almost set the smaller vehicle spinning.

Again he fought the shuddering steering wheel to keep control, and again he somehow won and kept on the winding downhill highway. There was a bang, as something came loose and fell from the back of the little car. That big radiator grille was beginning to fill his rear-view mirror once more, and the car behind him was twice as heavy, probably twice as powerful.

Weaving the Ford protectively, Gaunt felt his mouth dry as the two vehicles clawed their way round a shaking bend. Be pushed off the road here, and it could be a long way down through trees or scrub or rock.

It wasn't thinking time any more. He let his reflexes take over, and suddenly he was back in the hellhole that was Parachute Regiment combat training, the kind of hellhole where they used only live ammunition and where the training sergeant had been knitted out of razor-wire pickled in battery acid. They had learned to hate the man with a deep and total fervour, but the angry screaming of his voice had left some strange fragments of wisdom etched forever in Gaunt's mind.

One was simple. "When your enemy thinks he's winning, that's when he gets careless. That's your best chance to kick him in the crotch. So try! What the hell have you got to lose?"

Part of the answer was there already. He caught glimpses of it through the trees as it toiled up the winding road towards him. A big, bright blue truck, it was a massive eight-wheeler with a load under a blue canvas cover. A steady coughing of dark exhaust smoke was coming from the chromed exhaust stack mounted behind the driver's cab.

What he might be able to do—

It became what he had to do as the Mercedes thumped the Ford's rear and he heard more metal crumple while the rented car lurched.

The truck had vanished behind another patch of trees. But his Ford would meet it within the next minute—and as the big truck appeared in the open again the Mercedes behind eased back a fraction. It was as if the driver had decided to let the eight-wheeler pass before he finished things with Gaunt.

What Jonathan Gaunt had to do needed cold, computer accuracy— if he could do it at all. The approaching truck had an Austrian registration, he could see that the driver had a moustache and was wearing a woollen cap, that someone had wired a yellow plastic duck to the truck's roof . . .

There is only one certain way to induce a vehicle into a total rear-wheel skid, then take precise control. The control method is not the driving manual steer-into-your-skid way, which is for all sane drivers with any road room to spare. It is the other choice labelled Keep Away unless the driver is a tutored professional. Gaunt had been put through the sequence as a pupil around cones on an airport runway.

But never for real.

Like now—

Braking hard, he swung the steering wheel and felt the whole vehicle lurch and shudder on its suspension as rubber screamed and the coarse rear-wheel skid began.

Like now—

Foot lifted off the accelerator, he swung the wheel hard for a second time, but now against the skid—and the Ford began a wild spin. The Mercedes was there somewhere but he was too busy to care what it was doing.

Less than two seconds into the spin. Now. He hauled hard on the

handbrake to lock the rear wheels. The Ford bucked. Now. He released the handbrake as fiercely as he'd hauled it on. Now. Suddenly,
the little car was in a total, tyre screaming, sideways slide and its tail
was going to take the rocks on the nearside verge.

But the Mercedes was in much more trouble. The driver had
braked, had skidded, had steered wildly then had over-corrected as
he tried to avoid what had one moment been his certain kill but now
had become something lethal which threatened a head-on impact.

The grey Mercedes clipped the Ford's nose then swung across the
road while the blue truck tried to swerve. Gaunt saw the impact.
Then his Ford was continuing its slowing four-wheel sideways slide
until it crunched lightly, almost gently, into the rocks at the roadside.

His engine stalled, then the car was stationary. For moments he
didn't even try to move. His legs felt like jelly, he had to get used to
the fact he was still alive. He could hear the wind clawing round his
car's damaged bodywork and the exhaust was already beginning to
crackle as it cooled. Suddenly, a torrential lash of rain came out of
nowhere, raked everything around, then ended within seconds.

That was when Gaunt discovered his driver's door had jammed. He
opened it with a kick, clambered out into the chill of the hillside, and
was battered by a new shriek of wind.

He stared.

It wasn't what he'd wanted, it wasn't what he'd expected. The big
blue eight-wheeler had partly jackknifed across the road, blocking it.
Only the rear of the grey Mercedes was visible, protruding out from
the underside of the truck, behind the cab. The rest of the car was a
mangle of wreckage embedded under the truck's chassis.

The truck driver came out of his cab. A fat little man with the wool
cap still on his head, he was white-faced and shaking. He looked at
Gaunt, then turned and took a few reluctant steps towards the Mercedes. His mouth and that little moustache quivered, and he crossed
himself. Then he walked across to the nearest of the big roadside
rocks, leaned against it, and vomited.

A car was coming down the hill towards them. An Opel, it arrived,
braked and stopped, but Gaunt ignored both it and the weather as he
walked over to the embedded Mercedes.

He looked inside the wrecked car, then wished he hadn't. The steel
frame of the truck's chassis had acted like a giant guillotine, neatly
shearing off every part of the Mercedes above steering wheel level.
Both occupants were dead. The driver had been decapitated, and it

might have been better if his passenger had been. The passenger hadn't been a woman, but another man with long, blond hair.

Gaunt heard hurrying footsteps, looked round, then gave a small nod of recognition. It seemed natural enough that the first driver to arrive, coming from her unmarked police car, should be Dieter Vogt's copper-haired sergeant. She wore a civilian ski-jacket over a sweater and trousers, and she reached him with one hand nursing the holstered automatic pistol strapped to her right hip.

She saw what Gaunt had seen, then turned away quickly and drew a deep breath.

"Lieber Gott," she said in quiet, tight voice. She looked over at Gaunt, then at his car, and moistened her lips. "Are you hurt?"

He shook his head. "I'm all right."

"I radioed for help. An emergency team will be here soon." She had very green eyes, and she was staring at him in near disbelief. "I —I saw what happened."

Gaunt remembered her name. "And what the hell were you doing, Krissa?"

"Following you." She shrugged, her tanned, attractive face still pale. "I was supposed to keep an eye on this Fräulein Dennan. If I could, I was also to make sure you stayed out of trouble." A brief, harsh gust of wind and rain lashed the road, and she clutched the collar of her ski-jacket. It was white, with two broad red bands. "I didn't do either thing very well, did I?"

He didn't answer. The truck driver had taken a few steps towards them but then the man seemed to change his mind. He stopped beside his truck's radiator, sheltering there.

"I was slow." Her voice was bitter. "Even if our *verdammt* Kriminalinspektor Vogt often expects miracles. I was following you, because you were following the woman." Pausing, she looked back at the wrecked remains of the Mercedes. *"Ja,* and I knew about these people from yesterday. But I didn't realize it was the same car—not until I saw them try to put you off the road. I'm sorry."

Gaunt gave her a wry grin. "Look on the bright side, sergeant. I didn't get killed—and you should make a good witness."

Other vehicles were beginning to arrive, from both directions. They stopped short of the crash scene and some of the drivers made a cautious approach. Another blue eight-wheeler arrived. The driver jumped out and ran to where his companion waited. They hugged each other in relief.

"I didn't mean it to be this way," said Gaunt. Aloud this time.

Krissa looked puzzled for a moment. Then she understood, and shrugged.

"Bitte, tell that to my brother. He'll have to cope with the paperwork from this," she said in a dry, factual voice. "He doesn't like paperwork, not our Dieter." Then she saw Gaunt's expression and swore softly under her breath. "He didn't tell you? I'm our dear *Kriminalinspektor's* baby sister. I thought, as you were a friend—"

Gaunt shook his head.

"He keeps me hidden. All last winter he had me posted to one of the border ski-patrol teams." She glanced at her wristwatch. "Get used to waiting, Herr Jonny. This is going to take its own time to sort out."

It did. It was a process that began with the arrival of two more police cars, then a big four-wheel-drive emergency vehicle and its crew, closely followed by an ambulance and a medical team. The cars and trucks beginning to queue on both sides of the crash site were kept under control, the emergency crew screened off the smashed Mercedes with flapping, tied-down canvas as soon as they had taken a video tape of the entire location, and Gaunt had to watch as the battered, rented Ford was ignominiously shoved off the road. It was too damaged to be driven, it would have to be hauled away.

The medical team left. They had managed to find a live patient, the truck driver. He had decided he was suffering from shock, and was insisting on a hospital check. At the same time as he was taken away, the road was opened enough to allow a controlled flow of traffic through in steady dribbles.

Part of the time, Gaunt waited in the shelter of Krissa Vogt's police car. While the newcomers took over, she used the radio to pass some brief messages then produced a flask of coffee. It was hot, it was welcome, and though he caught those green eyes considering him carefully more than once, she said little.

But at least the weather improved. In a matter of minutes, with no particular warning, the rain and dark clouds vanished and the wind stilled. Once again, the air felt warm and there was blue sky and sunlight. The skyline of hills and their backing mountains firmed. There were insects and there were birds.

Then there was also Kriminalinspektor Dieter Vogt. He arrived in one car, driving alone, and was followed by another car filled with plain-clothes men. Some were technicians, who produced their specialist kits from their vehicle. Gaunt was left in isolation, Vogt talked with his sister, then all the new arrivals disappeared behind the canvas screen.

At last, Vogt emerged alone. He waited until there was a break in the single-file traffic going past, crossed over, and marched purposefully to where Gaunt was standing. His dark hair was tousled, his plump face pale but still resolute.

"The inside of that Mercedes is like a butcher's shop." Vogt made it a blunt, factual comment. "You were lucky—even if your car looks like it was attacked with a tin-opener." He paused and pursed his lips. "According to my sergeant—"

"Your sister." Gaunt nodded.

"*Ja,* my sister." Vogt grimaced. "I meant to tell you about her last night. I forgot, she says she told you—she often talks too much." He brushed a foot along the gravel-like soil they stood on. "Jonny, have I got your word that you're not holding back on this?"

"My word." Gaunt nodded.

"So." Vogt scowled across at the jack-knifed truck, the embedded car, and the canvas screen. "You were following the Dennan woman, this pair were doing the same—then they spotted you. After that, you've a witness." He sighed. "That piece of trick driving of yours seems to have been impressive—and effective. Luck?"

"Luck." Gaunt pointed towards the canvas screen. "What about them? Who were they?"

"They had some identification in their pockets. We'll need fingerprint checks with our records to be sure—you saw why." The dark-haired Bavarian hesitated, then relented. "Conrad Hass and Heine Norden, both in what the Americans like to call the "hired gun" league. Known criminals."

"Drugs?"

"Sometimes. Whatever work is going. Both based in Stuttgart—like our late friend Beck. Both armed. Norden"—Vogt drew a graphic hand across his throat—"that one, the driver, had a nine-millimetre Heckler and Koch automatic pistol. Hass had a Beretta, and there is a Mauser rifle with telescopic sights hidden under the rear seat. Professionals, Jonny. But nothing to tell us who was paying the wage bill."

"What about the car?"

"I said they were professionals," reminded Vogt wearily. "The licence plate details match with a grey Mercedes registered in Bonn. Except that particular grey Mercedes is still in Bonn, and the one we have here has different engine and chassis numbers."

Gaunt nodded. It was the way professional car thieves operated.

Steal a car to match one you already knew about. Just never let the match-ups meet. That way, police checks were deflected. It was a much more sophisticated affair than using a fake plate which in reality belonged to someone's farm truck. Any half-educated computer caught that one first time.

"But neither of them was our hotel thief?"

"Different trades, Jonny." Dieter Vogt paused as something caught his eye. For a moment his face brightened, and he pointed.

A large brown hawk was planing across the face of the hill, wings outspread, riding some minor thermal of air. Compact, hovering power, it suddenly folded its wings and went into an arrow-straight dive. It disappeared among the high rocks.

"Lunch," said Dieter Vogt enviously. "More than I've had today." Reluctantly, he shifted his attention back to what mattered. "Our immediate priorities are those fingerprint identification checks, and to get the weapons to ballistics. I also want to know where these two have been located—we've been trying for that since they were spotted yesterday, now we will try a lot harder." He looked directly at Gaunt. "What about Fräulein Dennan?"

"I know why she's here." Gaunt told him the story.

"Do you believe her?"

"Until I'm proved wrong."

"*Ja.* That's being reasonable. But are *Polizei* supposed to be reasonable?" Vogt sighed. "You say the men in the Mercedes were following her. We don't know why—"

"But the 'where' might be to see Bessie King."

"I would put money on it," growled Dieter Vogt. "I was at Scheckheim, with the SPO team. My plan was I'd go on from there to Bessie King's hotel and talk with her again." He stirred at the ground again with the toe of his shoe. "But when I telephoned to arrange it, the woman said she'd meet me at Scheckheim. Someone else was already coming to see her, then could drive her over."

"Someone who could be Joan Dennan." Gaunt nodded.

"Then they wouldn't have to return this way to get to Scheckheim. There's a shorter more direct route." Vogt scraped a thumb along the faint dark stubble on his chin, and gave one of his surprise boyish grins. "Jonny, I'll fix for your car to be collected, then I'll give you a lift to Scheckheim. On the way, we can talk about the very short, very simple statement you're somehow going to make to cover all of this."

"How short?"

"Very short," pleaded Dieter Vogt. "For my sake, okay?"

They crossed over to his car. On the way he spoke briefly to his sister, who listened, nodded, then gave Gaunt a slight smile before she turned away.

"About Krissa." Vogt was slightly embarrassed as they got into his car. "We've an agreement. When we're working, we're not family. There are times when it helps."

"What about afterwards?" asked Gaunt.

"Then she gives me hell," said Vogt.

He set his car moving.

The main road was clogged with delayed traffic, but once Vogt reached the Scheckheim turn-off they made good time. Very soon, Gaunt saw the test track boundary fence ahead and began spotting some of the features that he'd been guided round by Florian Beck just twenty-four hours earlier.

Yet now Beck was dead, and so were two other men.

He watched the road in silence and Vogt left him in peace. The security guard at the main gate was still replaced by armed police, but they were waved straight through, and Vogt pointed his car towards the SPO base.

"I forgot," he said suddenly, and slowed. "This is Thursday, right?"

"All day," agreed Gaunt politely.

"Danke." Vogt grinned. "Thursday afternoon is when they crash cars at Scheckheim—production cars as well as the *Erlkönige* disguised cars. We can go round that way. You don't mind after—ah— your own happening?"

"It sounds fun," said Gaunt sarcastically.

"It's also where we could find Bessie King and your lady accountant," said Beck practically. He winked. "Anyway, maybe you can pick up some tips for next time."

The car turned in the opposite direction, heading away from the SPO base. Then Vogt slowed again and they crawled past a line of cars of different shapes and makes, all waiting in a patient queue. Along the line, drivers stood gossiping beside their charges. There were mechanics in white overalls, technicians of all kinds, and a duty team of firemen ready around a fire tender.

"Over there," said Vogt, nodding ahead.

Gaunt saw what looked like a series of giant blocks of concrete, each block the size of a single-storey house, each with its own surround of tarmac, its monitoring bunkers, and its people.

A car was moving on one of the nearer tracks, travelling with cables linking it to a control console, picking up speed, with no one aboard, heading straight for one of the giant blocks.

"Here we go," said Vogt mildly.

Gaunt stared. The car was a gleaming British-made Jaguar, one of the top-range models with a price tag that went well beyond his salary for a year. It didn't slow, it didn't stop. It hit the concrete block head-on with a smash of glass and a crumple of metal, and technicians moved in. A low-loader truck was waiting to remove the damaged test vehicle.

"Thursday afternoons," said Vogt cheerfully. "It's a tradition."

He saw Gaunt's expression. "Thirty-five tonnes of concrete, Jonny. And you thought you had worries?" He shrugged. "They come here, they crash-test their own cars, they crash-test rival cars, they study the films and recordings."

"What happens to the wrecks?" Gaunt watched another car being lined up near them. It was a Nissan, but there wasn't a Japanese face in sight.

"More research. They get cut up, then scrapped." Vogt broke off. Further along, a catapult launcher banged and a Volvo pick-up was thrown sideways against another of the concrete blocks. "Anyway, some aren't all they seem—maybe no seats, or no trim. Maybe no window glass. Others"—he grimaced—"the whole works, they've got everything aboard. It makes no difference. This is the killing ground, survival time. They check their own ideas, or take a good look at what the other fellow has begun selling."

"Get me the scrapyard concession, and I'd be happy." Gaunt sighed as the Jaguar, newly winched on its low-loader, was quickly covered over. "I know a mechanic who does a nice line in rebuilds." Then he stopped there, nudged Vogt, and thumbed over to their left.

Dieter Vogt's guess had been correct. Two of the SPO test cars were there, and Joan Dennan's Volkswagen was parked beside them. She was standing in front of it and Bessie King was still in the passenger seat. Some of the SPO team were talking to them.

"Now," agreed Dieter Vogt.

The police car weaved its way back and round, stopped, then both men got out and walked over. Somewhere down the line an engine screamed to peak revolutions then faded back again. As it stopped, another engine began. The air smelled of exhaust fumes and a rider cruised past on a lightweight motorcycle with a six-pack of soft drinks under one arm.

Joan Dennan saw them coming. She gave Gaunt a wary smile of recognition, then looked at Vogt.

"This is the *Kriminalinspektor* handling the Beck murder inquiry." Gaunt went through the introductions, with Dieter Vogt wearing his totally formal, totally attentive face. Then Gaunt told them, "I'll leave you to talk. I want to speak with Bessie King—"

"But gently," murmured Vogt. "I'll take over when you finish."

There were still two people in SPO overalls at the Volkswagen's passenger window, but they faded back as Gaunt went round to the driver's door and opened it. Getting in behind the wheel, closing the door again, he faced the grey-haired woman.

"A few minutes, Bessie. A few things I want to ask," he said quietly. "All right by you?"

"Yes." She looked tired, but she gave a small, firm nod. The woman who would have married Florian Beck if he had lived still had the same basic air of stunned loss and grief as before. But she was trying. She was wearing a dark grey jacket and skirt over a white shirt-blouse. Her hair had been brushed, and she had used a faint touch of lipstick. Maybe the tears still weren't far away, but she was holding them in firm check. "Ask."

"Mostly, they're about Florian." Gaunt paused just long enough to see her nod again. "You knew he had some dangerous friends. Did he talk names?"

"Never names. Just places—he'd be in touch with the Frankfurt man, the Munich man, labels like that." Bessie King had somehow aged in the last few hours. One way it showed was in her voice. "He knew the risks, he said if he was careful then he was too small to matter." She looked at Gaunt more closely. "I heard that you'd been in a road accident."

"There were two men in the other car," Gaunt told her unemotionally. "They weren't so lucky. But they may have been involved in Florian's murder. There could have been others."

"Then damn them all," said Bessie King softly. There was a sudden burst of noise outside as another test car impacted on a concrete block, but she ignored it. Spreading her fingers apart, she rested both hands lightly on the Volkswagen's fascia. "I hope they burn in hell."

"Bessie." Gaunt touched her lightly under the chin and gently turned her face so that her eyes met his. "Hiding what you know isn't going to bring him back. You know what I'm talking about, don't you?"

"Yes." She sighed. "Maybe I was trying to protect him. But I can't, not any more."

"So go back before last night," suggested Gaunt. "How much did he know about the size of his Hartondee inheritance before I arrived?"

"In detail?" She shook her head. "Nothing. But someone else contacted him, and said that whatever he was told it was worth, he was to wait. There could be a better offer."

"Someone?" Deliberately, Gaunt looked out to where Joan Dennan was talking earnestly to Dieter Vogt. "Man or woman?"

"A man. Florian thought he was English or American."

"After the income tax calls?" guessed Gaunt.

She shook her head. "There were no income tax calls. Florian invented them—he was trying to find out from you who else could know what was going on."

"The same way he had one of his little friends break into my hotel room?"

"Willi." Bessie King almost smiled. She nodded. "I've met Willi. I know about his ammonia spray trick—but otherwise, he's frightened by his own shadow. Florian told him you weren't to be hurt, no matter what happened."

"I'm glad," said Gaunt caustically. He sighed, glanced out at the continuing, noisy bustle all around, and turned back to the grey-haired woman. "Then what about last night, Bessie? What's the truth?"

"I don't know." She said it earnestly, shifting in her seat so that she faced him squarely. "He took that telephone call when we were at the restaurant. Maybe"—she chewed her lip for a moment—"maybe I should have realized he was frightened, not just worried when he came back to the table."

"What was the call really about?"

She shook her head. "I told the police what he told me—that you wanted to see him, and it couldn't wait."

"Could he have been lying?"

Bessie King gave a small, resigned shrug. "One thing you have to understand about Florian is that I got used to him being a liar. Outside of his work, the truth didn't matter too much to him—particularly if it got in the way."

"One minute he was talking marriage with you," reminded Gaunt, letting the words sink home. "The next, you're being talked into being dumped back at your hotel. Something happened, Bessie. Who would frighten him enough to make him act that way?" He saw the question failing, changed it. "Or was there anyone he could feel he could rely on, would go to meet—maybe about something he didn't want you to know about?"

"It was important." She chewed her lip again. "It wasn't work—the SPO car tests were going well. He'd talked about our own futures, and he seemed happy. It—it just had to be something about this damned Scottish legacy." Suddenly, Bessie's voice was tight and bitter and there was anger in her eyes. "That money was like a dream come true —nobody told us it would turn into a nightmare. It's going to be my nightmare, for the rest of my life."

"I know about nightmares." Gaunt made it a harsh, flat statement. She sighed, then unexpectedly went back to his question.

"If it was important, he would trust Willi—"

"His hotel thief?"

Bessie King nodded. "Willi Dorn. He may be hard to find. But your police inspector friend should know his name and can try."

"He will," promised Gaunt. "But what about you, Bessie? What will you do?"

Bessie pursed her lips and spent a moment looking out towards the line-up of cars and the people in overalls moving around them. "Stay with the kind of life I know about, at least for now. I'm Irish. When it matters, we're a practical people—and that means I won't rush into anything new." She nodded where Joan Dennan and Dieter Vogt were still in earnest discussion a short distance away. Vogt was frowning. "She asked me the same thing."

"I didn't tell her to see you." Gaunt said it grimly. "I'm sorry, Bessie."

"No need." She gave that same odd half-smile again and let herself settle deeper into the seat. "She told me she wanted to help, any way she could—and why she'd come out here. I'm not soft-hearted, Jonny —and neither is any young woman who gets to be a chartered accountant by profession. But I know she feels that if she hadn't started this, in the beginning, then Florian would still be alive."

"What did you say?"

"I told her not to be a fool." Bessie King left it there. Someone from one of the other test teams was tapping on the window, looking in. She glanced at Gaunt. "Is there anything else?"

He shook his head, reached for the door handle, and left her. Out in the open the noise and hustle were continuing all around. He heard a roar of laughter and saw where someone's car had just finished its test impact into one of the concrete blocks. It hadn't so much crashed as disintegrated. One front wheel was bouncing on the tarmac some distance away, the other had torn loose and was spinning like a top.

"Herr Gaunt." An apologetic voice brought him round and he saw one of the SPO technicians he'd met the day before. The man came nearer and gave an embarrassed gesture. *"Bitte.* The way we're keeping working means no disrespect to Florian Beck. We liked him, but none of us was a close friend—except for Frau King, of course. We have to finish these tests on schedule, or it costs a lot of money."

"I understand." Gaunt nodded, and the man made a quick retreat.

Dieter Vogt was still with Joan Dennan. The dark-haired Bavarian ended their conversation as Gaunt arrived, and thumbed towards the Volkswagen.

"How is she?" he asked.

"Wanting to tell you a few things," said Gaunt obliquely.

Vogt raised an interested eyebrow. "The things we wondered about?"

"Some of them," agreed Gaunt. "But—"

"Go easy on her?" Vogt sighed and gave a slight wink at Joan Dennan. "Do I look like I'd growl and show my teeth? I'll be gentle— that's a promise."

He left them, striding off towards the Volkswagen, and Gaunt considered Joan Dennan quizzically.

"You didn't waste any time getting out to see Bessie King." He saw her flush, and took some of the edge from his voice. "Joan, nobody's blaming you for any of this."

"Thank you." She thawed a little.

They were both silenced as another car engine accelerated to a screaming peak of noise. After a long, almost deafening howl, it came to a sudden halt again and an ominous cloud of dark, oily smoke began rising skywards.

"What about the *Polizei?"* Gaunt indicated the Volkswagen, where Dieter had begun talking with Bessie. "Any problems?"

"No." She shook her head. "He was nice about things."

"Don't let him hear that." Gaunt chuckled a little. "It wouldn't please him."

"He also told me about these two men—that they started off following me. I asked him why—"

"And we don't know," said Gaunt flatly.

"But it had to involve Florian Beck?"

"Beck, yes." Gaunt heard the tension in her voice, saw the question that was coming. "But it doesn't have to have been about the Hartondee shares. He had his own problems."

"Bessie told me." Joan Dennan stood silent for a moment, then took a deep breath. Suddenly, she was the professional accountant again, her manner crisply businesslike, the faint mid-Atlantic accent back in place. "There's nothing left for me in Bavaria with Beck dead. I suppose my boss and the Hartondee board will need to wait until your Remembrancer decides if there's anyone else entitled to inherit."

"Which could take long enough." That wasn't necessarily true, but Gaunt decided to err on the cautious side. In more ways than one, it could do no harm. "There might be someone waiting under a stone somewhere. It might end up the way I warned you."

"Royal housekeeping money." Joan Dennan grimaced at the thought and brushed a strand of hair blown over her eyes by a light gust of wind. "Anyway, I'll probably get a flight back tomorrow."

"Edinburgh?" asked Gaunt.

"There's an early flight from Munich to London." She nibbled at her lip, thinking. "There's someone I'd like to see in London, then I can get an afternoon Heathrow–Edinburgh shuttle. I'll probably do it that way."

"I'll be in touch," said Gaunt.

"I'm relying on it." She gave him a wry smile. "I need all the help I can get. You kept that card I gave you?"

He nodded.

"Let me see it." Gaunt produced the card and she took out a small ballpoint pen, then wrote quickly on the back of the card. "That's my home phone number. It's not in the book—some of my clients think a female accountant should be available for some non-deductible after-hours activities. I'm not." Joan Dennan put the pen away and gave him back the card. "I'm not usually around at weekends. Otherwise—I mean it. I want to stay with this."

"Where will you be this evening?" he asked.

"Your police inspector friend wants a formal statement. After that, I've promised Bessie King I'll be with her." She paused. "When will you head back to the Remembrancer's Office?"

"Some time over the weekend." He still wasn't certain himself.

"Good." Joan Dennan sounded relieved. "Your police inspector says he'll be glad when I leave—and that I shouldn't take any risks while I'm still here." Suddenly, surprising him, she clutched his arm. "Maybe you should do the same, Jonny."

"Maybe I will," he agreed.

She said something in reply, but her words were lost in the noise as the next test vehicle slammed into the nearest concrete block.

It was another fifteen minutes before Vogt emerged from the Volkswagen. He looked round, saw Gaunt, and beckoned.

"You were right. She admits she lied, she swears what we're getting now is the truth." Vogt's chubby face was angry. "But I did like I promised you, I treated her gently."

"What about this tame thief, Willi Dorn?"

"Dorn is the man I'd thought about all along. He won't be easy to locate." Vogt looked back at the Volkswagen and swore under his breath. "Women! They're just naturally devious."

"Does that include the one you're planning to marry?" asked Gaunt mildly.

"Maybe not all women," said Vogt uneasily. "Most. Or some. Better?"

"Safer," suggested Gaunt.

"*Ja.*" Vogt sighed. "The one thing she asked me was when we'd be able to release Beck's body for burial." He shook his head. "It could take time. I told her that, and she didn't like it."

A new burst of activity was going on near them. The last test-crash vehicle was being hauled away, while a girl with a video camera kept recording. The car had no maker's badges. From the state of the wreckage, the precaution was probably justified. Gaunt looked around for Joan, and saw she had already returned to Bessie at the Volkswagen.

"I'm almost finished here," said Vogt, as if reading his mind. He looked around himself, then waved, and shouted. "Franz!"

The big, middle-aged sergeant usually seen with him trotted quickly towards them. Drawing the man to one side, Vogt spoke briefly. Franz listened, asked a question of his own, nodded at Vogt's answer, then strode off again.

"Do I ask if he's your brother?" asked Gaunt.

"Having a sister like Krissa is enough." Vogt grinned at the thought. "Franz will mop up the statements we need around here—the ones we haven't got already. None of them are going to be much help—the security around here has more holes in it than a rabbit warren." He paused and sucked his lips. "I'll get Krissa to deal with the two women later. That leaves you—and I'll deal with you. There's something I want you to see, then I'll drive you back to Rottach and we can sort things out."

Gaunt nodded his thanks. They walked back to Vogt's car, got aboard, and he set it moving. They travelled only as far as the main gate, then stopped again. Gaunt followed Vogt over to a brick single-storey office building, in through a door, and past a worried-looking security guard. A supervisor appeared and led the way into an office where a television screen was already showing a freeze frame of the Scheckheim main gate by night. The shot was timed at a few minutes after midnight.

"Watch this, Jonny," said Vogt unemotionally. "You'll find it interesting."

He signalled the supervisor, the man tapped a switch, and the picture on the monitor came to life. A vehicle was approaching the gate from outside, headlights blazing. As it neared the gate, the barrier pole went up—and Florian Beck's old Porsche swept through without slowing. It was impossible to say who had been driving. It was equally impossible to say if anyone else had been aboard.

"Danke," said Vogt curtly.

The picture froze again. The supervisor gave an apologetic shake of his head.

"Scheckheim's security was not at its sharpest last night," said Vogt. "Certain people have already been disciplined."

From the way the supervisor's mouth tightened, Gaunt had the impression that was an understatement. But the security video camera on the main gate had been recording all the hours of darkness. The tape had already been checked and rechecked. Every vehicle it recorded was known—even if most had simply been waved through.

"We're impounding the tape as evidence." Vogt scowled at the supervisor again. "The reason security was slack last night is simple. There was a *verdammt* football match on TV, then a John Wayne western. They were too busy watching to care about anything as unimportant as work."

The supervisor avoided looking at them and said nothing.

They left him and went back to Vogt's car. Before they started off, the Bavarian reached into the glove box, produced a chocolate bar, broke it in half, and gave one part to Gaunt.

"My lunch," he said bleakly, stuffed his half of the chocolate bar into his mouth, and set the car moving again.

It was 5 P.M. by the time they reached the little police station at Rottach. Then the inevitable procedural routines common to police anywhere took over.

Dieter Vogt had a backroom office which apparently doubled as the local mountain rescue team base. Large-scale maps covered most of the wall space with spectacular photographs of alpine peaks pinned up around them. There were lists of emergency telephone numbers, there were call-out team roster sheets, and someone's old climbing boots protruded from under a cupboard. Vogt cleared a chair for Gaunt by dumping its pile of paperwork on the floor, shouted to a passing orderly to bring them coffee, slammed shut an opened window which overlooked the *Polizeiamt's* rear yard, and fed a clean sheet of paper into his typewriter.

"We can start where your previous statement ended. We can call it Part Two," he suggested acidly. "That way, it makes life easier for us both. Agreed?"

They began, then the telephone rang. The call was from the police ballistics laboratory in Munich. They had received the Heckler and Koch pistol recovered from the wrecked Mercedes. It still had to be test-fired, but was almost certainly the gun used to murder Florian Beck.

They managed another couple of sentences of Gaunt's statement, then the telephone rang again. The bodies of the two dead men, recovered from the Mercedes, had been delivered to the Rottach district mortuary. How soon did Vogt need an autopsy report?

As Vogt finished that call, the orderly arrived with coffee and a mound of thick meat sandwiches. They managed a little more of the statement before a messenger brought in a telex slip. Willi Dorn, hotel thief, was absent from his usual locations around Munich. He had disappeared some time the previous week, after telling friends he was doing "a favour for a friend."

Then it was back to the statement again, and it went on that way. By the time the last sheet came out of Vogt's typewriter and Gaunt signed it, they had positive fingerprint confirmation. The two dead men were the Stuttgart professionals, Conrad Hass and Heine Norden, matching the papers they'd been carrying. But Stuttgart also reported back that both Hass and Norden frequently operated in the Munich area, and that Munich was now trying to locate where they might have been living.

There was more—it just seemed to keep coming. A *Bundeskriminalamt* technician appeared, in his shirt sleeves and drinking soup from a mug, and solemnly took Gaunt's fingerprints for elimination purposes. With a general clatter of noise, a truck off-loaded the torn metal which had once been the grey Mercedes. Now wrapped like a parcel in anonymous black sheeting and yellow nylon climbing rope, it was dumped in a corner of the rear yard. Vogt's sister had driven back as an escort. Gaunt saw her park beside the other police vehicles, and within a couple of moments she came into her brother's office.

"Krissa?" Dieter Vogt made it both a greeting and a question.

Sergeant Krissa Vogt looked at her brother, then at Gaunt. She dumped a clear plastic evidence bag on Dieter's desk and helped herself to one of the last of the sandwiches.

"I brought everything from their pockets, and everything personal from the car." Her strong white teeth took a first bite at the sandwich, and she chewed for a moment. *"Ja,* and it was messy."

"When you stop eating I'll start worrying," said Vogt with a grin.

He took a large sheet of clean paper, spread it on the desk, then emptied the bag over it.

There were two wristwatches, one of them with a smashed glass and casing. There were two wallets, there was small change, there were keys, a springblade knife, and a small bone-handled pocket knife. There were handkerchiefs, a short length of string, and all the other normal, everyday items that could have been expected. Some had dried stains that looked like blood. There were other stains that Gaunt decided not to ask about.

Vogt glanced up at his sister. "Krissa, anything here we didn't find first time?"

"More money." She leaned forward and used the sandwich as a pointer at a wad of high-denomination banknotes. "Ten thousand Deutschmarks—hidden under the front carpet, passenger side."

"Why carry that much around?" Vogt scowled.

"Expenses?" suggested Gaunt.

The telephone rang again. Vogt sighed, scooped up the receiver, listened, raised a startled eyebrow, then reached for a pencil and notepad.

"Bitte . . ." He made the caller start again and began scribbling as he listened. The scowl stayed, but became puzzled at the edges. At last he thanked the caller, hung up, and just looked at his hands for a moment while he cursed softly and carefully.

"Trouble?" asked Gaunt.

"Ja. What have you got me into, Jonny?" asked Vogt sadly. "Did I ever do you any real harm?"

"Dieter—" Krissa made it a plea.

"Get my car round front," said Vogt. He indicated Gaunt. "I'm taking him with me—he might be useful." He tore the top sheet from the notepad and stuffed it into his pocket. "While we're away, I want everyone trying for Willi Dorn, I want everyone pushing for any recent sightings of Hass or Norden or their car—or who was with them."

"We've got one already?" guessed Krissa Vogt.

Vogt nodded, wrote quickly on the notepad again, and shoved it towards her. "That's where we'll be. A next best to positive identification, and they were there twice. Each time, they met with the same people." His gaze switched to Gaunt. "A man and woman, middle-aged, looked like tourists, driving a Volkswagen—both believed English."

Gaunt and Krissa stared at him.

"Get that car round front, sergeant," snarled Vogt. He sat silent while his sister went out, then used a finger to stir through the collection of items in front of him. "Jonny, I wish you had found your *verdammt* Hartondee heir somewhere else—anywhere else. What makes these shares so special?"

Gaunt shook his head. But he was going to have to find out, as soon as he could.

It was dusk outside, darkness closing in from the hills. They didn't have to travel far, just a few kilometres along the road which wound beside the east shore of the Tegernsee. Where they stopped, there was only a small restaurant and filling station. The restaurant had half a dozen tables and the filling station amounted to three pumps, one of them for diesel. It was a husband and wife operation, with their house located behind the restaurant.

The woman was a little, bird-like person with a chirping voice to match. But she did the talking while her husband, tall and good-looking but suffering from what looked like the aftermath of a stroke, contented himself to regular nods of agreement.

The two men with the grey Mercedes had visited the restaurant twice—the woman remembered the car, which she'd admired, and the fact that one of the men had such long, fair hair. Each time, the middle-aged English couple had been there. The first time, the men from the Mercedes had only shared a table for a short time with the English couple. That had been three days before. The day after that— which meant the day Gaunt had flown into Munich—they had met again, for much longer.

Why did she think the middle-aged couple were English?

"Why, Inspektor?" The woman blinked, paused, then chirped

again. "When they were leaving the second time, the man bought some cigarettes. He paid in change from his pocket—some of it was English money. He apologized for the mistake. So I asked if he was English, and he laughed and said yes."

Vogt tried for descriptions. Wife and husband agreed that the couple had been aged in their mid-forties. The man had a moustache, the woman wore glasses. Beyond that, the descriptions could have fitted a considerable percentage of the middle-aged adult population of Western Europe.

The couple had customers waiting. Vogt thanked them, and Gaunt stopped on the way out of the little restaurant to pick up one of the free books of matches lying in a bowl at the cash desk.

"Herr Gaunt"—the woman was over beside him again—"one other thing I remember. The man the Englishman"—She nodded to a pay-phone booth near the filling station pumps. "He used the telephone each time he was here. I had the feeling they were local calls."

"You could be right," said Gaunt.

He was thinking of Florian Beck, and some of the strange telephone calls the engineer had received in the days before his murder.

They returned to the police station, where the messages waiting included a ballistics report confirming that the Heckler and Koch pistol found on Norden's body was the weapon used to kill Beck. Another said that there had still been no sighting of Willi Dorn.

There was also a note, written in large capitals, from Sergeant Krissa Vogt, addressed to her brother. It was short and pointed:

"Gute Nacht."

Gaunt and Vogt shared a pot of coffee. They talked, they discussed, they argued. Then suddenly it was almost midnight.

Jonathan Gaunt shook his head at the offer of a lift and walked in moonlight the few minutes' journey back to the Gasthaus Rotwild. He was glad to get up to his room, he hardly noticed the view out across the calm silver of the Tegernsee, and he spent some time nursing a beer he'd brought up from the reception lobby and just thinking —or trying to think.

He gave up at last, used the last of the beer to wash down one of his painkiller tablets, undressed, and got into bed. When he slept, the usual nightmare only came once, and not too vividly. He was barely awake before he had dozed off again.

The next time he wakened, there was daylight and someone was shaking him. When he propped himself up on his elbows and forced open his eyes, Krissa Vogt was standing over his bed. She was in police uniform, she showed signs of having dressed quickly, and the expression on her face wasn't happy.

"Dieter wants you," she said simply. "They've found Willi Dorn."

Gaunt looked at her, and guessed. "Dead?"

Krissa nodded.

It stopped mattering that, as usual, he'd gone to bed naked. It was the second morning running he'd been handed this kind of news. He hauled himself out of bed, and the sergeant calmly ignored him as he padded over to where his clothes lay on a chair.

Or maybe she didn't.

"Jonny." Gaunt was pulling on his jacket before she spoke. "How did you get that scar on your back?"

"When I was army."

"Dieter told me." She gave a slight nod, satisfied. "I've a car waiting. Dieter called me out, and told me where we've to go. That's about all I know."

The *Gasthaus* staff were just starting the new day's routine as he followed Krissa Vogt out to her car. It was a quiet, still morning with only a few clouds, it was only around 7 A.M., and the roads were almost deserted.

They travelled for a distance on main roads then plunged off on a network of smaller roads which climbed high into the hills. They travelled far enough and climbed high enough for the Tegernsee to be just a patch of water far below, passing only an occasional small farm or a woodcutter's chalet. Cows with bells round their necks stared at them from handkerchief-sized fields carved out of slopes.

"Here," said Krissa suddenly.

They pulled off the road beside a cluster of other police cars outside a small cabin with wood-beam walls and a timber roof. Lights burned inside and the policeman who opened the door to them nodded a greeting and waved them through into a small lobby.

"In here, Jonny," said Dieter Vogt, emerging from a room.

Gaunt went into a plainly furnished kitchen. Police floodlamps lit every corner starkly, but particularly focused on an area beside an unlit stove.

Willi Dorn had been a slight, mousy-haired individual with a sharp, thin face. He had been wearing denims and a dirty white shirt, and his hands were still tied behind his back. He had died on the stone-slabbed floor, his body curled into an almost foetal position. The front of the shirt was dark with blood.

"Shot twice in the chest," said Dieter Vogt. "Our doctor has been and gone—she has a patient having a baby in the next valley. But she reckons it happened some time early yesterday." He shrugged. "A smaller-calibre weapon than the Heckler and Koch. I'd put my money on the Beretta we found."

"How did you locate Willi?" asked Gaunt.

"Routine and luck—the usual combination," said Vogt. "Farmers rise early. One of our early-shift cars stopped a farmer on his way to work, spoke to him, and heard about this place—the farmer owns it, rents it out. Someone who sounds like Florian Beck took it for a week, he'd seen a Porsche up here a couple of times, then a grey Mercedes yesterday. Our early shift car came up to have a look." He shrugged. "They pressed the alarm buttons."

Jonathan Gaunt walked two paces nearer the dead man and looked down at him. Willi Dorn had had dentures. His top plate had slipped halfway out of his mouth, partly distorting his face. The small-time hotel thief had become caught up in something he probably hadn't understood. It had cost him his life.

"Dieter." Gaunt said it quietly. "Do you get the feeling that some of this wasn't the way it was planned?"

"Because of a couple of pistol-happy idiots?" Vogt shrugged. "Have you ever seen him before?"

"No."

Vogt sighed. "I wondered. That middle-aged couple we heard about —you had a couple like them staying in your *Gasthaus* for a few days. They left yesterday afternoon."

Gaunt remembered the couple who hid behind newspapers. "He didn't have a moustache. Your man did."

"A man can buy a moustache. Just like a woman can buy a wig." Vogt considered the box of cigars. "Maybe Dorn broke into more rooms than we knew about. Maybe someone panicked when they found out."

"Maybe." Gaunt couldn't argue.

"Maybe." Dieter Vogt nodded to himself. "You were thinking of going back home this weekend, weren't you?"

Gaunt nodded.

"It seems like a good idea," said Vogt.

Krissa Vogt seemed ready to speak. But she didn't. She contented herself with a small, sympathetic grimace.

It was only his third morning in Bavaria—and in that time, four people had died.

CHAPTER 4

The Queen's and Lord Treasurer's Remembrancer has his department in a grey granite office block in Edinburgh's George Street, close to the banking and business heart of Scotland's capital. The building has a small, highly polished brass nameplate at the main door, and anyone who has genuine business with the Q and LTR is supposed to know where to come. Anyone who strays in by mistake is politely seen off again by the security staff.

George Street always has a certain quiet style. It also always has cars queuing and fighting for every parking space that happens along its length, just as it has hungry, prowling patrols of traffic wardens. The result is a driver population who unite in cursing the elected city councillors for their apparent dislike of anything that came after the horse and cart.

Jonathan Gaunt arrived at the Remembrancer's Office on the Monday morning, but later than he had intended—too late for any hope of easy parking. He had flown back from Bavaria on the Sunday evening and it had been good that when he wakened on the Monday he was not only in his own bed, but the world outside seemed bright and calm and pleasant.

Things had stayed that way until he left his small bachelor apartment on the west side of the city. Then he discovered that someone had tried to break into his old, rebuilt BMW during the night. Someone using the fashionable method of a short, sharp screwdriver held stiletto style in a thick glove had smashed one of his side windows. The screwdriver had been left behind on the floor and there were traces of blood where the thief had cut himself while attempting to steal the car's radio.

But the culprit had been disturbed halfway through. A night-shift cop who had chased a teenager had left a note in the car inviting Gaunt to call at his local police station.

That could wait. Gaunt drove round to the nearest glass replacement depot and joined the queue of other weekend hard-luck stories. By the time the new glass was fitted and he got to George Street, parking was at its mid-morning peak.

He won a sudden slot from under the nose of a tweed-clad woman driving a Nissan station wagon. She swore at him, and the two doberman dogs in the Nissan's rear seat snarled and showed their teeth as she drove off.

It left him feeling perversely better as he went into the Remembrancer's building. He nodded his way past the security guard, then went through the surprisingly bright and modern open-plan main area and on to his cubbyhole of an office two floors up. A box of Bavarian hand-made chocolates he'd brought back for the witches' coven in the typing pool did him no harm and won him a mug of coffee.

But someone couldn't leave it there. Gaunt was back in his office, taking a first glance at the small pile of mail and telephone message slips lying waiting on him, when he heard footsteps clicking their way along the corridor.

"You're late," accused a voice.

"You noticed." Gaunt looked up at the tall, smartly dressed brunette standing in his doorway, and smiled to annoy her. "That's nice, Hannah."

"Then I'm glad," said Hannah North with matching sarcasm. She was in her very late thirties, and was private secretary to Henry Falconer, the senior administrative assistant. Coming into Gaunt's office, she considered him with faint disapproval. "I suppose we should be surprised you're back in one piece. You were lucky."

"Very lucky," said Gaunt. Within agreed limits, he could relax when he talked with Hannah North. "I was coming to see Henry."

"He wanted to see you." She glanced deliberately at her wristwatch. "But he had to go out. He had an appointment to keep with a banker—someone who might know something about this Hartondee company."

"That might help. Right now, anything could," said Gaunt.

"He knows it." Hannah North frowned at any implied criticism. She could be relied on to defend Falconer in any situation—even, when required, defending him from his wife. That was a woman Gaunt had met only twice, and once would have been enough. Falconer did not have an easy time at home. "He said to tell you he wouldn't be back in his office until afternoon, but that you could meet him for lunch—that you'd know where."

"I know."

"He also wants you to pay a visit to Hartondee's accountancy firm —try for another talk with this Joan Dennan woman, and with her boss. Any other cases you're handling can wait. This one has priority."

"What about upstairs?" Gaunt pointed towards the ceiling, in the approximate direction of the office occupied by the seldom seen but never far distant Remembrancer. "How does he feel?"

"Not pleased." Hannah North shrugged a little, then saw the bottles Gaunt had placed on top of a filing cabinet. "Is that the wine Henry wanted—the Franken Thungersheim?"

"Priority Franken," Gaunt said dryly. "Enjoy it."

"We"—Hannah North caught herself in time—"I expect he will." She had her own special kind of understanding with Henry Falconer, one they fondly imagined few people knew about. But though Henry Falconer and Hannah North might hold hands in private they didn't go to bed together. Somehow, it had always, touchingly, been that way.

"Take the wine along with you," said Gaunt. He watched her collect the bottles. "Hannah, have we another possible Hartondee heir lined up?"

"Not yet. We didn't have a reserve—but we're trying."

"How much do we know about Gladstone Baxter Accountancy?"

"About the firm, about Gladstone Baxter himself—or about their Ms Dennan?" An amused glint showed in Hannah's eyes. "Joan Dennan is some kind of relative of your stockbroker friend Milton—"

"She told me," said Gaunt stonily. "John Milton's wife's cousin."

"You know the saying," murmured Hannah. "We can pick our friends, not our relatives." She relented. "Joan Dennan seems to be exactly what she claims—someone trying hard to establish herself professionally in a field which is still mostly male-dominated. There's nothing known that says differently."

"But the firm—and her boss?"

Hannah North frowned. "As a firm, they keep a mainly low profile. No apparent star-studded clients on their books, they don't make waves when it comes to Inland Revenue situations. You could say the same about Gladstone Baxter." She paused. "Except—"

"Well?" encouraged Gaunt.

"Gossip. Gladstone Baxter is rated as being someone who knows all the tricks, both sides of the law. Maybe he has never been in real trouble, maybe Gladstone Baxter Accountancy is a good firm for someone who wants to gain some solid experience—but Baxter is the kind who has to end in trouble some day."

"Says who?" challenged Gaunt.

"The Fraud Squad," said Hannah North. "Henry asked." She turned to go, then looked back. "That reminds me, Jonny. Go easy on your expenses for Bavaria. The Remembrancer is on another economy prowl."

"Vouchers for everything," agreed Gaunt. "Amen."

He checked the waiting mail and message slips again after she'd gone. John Milton had telephoned after Gaunt had left for Bavaria, but there had been no message. He just wanted it noted he had called. The others seemed routine enough, the mail appeared equally dull. Sighing, he put an internal call through to Companies Branch in their basement cavern.

Three minutes later, a Companies Branch girl arrived and laid a file marked "Hartondee" in front of him. She gave what was meant to be an enticing intriguing smile that failed, then drifted off to gossip with the typing pool coven. Gaunt opened the file, sipped his almost cold coffee, and began reading.

He finished half an hour later, closed the file, shoved it to one side, and swore to himself.

It all looked perfectly ordinary. There had to be hundreds of small Scottish companies which could have presented the same paper picture as Hartondee. It didn't feature in any stock market quotes, it always filed its company returns on time. The chairman and managing director, Renton Handel, was a failed politician and a name always recognized as available for any company board for a suitable fee. Another name was vaguely familiar, a titled Highland landowner who usually saw the world through a drink-induced haze.

Joan Dennan had said that Hartondee had left animal feedstuffs far behind, that their interests were in property management and financial services. By their company returns, they were doing very nicely, thank you. Turnover and profit had been rising year by year, the latest set of figures showing a before-tax profit well in excess of two million.

But was that enough to justify the four hundred thousand pounds they'd been ready to offer Florian Beck for his surprise inheritance— an inheritance that had begun when Beck's great-grandfather had invested the sum of ten pounds all those years ago?

It was hard to believe. Scowling to himself, he picked up the telephone again and tapped a number he knew so well he didn't even have to think it. The number connected, buzzed twice, then was answered. It was John Milton's private office line, and the stockbroker had a near fetish about not making people wait.

"It's me," said Gaunt without preliminaries. "You're a traitor."

"Not really. I'm just scared of my wife," said Milton apologetically. "My wife and her cousin—sorry about it, Jonny. I did try to warn you by phone, but you were on your way by then. I hear things got rough."

"Who told you?" asked Gaunt.

"Joan. Not my Joan, her cousin Joan—" Milton paused for a moment, as if to let Gaunt sort it out. "She called us on Saturday, to say she was back—Cousin Joan, I mean."

Gaunt grimaced at the telephone. But John Milton was a friend quite apart from being the kind of stockbroker who had a sense of humour and who claimed that with a pocket-money-sized client like Gaunt, only laughing kept him sane.

"How much do you trust Cousin Joan?" asked Gaunt.

"Wife's Cousin Joan," corrected Milton. "She's an accountant. I've told you before, never trust an accountant. She's working for a thin-ice-style accountancy practice, but that's the best way to get experience—as long as the ice doesn't crack. At personal level, she's all right." His voice took on a dry edge for a moment. "Off limits, Jonny. But all right."

Gaunt didn't push it. "Second question, because you have to know more about it than I do. What's so important about a firm like Hartondee?"

"Anyone who can answer that gets a gold star," said Milton gloomily. "He could probably also make himself some money—the kind of thing I'd like to see you do sometime."

"Very funny." Gaunt made it a warning.

"Don't you think I've been trying to find out?" There was indignation in Milton's raised voice, then he quickly lowered it again. "Look, Jonny, Hartondee is one of those companies where the first question to ask is who really owns it. We're not talking nominee shareholders. We're not talking about Renton Handel and a toytown board of directors anyone could buy for the price of a pack of dog biscuits."

"The paperwork says they're into property management and investment," said Gaunt. He had picked up a pencil and was doodling on the cover of the Hartondee file as he spoke. "Surely—"

"Surely, nothing," countered Milton. "There's an alleged office through in Glasgow, with a good address—except that Hartondee uses two rooms and rents the rest out to an insurance company. The staff are a trio of pensioners who make coffee, take their pay, and don't worry about what they're really supposed to be doing." He anticipated Gaunt's question. "Yes, there's a branch office—in London. A room in a basement at one of those Middle East banks where it costs a fortune to walk in, then another fortune to leave intact."

"But it's all legal?" Gaunt saw that what had started off as a shapeless mess had somehow become a cartoon pirate ship flying the skull and crossbones flag.

"It's all legal," agreed Milton sadly. "There are plenty of others like it, Jonny—some big, some small. Sensible little people like you and me stay clear once they realize what they could be getting into."

"I can't." Gaunt added a quick little row of cannons along the hull of the pirate ship. "Have you told Cousin Joan any of this?"

"Wife's Cousin Joan," emphasized Milton again. "No, not in detail. Why make trouble for her? You're different."

"Thank you."

"Look, come over tonight if you want to talk about it," suggested John Milton. "But do me a favour. Don't park outside my house, and use the back way in."

"Why?" asked Gaunt, surprised.

"Because I've already had the feeling I've been checked out by someone since I started asking about Hartondee," said the stockbroker patiently. "So I'm keeping a low profile. Just do it, will you?"

They fixed a time, just after dusk, then Gaunt said goodbye and hung up. He had added smoke coming from the little cannons on the pirate ship. Companies Branch wouldn't be pleased when they got their file back. Carefully, he put it to one side then brought out Joan Dennan's business card from his inside jacket pocket. He'd tried her home number the previous evening, but it was still the weekend. As she had warned him, there had been no reply.

The chartered accountancy office was different. Immediately he tapped out the Gladstone Baxter number it was answered by a switchboard. Gaunt asked for Joan Dennan, gave his name, and waited. But it was a man's voice that came on the line.

"Joan is out, Mr. Gaunt." There was the faintest pause, as if he were being given time to accept it. "She told me about meeting you— how can we help the Remembrancer's Office? I'm Gladstone Baxter."

"You're the next name on my list now I'm back," said Gaunt unhurriedly. "I think we should talk, Mr. Baxter."

"About Hartondee?" The man at the other end took the suggestion calmly. "Well, I don't know when Joan will be back—"

"You and I," suggested Gaunt. "Today."

"I'm free right now," said Baxter. "Come round."

"I will," said Gaunt.

He thanked the man, replaced his receiver, stuffed his hands in his trouser pockets, and his grey-green eyes were thoughtful as he sat back. He still needed a moment every now and again to slot things in place.

It was three full days since Willi Dorn's body had been found in that lonely Bavarian cabin, three days that had merged into mostly bustle without anything in particular happening that mattered.

Friday had been swallowed up by the aftermath of Willi Dorn's death. Eventually, when he'd got back to the *Gasthaus* late in the evening, there had been a telephone message waiting for him to say that Joan Dennan had called from Munich airport. By the time he read the message, she was probably back in Britain.

He'd originally planned to leave on the Saturday. But that was before the complex web of West Germany's police system had caught up with him. He had to give new statements to new faces, two men from the Federal *Bundeskriminalamt*. The BKA men had taken him back to the beginning of everything. In between times, Dieter Vogt appeared regularly to complain about other new arrivals and new demands.

In most ways, there was only small progress. The bullets that had killed Willi Dorn had been matched as fired from the Beretta pistol found on Conrad Hass after he died in the wrecked Mercedes. There had been three more apparent sightings of the middle-aged English couple, who had been travelling as a William and Mary Hamilton from London. They had said they were tourists, they had a car which had been hired in Munich.

The main fact that mattered about them was that they still couldn't be found.

Things had finished too late for Gaunt to catch a flight out of Munich that night. But Lufthansa had a Sunday mid-day service from Munich to Heathrow, and Dieter Vogt arranged Gaunt's ticket, then assigned his sister to drive him to the airport.

Except that when Krissa got Gaunt there, the flight had been delayed two hours for "technical reasons."

Leaning further back in his chair, Gaunt grinned at the memory. "Technical reasons" could mean anything including an engine falling off. But it also meant that the copper-haired sergeant, out of uniform, had agreed there was time enough for them to make a visit into the city. They'd eaten in a restaurant close to the twin domes of the Liebfrauenkirche, then afterwards she'd been relaxed enough to take his arm while they went exploring.

Eventually, as they walked down a lane, literally heading back towards the car he'd seen the grubby window of a small antique shop —the kind where the antiques were mostly second-hand junk. A small bundle of old 78 records had caught his eye, and he'd hauled Krissa in for a moment.

When they came out, he'd bought two rare American jazz classic recordings and could hardly believe his luck. One was an original Thelonious Monk piano number, the other was an early Jelly Roll Morton, and how they'd ended up with the dealer was something the man couldn't remember.

Then Krissa had had to drive hard to get back to the airport in time. She had given him a hug and a grin as they parted, and he had gone off showing the orange Lufthansa ticket for the Heathrow flight.

At Heathrow, he changed terminals and walked on to an Edinburgh shuttle flight that was about to depart. Five hours after leaving Munich he was opening the door of his two-room apartment.

The way things had been tidied and dusted, he knew his twice-weekly cleaning woman had been. The stacked mail included an electricity bill, three junk circulars from people who wanted him to borrow money from them, and a postcard from Patti. His ex-wife, her second husband, and their new baby were holidaying in Majorca, enjoying the Mediterranean sunshine. Only Patti could have innocently finished a postcard message to him by writing "wish you were here."

Gaunt had the two jazz 78s and he didn't feel like going out. He'd microwaved a freezer meal of steak and mushroom flake-bake, then switched on his Japanese rack system and fitted a freshly sharpened hardwood needle to the converted pick-up arm. He ate to the scratchy but playable Thelonious Monk, treated himself to a straight, amber-clear Glenlivet malt whisky from the duty-free bottle he'd brought back with him, then sipped to the joy of a Jelly Roll Morton which had been pressed before he was born.

Then he had another whisky and played them both again.

He slept like a baby that night, without need of painkillers.

The Gladstone Baxter Accountancy offices were on the ground floor of a new block of offices near the Haymarket, where one of the benefits included parking space. Gaunt got there at noon, left his old BMW in the gap between a Rolls-Royce and an upmarket Honda sports, and went inside.

They'd been expecting him at Gladstone Baxter's reception desk. A two-second call on the internal telephone, and he was being piloted through a general office where the typing pool were using word processors and an open-plan lay-out gave him glimpses of people working at computer terminals behind shoulder-high wood partitions.

But Gladstone Baxter's personal office, located at the rear, was one of the few private areas and had a mahogany-veneer door.

The plump young girl who had guided him through smiled at him, tapped on the door, opened it, and ushered him in.

"Glad to meet you," said Gladstone Baxter, limping across the room towards him. "Hell, I don't expect this kind of punctuality from anyone these days!"

"It's a new civil service rule," said Gaunt mildly. "Next month, we start having Happy Hours."

Gladstone Baxter allowed himself a controlled bark of a laugh. He was a man in his early fifties, thin and totally bald, wearing rimless spectacles. He was dressed in a dark blue business suit with a pink shirt and a grey tie, and had a face shaped like a large pink football, with a small mouth and very small ears.

"Sit down," he invited, indicating a chair to one side of his desk. He limped back round to his own chair, which had a walking stick hooked over its back, and saw Gaunt settled. "Coffee?"

"No thanks."

"Nothing, Emma." Baxter shook his head at the girl still at the door. She left them. As the door closed, the man resumed his own seat and spent a moment building a steeple with his fingertips. "Joan telephoned out to Bessie King in Bavaria this morning. Mrs. King told her about the other death, this man Dorn. Bad—all of it, Gaunt."

"Like you say," agreed Gaunt politely.

"But nothing to do with us," said the thin-faced man primly. "You can't help it and I can't help it. Florian Beck kept bad company. I think we can agree on that. So—" Small, hard eyes looked at Gaunt through the rimless spectacles. "What brings the Remembrancer's Office visiting, Mr. Gaunt? No prizes for guessing Hartondee?"

"None." Gaunt matched the accountant's faint, unemotional flicker of a smile. "You've handled Hartondee's books for a long time—"

"Fifteen years." Baxter gave a guarded nod.

"Handled them personally?"

"Yes." Gladstone Baxter nodded again, this time in the direction of the walking stick hooked to his chair. "Until this year. You've been told why Joan had to take my place."

"You knew about those sleeping shares?" asked Gaunt.

"Always." Baxter waited.

"But you didn't do anything about them?"

The man's round face didn't alter. "I carried out my client's instructions, Mr. Gaunt. I did nothing. The original transaction was informal —less than informal, not much more than a cash loan out of one man's pocket into another. The debtor, the original Hartondee proprietor, voluntarily converted what was a debt into a shareholding. It remains that way, it has grown as Hartondee has grown."

"But quietly," suggested Gaunt.

Baxter shrugged. "My client's instructions, Mr. Gaunt. Unusual, but legal."

"Then Joan Dennan discovered them."

"Yes." The accountant allowed himself the luxury of a scowl. "She wasn't aware of the full situation."

"And now Hartondee aren't pleased?"

"Mr. Gaunt, they are mad as hell," said Gladstone Baxter softly. "But if they want, they can afford that luxury. Everything had always been suitably documented. Now"—he shrugged—"they want the matter settled, ended. They haven't tried to impede the Remembrancer's actions. They were glad when he found this man Beck."

"And, naturally, they're sad that we lost him," said Gaunt stonily.

"Meaning?" Baxter's eyes narrowed.

"Meaning different people seem very interested in getting the Hartondee shares." Gaunt saw the man stiffen. "More than interested —and we want to know why. What's Hartondee about, Baxter? Who runs it?"

"There's a managing director—"

"And even a board of directors," said Gaunt. "Nice, distinguished rent-a-mob names that look good on headed notepaper—all of them. But who speaks for Hartondee when it matters? Do you?"

"No." Baxter shook his head. "I'm an accountant, Hartondee is a client." He paused and sucked his lips for a moment. "Hartondee's offices—"

"Are a joke," said Gaunt mildly. "Try again."

"You didn't let me finish," said Baxter. His manner had become wary, almost defensive. "There is someone."

"And I want to meet him."

"All right." Baxter opened a desk drawer, took out an address book, opened it briefly, then wrote on a notepad. When he'd finished, he ripped off the sheet and passed it over. "Hartondee's executive secretary and company lawyer is John Darnley. Try him if you want, Gaunt. I can't say how he'll react."

"Thank you." Gaunt glanced at the sheet. Whatever kind of lawyer Darnley might be, he operated from an expensive office address in Edinburgh's Queen Street. "You've a phone number for him?"

"Yes."

"Call him."

"Now?" Baxter blinked.

"Now. Say I want to see him. Today."

The accountant's mouth tightened. Then he nodded and left his office, closing the door firmly behind him. He returned within a couple of minutes, leaving the door open this time, standing beside it, the message clear.

"I've spoken with John Darnley. He can spare you a few moments —but if you want to make it today, then it has to be straight away." Gladstone Baxter's manner stayed cold, yet held some relief. "He has a full afternoon schedule."

"Fine." Gaunt rose from his chair and moved towards the door. He smiled. "I appreciate the help."

"Any time," said the accountant.

"When do you expect Joan Dennan to be back?" asked Gaunt.

"Not today," said Baxter shortly. "She's working out of town. Goodbye, Mr. Gaunt."

As Jonathan Gaunt left, the door slammed shut behind him. Gladstone Baxter didn't seem to be enjoying his morning.

The sun was still warm and bright, and it was only a few minutes' drive from Haymarket to Queen Street. Gaunt parked the BMW as near as he could—which was in the next street—then walked round while the first of the early lunch-break workers began to emerge.

Darnley's law firm was one of three businesses on the second floor of a tastefully modernized Victorian building built of red sandstone. There was a doorman at a desk in the entrance hall, there was a small pond with a fountain and some bored-looking goldfish, and the names of other firms on the directory board beside the elevator showed Darnley kept exclusive company.

Gaunt took the elevator up, got out at the second floor, then stopped outside the frosted glass door that said "John Darnley, Solicitor and Notary." The names of half a dozen companies were listed in smaller print beneath. But Hartondee wasn't one of them. He went in, to a small office suite which had thick wall-to-wall carpeting and rich furnishings. A blonde secretary wearing a tailored grey two-piece broke off tapping at her word processor to greet the visitor.

"Mr. Gaunt?" She smiled as he nodded. "You're expected."

He was taken through a mahogany panelled door into another richly furnished room. There was a desk in one corner, but a tall man rose from one of a group of leather armchairs arranged around a circular glass table which had a telephone but which was bare of papers.

"I'm John Darnley," said the man. He had a thin smile, a laconic voice, and a dry handshake. "Gladstone Baxter says we're giving your department some problems. Sit down, tell me about them."

Gaunt settled in one of the armchairs and John Darnley chose the chair exactly opposite. The Hartondee executive secretary was younger than Gaunt had expected—probably in his mid-thirties—and had the build of a weekend football player. That went with prematurely grey hair and bushy eyebrows, a narrow face and a beak of a nose. He was wearing a blue pinstripe business suit with a white shirt and a plain blue tie. A gold watch peeped out from under one shirt cuff, and Darnley drew out a slim gold ballpoint pen from an inside pocket, then nursed it between his fingertips.

"You had difficulties in Bavaria, Mr. Gaunt," he said in that same laconic voice.

Gaunt nodded. "People kept getting killed."

The narrow face gave an amused twitch. "So you come back to Edinburgh and frighten the daylights out of an innocent like Gladstone Baxter—a poor harmless accountant?"

"Did I?" Gaunt left it there. "He told me you talk for Hartondee."

"Only when Hartondee wants it that way." Darnley gave the gold pen a final twirl, then tucked it away. At the same time his manner hardened. "Here's what you can report back to your Remembrancer. As a company, Hartondee always acts within the law. But my shareholders prefer privacy, and they intend to keep things that way—unless we're dragged into a court of law. If that should ever happen, we'd still fight—and demand compensation. Do I make our position clear?"

"Who gives you instructions?" asked Gaunt.

Darnley smiled. "My board of directors, Mr. Gaunt."

"Who tells them?"

Darnley's smile widened. "The shareholders."

"Who could be nominees?"

"It's possible," murmured Darnley. "I—ah—certainly speak for some private trust funds."

"Very private?"

Darnley nodded.

"So you tell the Hartondee board what to do, then they tell you to do it." It wasn't unique. But it still made Jonathan Gaunt feel that his head had just run into a brick wall. "One other question?"

Darnley glanced at his gold wristwatch. "One."

"How big a slice of Hartondee are we talking about?"

"In terms of the Peter Church shares?" The narrow face didn't alter. "They've grown with the company. Today—well, we're still talking five per cent in voting terms." Pausing, he used the internal button on the telephone beside him. It was answered, and he said, "Martha, has my lunch arrived?"

Putting down the telephone, Darnley glanced at Gaunt, then rose, went over to his window, and looked down at the street. He stayed that way until there was a knock at his office door, then turned as his blonde secretary came in. She was carrying a silver tray with a white porcelain teapot, matching china, and what appeared to be a smoked salmon salad.

"Thank you, Martha." He indicated he wanted the tray over at his desk. "And Mr. Gaunt is leaving."

"Enjoy your lunch," said Gaunt, rising.

"I will," said Darnley. "We've a little restaurant round the corner. Try it some time."

"Maybe," said Gaunt. Their eyes met and he let Darnley be the first to look away. "Thanks for your time."

"My pleasure," said Darnley. "Goodbye, Mr. Gaunt."

He left the lawyer's building and stopped outside for a moment, looking up. Peter Church's tiny ten-pound investment now equalled five per cent of Hartondee's holdings—but what did that mean in real terms? Speaking to Darnley had still left just about everything unchanged. It was as if he'd been dumped in a maze, without any hint which way was in or which was out—or if he was going anywhere at all.

As he looked up he thought he caught a flicker of movement behind one of the second-floor windows which was probably the one at Darnley's office. Then it had gone. Maybe the lawyer was amusing himself between morsels of smoked salmon. Gaunt scowled at the thought, then started back to his car.

There were three of them suddenly ahead of him, young drunks wearing denims, grubby T-shirts and boots. They were shouting and laughing as they ploughed a way along the busy pavement towards him, and one waved a can which splattered beer over some girls who couldn't get clear in time. Another of the drunks yelled his amusement, his two friends began a drunken dance together, and most people around were trying hard to avoid them.

They were heading straight towards him—and they were almost there, still laughing, still shouting, before Gaunt realized the drunk part was an act. They were clean-shaven, they had mean eyes, and as the thug with the opened can of beer threw it aside, a set of bright metal ring-pulls gleamed around the knuckles of his right fist. Then they came jostling in, a boot grazed Gaunt's shin, and someone else backhanded him across the face.

"Nothing personal, pal," said the young thug with the ring-pulls fist, bringing it up to strike. He had very short dark hair and a healed razor scar down one cheek. "Stop bein' a nuisance to people, right? An' make this easier—"

Jonathan Gaunt locked his hands together, brought them up in a two-armed blow which knocked the dark-haired thug's glinting fist aside, took one step forward, then followed it with a hard, precisely timed head-butt straight into the grinning face. He heard a scream of pain, but he was already turning, avoiding a high kick coming in at his stomach from another of the trio. Nobody in his right mind would have tried that kick. Grabbing the thug's ankle, Gaunt lifted and twisted in a way that used the man's own eagerness like a lever. With a yowl, the man was twisted off his feet then crashed down on the concrete.

That left number three, who had short ginger hair. Licking his lips, he backed away and glanced frantically at his two companions. The man Gaunt had butted was nursing his head in his hands, the other looked dazed, neither seemed to want any further share of the action.

"Back off, mister, just back off, right?" Ginger Hair's voice was shrill and he began to retreat, a hand darting into a pocket of his denim jacket. He gave another wild glance around, then his hand came out of the pocket. The sun glinted on the thin menace of a visibly dirty hypodermic needle as he flicked away the old bottle-cork which had been guarding the tip. "Or do you want to take a chance on who used this last time—do you want that?"

Gaunt halted while the needle waved in front of his face. The first two thugs were making a rapid stumbling retreat, and a small audience had stopped around, all staring. But they'd heard the threat and weren't going to intervene. Unless you were brave, unless it really mattered, you now thought twice about it in a city like Edinburgh—if you'd sense.

Police sorted out this kind of thing. Other people didn't.

The needle flickered a new, wide, defiant arc. Then, suddenly, the frightened thug was running after his two friends. In seconds, all three had vanished from sight. Someone from the crowd asked Gaunt if he was all right. Someone else asked about calling the police.

"No police," said Gaunt. "Forget it."

It would have been a waste of time. The trio had gone, they would have been hard to find. They were the kind who came in bargain offers, hired by the hour. They probably hadn't known who was paying them, they had just been pointed at him and been told to beat him up. Beat him up or cut him up—Gaunt thought of those ring-pulls and felt a momentary chill.

"They shouldn't get away with it," protested an elderly man.

"No," agreed Gaunt. "They shouldn't." He took a deep breath and looked back along the road to the Victorian building where John Darnley had his office.

Then he went on to his car.

Princes Street Gardens is a broad, beautiful carpet of carefully tended flowerbeds and lawns that slope down in front of the Scottish capital's main shopping street. The Gardens are overlooked by the great medieval bulk of Edinburgh Castle on its high rock. There are statues, there is a bandstand. Almost unbelievably, the busy main Glasgow–Edinburgh railway line runs through the middle of it all in a deep, well-camouflaged cutting.

It was warm and pleasant along the footpath on the first level of the slope below Princes Street and its traffic. The breeze flirted with the skirts of light summer dresses as the main lunch-break tide of workers from shops and offices walked and talked or just lazed around the Gardens area. The bandstand was empty, but some of the

wanderers were providing their own music from radios or tape play-
ers. When Jonathan Gaunt arrived one of the wooden benches near
the long sweep of the Scots-American War Memorial was vacant and
he settled there. The memorial dated back to World War One, and just
beside it was the latest addition to the Gardens, the Falklands Memorial Border. It was a mass of tulips in full crimson bloom.

Gaunt was a couple of minutes early and his back was beginning
one of its familiar low-grade aches. He was glad to relax against the
varnished wood and do nothing except watch the girls go by. Then
his attention strayed up towards the dark, dominant castle. From
being Scotland's stronghold, it had become the country's number one
tourist attraction. That was why a new tunnel was being carved out
of the volcanic rock, to give vehicle access which avoided the old
drawbridge route.

They were finding things as they dug, from proof of human occu-
pation in the first century A.D. to signs of the Roman military who
had come along later. Not far from the main gatehouse, they had
uncovered a pit which held a neat row of thirteen human skeletons.

Forensic pathologists said they had all been tall and robust adult
males, under the age of thirty-five—soldiers who had died in an epi-
demic which had hit the enclosed garrison in the mid-seventeenth
century. The castle was probably still hiding other forgotten secrets.

There was a harsh, sharp boom from the castle ramparts. It reached
Princes Street, then echoed back. Like most of the population of Edinburgh within earshot, Gaunt automatically checked his wristwatch.
The One O'Clock Gun was an institution, maintained by the military
to split-second precision—he grinned, catching sight of a bulky figure
now coming down from Princes Street towards him. Henry Falconer,
the senior administrative assistant to the Queen's and Lord Treasurer's Remembrancer, was wearing a dark grey suit and his usual,
Windsor knotted golf club tie and was carrying a government-issue
briefcase.

"A reasonable day." A trickle of sweat was running down Falconer's broad, middle-aged face, but his jacket stayed fastened. He sat on
the bench, carefully placing the briefcase between them. "I telephoned Hannah. She said you eventually got in."

"She welcomed me back," said Gaunt.

"Naturally." Falconer opened his briefcase. "She also told me you
remembered my wine. You enjoyed Bavaria?"

"Apart from the body count."

"I took that for granted." Falconer reached into his briefcase.

"Lunch? I brought for two." He took out two large beef, tomato, and rye sandwiches, then a coffee flask, two paper cups, and two large red apples. An alarming springblade knife completed his preparations. "About my bottles of wine, Jonny—I—ah—wouldn't like the Remembrancer to find that kind of thing in your expenses—tell me later what I owe you and I'll pay, as we agreed."

"It would be a bad day," said Gaunt solemnly. He opened the coffee flask, poured coffee into both cups, took one, and left the other for Falconer. "Henry, do we know what the hell is going on yet?"

"Too early." Falconer took one of the sandwiches and tried a first, tentative nibble. He rolled the result in his mouth, seemed satisfied, and looked happier. "But something our revered Remembrancer calls a 'waft of quality corruption' is hanging over happy Hartondee—past, present and maybe future. What do the Bavarian authorities make of it all?"

"They wish we'd stayed at home," said Gaunt.

"If I was Bavarian, I'd agree." Falconer sampled the coffee. "Very good—but then, Hannah made it up. You seemed to build a good relationship quickly with your Kriminalinspektor Vogt. Was there a reason?"

"We once played soldiers together for NATO."

"Join the army, meet interesting people, think about shooting them." Falconer took another nibble at his sandwich, then broke off a large crumb of the bread and tossed it at their feet. One of the Gardens' resident flock of pigeons grabbed the crumb and strutted off. "How did things go for you this morning?"

Gaunt told him. Falconer's face stayed impassive, but his eyes were thoughtful. "First we've an accountant, now we've a lawyer. Did you know that Robert Burns once mentioned lawyers in a work—then someone said he'd probably be sued, so our National Bard struck it out?" He closed his eyes for a moment, searching his memory. " 'Three lawyers' tongues, turn'd inside out, Wi' lies seam'd like a beggar's clout—' rather apt. It would have been in *Tam O'Shanter.*"

"Yes, they'd have sued." Gaunt bit into his own sandwich. "What about Darnley?"

"I've heard of him. Expensive, exclusive, plenty of skeletons stowed in his cupboards." Falconer shrugged. "That doesn't necessarily make him a villain—just a good lawyer. We can check. There might be something about the other companies he represents." He frowned. "But I'm unhappy about your three thugs—particularly the lout with the hypodermic needle. That I don't like."

"He could have been faking."

"Which would make it ten times worse," snapped Falconer. "Haven't most of these poor devils who are for real got enough problems already?"

Gaunt didn't answer. But he knew what Falconer meant. Every city had its down sides. One of Edinburgh's was the way in which too many of its drug addicts still shared hypodermic needles despite all the public pleas and publicity. The cruel said it was the kind of problem that would go away—eventually they would all be dead. That didn't help.

"I'm going to see John Milton tonight," he told Falconer.

"Will his wife's cousin be there?" asked Falconer. "I heard about that too. I'd feel slightly happier if I knew what that damned female was doing." He seemed surprised to find he had finished his sandwich. Taking the springblade knife, he clicked it open and peeled one of the apples in a long, single rope of red. Then he took a slice from the apple and ate it from the tip of the knife. "Do you trust her?"

"I don't untrust her," said Gaunt carefully. "Not yet."

"Fair, I suppose." Falconer sliced another piece of apple, saw the same pigeon was back, hesitated, then scowled at the bird but fed it. "We've two main fronts to attack. First, what is it about those Hartondee shares that suddenly makes them so special? Second, since we—ah—were so unfortunate with Florian Beck, we need another heir."

"Do we have anyone in mind?"

"We've a possibility that turned up when we were researching up Florian Beck," said Falconer. "I made a check at New Register House this morning, they're running a couple of additional suggestions through their computers for me this afternoon—and I think I'll ask Hannah to try following through if I'm right." He paused and gave the pigeon the benefit of some crumbs from his lap. "The way you'd expect, the family name tells us we don't have to go back too many generations—great-great-grandfather is shut-off time."

"Meaning?" Gaunt blinked at him.

"I forgot. You still haven't been long enough in this job to know a boundary fence when you see one." The big man sighed. "Jonny, most times if you meet someone named Church or Kirk in Scotland it means that there's an abandoned baby somewhere back in their family tree. Simple fact—churches were always prime locations for abandoning the unwanted newborn. It can still be that way. Churches are usually dry, sometimes warm, the people are usually decent. But what is the Reverend who has to christen this nameless child going to choose as a surname?"

Gaunt understood. It was obvious. "Church—"

"Florian Beck's great-great-grandfather James Church had his birth registered in Aberdeen in 1850," said Falconer unemotionally. "Parents unknown, because he was found in an unmarked shoebox which was left in a church. I don't know the size of church or the size of shoebox, but the fact he was found is in police records for the time —which saves us some work. No parents ever traced, we can't go further back."

Then, eventually, the adult James Church married and had a son who was named Peter. The Peter Church who would later make his modest investment in the young Hartondee company.

"You said we'd another possibility left," said Gaunt slowly. "Like what, Henry?"

"Just someone—we may be right, we may be wrong. Leave Hannah to give the family tree a new shake. Let's see what falls out of the branches." Falconer finished his lunch, gathered up their leftovers and dumped them in a nearby rubbish basket. When he came back he packed the flask into his briefcase then sat back and gave a smile at a middle-aged woman who was passing. "Lovely day."

"Pervert," she said coldly, and quickened her pace.

"I thought she was someone I knew." Falconer was embarrassed as he faced Gaunt again. "Maybe Hannah is right—I should see someone about my eyes." He recovered. "Now, the other main front— what makes those Hartondee shares special? John Darnley says we're talking five per cent of the company?"

Gaunt nodded.

"A voting five per cent can make all the difference in many a gory takeover," mused Falconer. "Hartondee could be like the proverbial iceberg—what we see could be tiny compared with what's hidden. I told you we had some outside interest in buying them. Did I also tell you that the people involved are being as elusive as the devil on Sunday about who put them up to it?" He didn't expect an answer. "We're back into the nominees' world—where nobody is totally real. All we have for sure is that there are at least two real interests—three if you add the Edinburgh connection, where the Dennan girl is being stuck at the sharp end. The other two are both working out of the London merchant banking world. But it doesn't stop there."

"Then where?" Gaunt knew he was expected to ask, saw from the glint in Falconer's eyes that they'd made some small progress.

"One might be Anglo-American. The other is a deeper cover—a Swiss bank that has a long history of running smokescreen operations for a couple of Spanish financial houses."

"Yet they're chasing Hartondee?" Gaunt found it hard to believe.

"Why not? A little key can open a big lock," said Falconer. He sniffed his distaste. "Ask your stockbroker friend Milton." A new thought struck him like a rebound. "Milton or his wife's cousin—do we know where Joan Dennan has gone, or why?"

Gaunt shook his head.

"Keep trying," advised Falconer. He sat for a moment, thinking, while a shadow chased its way across the Gardens as the sun was briefly covered by a wisp of cloud. "Where's your car? Somewhere near?"

"Near enough." He'd squeezed the BMW into the last space in a line of illegally parked cars in Kings Stables Road, on the west side of the Gardens.

"Good." Falconer rose ponderously to his feet and beckoned. "We'll both pay a new surprise call on this John Darnley. Rattling Hartondee's lawyer a little more might do some good, and can't do much harm."

When they reached it, the BMW had acquired a parking ticket. So had every other car in the line. Falconer smiled gently, removed the ticket from under the wiper blade, folded it, and handed it to Gaunt.

"I did bring lunch," he reminded.

They set off on the short drive, and traffic was light. When they reached Queen Street, Gaunt slowed the car to a crawl and began looking for a place to stop anywhere near the Victorian office block where Darnley's office was located. Then he swore under his breath, ignored a space immediately outside the building, and kept the BMW moving.

"What's wrong?" asked Falconer, puzzled.

"Wait." Gaunt saw another space on ahead, and stopped the car there. But he kept the engine running as he looked back.

He'd been right. Two men who had just left the Victorian block were walking across the road. One was using a walking stick and had a limp. As he watched, they got aboard a blue Volvo station wagon. The driver was Gladstone Baxter, his passenger was John Darnley. If Hartondee's accountant and Hartondee's company secretary were going somewhere together while so much was going on, it had to be interesting. Darnley had been carrying a small suitcase.

"Well?" Falconer was impatient.

"A complication, Henry." He explained, still looking back towards the Volvo, which was starting up.

"Damn," said Falconer uneasily. "Damn, damn—"

"No problem," soothed Gaunt. As the Volvo began moving, heading away from them, he let the distinctive blue shape blend into the traffic flow for a moment. Then he saw his chance, flicked the BMW into gear, and took it in a fast, harsh U turn which made Falconer gasp and drew a horn-blast from a startled van driver. But they were round, they could still see the Volvo, and this was Edinburgh, not Bavaria. "Now we stay with them—right, Henry?"

Henry Falconer swallowed, but nodded.

Within a minute, Jonathan Gaunt began to have a suspicion that he knew where the Volvo might be heading. Within five minutes he knew he was right. They were on the main route for Edinburgh Airport.

In all, it was a twenty-minute drive. There was moderate traffic in both directions, and the two men in the Volvo had no particular reason to notice the small black BMW always about half a dozen cars behind them.

At the airport there was plenty of space in the parking areas. They saw the Volvo park in one line of vehicles, and Gaunt slotted the BMW into another line about a hundred yards away. Then they watched while Baxter and Darnley began walking towards the long, low terminal building. Darnley, the taller of the two, was carrying his small suitcase and walked with a long stride. Beside him, limping on his stick, Gladstone Baxter had to hurry to keep up but still seemed to be doing most of the talking. The sunlight glinted on the man's spectacle lenses each time he turned to his companion.

"Now." Gaunt nudged Falconer as the two men neared the terminal building. "Our turn, Henry. You first—they don't know you. But I won't be far behind."

They climbed out and began walking, Gaunt letting Falconer stay several paces in the lead. Darnley and Baxter had gone into the terminal building and could be seen heading towards the check-in desks. Falconer went nearer, then loitered and glanced back. Gaunt nodded. Only John Darnley seemed to be travelling. He had checked in at the London shuttle flight desk, and the public address system was already calling the flight.

Moments later the public address system was busy again and at the same time the terminal area was suddenly flooded with people. Three flights had apparently landed one after the other and their passengers were pouring out of the arrival gates. Some were meeting friends or relatives, others had luggage trolleys and were heading for the exits, a number had that dazed expression which marks air travellers still trying to accept they've arrived.

Gaunt lost all sight of Darnley and Baxter in one tightly packed swirl of people. Then, as the swirl cleared, he realized that Henry Falconer had also vanished. He began searching. But another couple of minutes passed before he saw Falconer, beckoning urgently. Gaunt made his way over.

"They're in there." Falconer pointed at the entrance to one of the airport bars. "At a table on the left, halfway down. They seem to have met people they know—a man and a woman."

"You're sure?" Gaunt was puzzled.

"I've seen them," said Falconer impatiently.

A partition screen of decorative greenery filled part of the bar entrance-way. Gaunt got there then eased forward, using it as shelter.

"You're blocking the way, friend," boomed a cheerful voice behind him. "Move, will you? We've only enough time for a quick wet!"

A small tidal wave of people came past Gaunt, all heading for the bar counter, all carrying identical red flight bags which said España Holidays and clutching boarding passes for their flight. He tried to grin, went with them, then looked to his left. There was an empty table about halfway along the bar area. There were still two empty glasses lying on it. Then Falconer was beside him, cursing softly. Because there was another way out of the bar, where a door was still swinging.

"They were there," protested Falconer. "With those people—"

"Then they're still around." Gaunt grabbed Falconer's arm and hustled him towards the door.

It led into another busy, brightly lit airport corridor with signs that said Flight Departures. They hurried along, into an even more crowded area where there was a barrier and new signs that said Passengers Only—and Gaunt grabbed Falconer's arm again, this time to bring him to a halt. Gladstone Baxter and John Darnley were part of the crush of people around the barrier, in conversation with a man and woman while travellers flowed past them and through the screens to the security check desks.

There was a sudden surge in the people around and some angry protests as two agitated passengers, late for a flight and carrying a mass of hand luggage, elbowed their way through. When they had passed, Baxter and Darnley were still ahead but the couple who had been with them had gone and more people were flowing out of sight through to the security desks. Gaunt looked around, but couldn't see them anywhere else.

"Jonny." Falconer gave him a warning nudge.

Accountant and lawyer had parted. Baxter was heading in their direction, Darnley was going through towards the security desks. There was a Scottish Tourist Board display case beside Gaunt. He faced it, also using Falconer's bulk as a shield, while Baxter limped past them in the direction of the exit signs. Falconer took a half-step to follow, but stopped again when Gaunt didn't move.

John Darnley had now vanished from sight. But it was the couple they'd seen with him, the couple who had already disappeared from view, who mattered more.

Gaunt moistened his lips as he realized it. There had been only that one brief glimpse. The man no longer had a moustache, the woman didn't wear glasses, they both looked younger. But they could have been William and Mary Hamilton, the alleged tourist couple he had last seen at the *Gasthaus* beside the Tegernsee.

Could have been. He hadn't any kind of reason to back the notion.

Even if he had felt more sure, what could he do about it—and, if John Darnley decided to take a shuttle flight to London, was it anyone else's business?

Falconer touched his arm. "We've still got Baxter."

"Forget him," said Gaunt sadly. The public address system was making a final call for the London shuttle. Other flight numbers began to be called. He needed time to think and time was the one thing he didn't have. "Henry, do you know anyone here?"

Falconer frowned and hesitated. "If you mean so we can get past security—"

"No." He hadn't enough time for that. "Can we check if there's a William and Mary Hamilton on the passenger list for the London flight?"

"Wait in the bar," said Falconer with a bland assurance.

Gaunt did. Ten minutes later, as the flight information boards showed the London shuttle had left, Falconer returned. He shook his head.

"No Hamiltons so far listed for any flight today. Darnley reserved his London flight by telephone this morning. Anything else while we're here?"

Gaunt shook his head. But he had missed something. It was there, it was nagging at his mind, but he had missed it.

"Then we'll get back," decided Falconer. "It's pick and shovel time again."

CHAPTER 5

For the moment they had to decide they were finished at the airport. Henry disappeared briefly to thank his anonymous friend, then they drove back to the city.

It began raining. One solitary dark cloud in an otherwise clear sky seemed to follow them all the way, and the only parking Jonathan Gaunt could find for his BMW was half the length of George Street from the Remembrancer's building. George Street is not a short street and the rain had become a downpour. By the time Falconer had snarled his way past the security guard and into shelter, he looked as though he should be hung up to dry. Gaunt felt pretty much the same.

"Come through when you're ready," said Falconer curtly, and disappeared in the direction of his room in a trail of damp footprints.

Gaunt went up to his own small office, used both hands to comb back his wet, unruly hair, and made pathetic noises at the typing pool coven. They were amused enough to send one of their junior cauldron-stirrers through with a chipped stoneware mug of coffee. Then he closed the door and used his telephone.

The way he'd agreed with Falconer, his first call was to Gladstone Baxter's office. Once again he asked for Joan Dennan but once again it was Baxter who came on the line. It meant that Baxter must have gone practically straight there from the airport. Just as important, either he was a good actor or the accountant's chill, slightly impatient voice meant the man didn't know Gaunt had followed him.

"Don't you ever listen?" asked Baxter curtly. "I told you this morning, Joan is out. Out of town, being paid to work."

"To work on the Hartondee account?"

"Possibly. She'll be in touch with your people if and when we think it necessary." There was a pause, as if Baxter was doing some fast thinking. His manner mellowed. "Was your meeting with John Darnley useful?"

"In parts," said Gaunt.

"He called me later and said he hoped it had helped," said Baxter smoothly, and compounded the lie. "Then he rushed off to a meeting somewhere." There was another pause on the line and Baxter switched tactics again. "Understand one basic fact in all this, Gaunt. Hartondee may have stretched company law a little, but don't waste your time trying to prove any law was broken. That didn't happen."

Gaunt thanked him, hung up, had a gulp of typing pool coffee, then called the next number on his list, John Darnley's office. The voice that answered was Darnley's middle-aged blonde secretary and he played it carefully. The woman had impressed him.

"You'll remember me, Martha," he said easily. "Gaunt, from the Remembrancer's Office. John Darnley told me he would be out this afternoon, but I've got to ask him something. It could be important. When will he be back?"

"Back here?" She sounded mildly surprised. "Not for a couple of days, maybe more. He had to take an afternoon shuttle flight down to London, Mr. Gaunt. Didn't he explain?"

"We didn't have too amicable a meeting," said Gaunt. He thought he heard a chuckle from the other end. "But can you contact him?"

"No, I'm sorry."

"But if you know where he is—"

"I don't, Mr. Gaunt." She stopped, then seemed to feel some kind of an explanation was due. "He makes his own arrangements. They stay private. He doesn't tell me and I know not to ask."

"Will he contact you?"

"He might. I wouldn't expect it." Darnley's secretary spoke with a degree of resignation. "I can't think why he should."

"Does this happen often?" asked Gaunt.

"Now and again." The woman could sympathize. "He lives on his own, and there's no one else to consider. I didn't know about London until he came in this morning."

"You can't even suggest where he might be?"

"I don't own him, Mr. Gaunt," said Darnley's secretary patiently. "But the first chance I get, I'll let him know you called. That's a promise."

She said goodbye and hung up.

That left one person to contact. Gaunt drank more of the coffee, then got out Dieter Vogt's police number at Rottach. It was a long string of numbers to tap, beginning with the international trunk code for West Germany, then the Munich area code. But a couple of relay beeps and a short burst of ringing tone later he was connected to the Rottach police switchboard. Another minute and Dieter Vogt was on the line.

"You've saved me a call." The young Bavarian *Kriminalinspektor* sounded cheerful and the line was good enough for him to have been in the next room. "We've had some luck you should know about—"

"If it's good, I could use it," Gaunt told him. "No guarantees, but there's an outside chance I've just seen your William and Mary Hamilton—then lost them again."

"Wie bitte, Jonny?" Dieter Vogt made it near to a yelp. "What happened?"

Gaunt told him.

"Like you said, you couldn't be sure." The Bavarian sighed. There was a brief pause, the murmur of another voice in the background, then Vogt was there again. "That was Krissa. She says hello, and when are you coming back?"

"When I can." Gaunt smiled at the thought of the copper-haired Krissa Vogt. "Once this mess is finished."

"Ja. She says she could use a partner at my wedding," said her brother dryly. "Jonny, this English couple Hamilton have vanished as far as I'm concerned. We believe they got into Switzerland—but things are better in another area. You remember how we found some items Beck had hidden, including his little address book?"

"I remember."

"The *Bundeskriminalamt* have been leaning on some of the people named in that address book. And when the BKA lean, they lean hard."

"I've heard," agreed Gaunt. West Germany's Federal police had no particular reputation for delicacy. "What did they get?"

"That your Hamiltons were certainly working with Conrad Hass and Heine Norden, the two killed when the Mercedes crashed. The Hamiltons were sent in to be part of the background, Hass and Norden were there to frighten or whatever else was required."

"Who says?"

"Two different sources, one mine, the other BKA." Vogt left it there. "It comes down to this. Hass and Norden were hired for the job at very short notice. They were told that they had to get down to the Scheckheim–Rottach area. The target was Florian Beck, they were to contact an English couple—your Hamiltons. They'd get their orders that way."

"It makes sense," said Gaunt softly. It also shaped its own question. "Who did the hiring?"

"A *Britischer*, tall and in his forties, well dressed." Vogt gave an annoyed grunt. "He called himself Mr. Smith, which doesn't win any prizes. When he came to see Hass and Norden, he gave them a name that Norden knew, some big-league London criminal who had told Smith about them. Smith was willing to pay them over the going rate, then a bonus on completion."

"When did he appear on their scene?"

"That's vague, like everything else. We're working with people who stay alive that way." The Bavarian sighed over the line. "But this *Britischer* Smith, the man we really want, made it clear that Florian Beck was not to be touched without orders and there were to be no mistakes." He paused. "That's it, Jonny. For now, at any rate. I'll stay in touch."

"Do that," said Gaunt almost absently. A wild possibility was racing through his mind. "Dieter, does Spain come into it anywhere?"

"Spain? *Nein*—though I'm going there on my honeymoon." Vogt was puzzled. "Why?"

"I'll let you know," said Gaunt. He was thinking of the wave of charter flight passengers at the airport bar, with their España flight bags. There had been more than one Spanish destination flight on the departure boards. "I might have a better name than Smith."

"*Ja bitte.*" Vogt made it a plea. "And don't forget what I asked about you and Krissa at my wedding, okay?"

Gaunt promised, said goodbye, hung up, sat for a moment just frowning at his desk and thinking. Then got out of his chair and went through to see Henry Falconer.

As usual, Hannah North was at her desk outside the senior administrative assistant's office. But for once she just waved Gaunt on towards Falconer's door. He went in and Falconer was standing at a table near the window, studying a large road map.

"Sit down," he instructed. "I need another minute."

Gaunt settled in a chair near Falconer's desk, and waited. It was a big, simply furnished room. All civil servants of Henry Falconer's grade had that size of desk, that size of personal filing cabinet, that framed photograph of the Queen on one wall, and the other basics. Falconer had added one or two personal touches, mostly things his wife wouldn't allow him to keep at home. That included the majestic old grandfather clock which ticked slowly in the far corner. It had one of the prized Midlothian painted faces and was a family heirloom. But it had still been banished. There were three telephones on the tidy desk.

"Sorry." Falconer had finished with the map. He folded it, tucked it into his briefcase, then sat behind his desk. "So that you know what's happening, Hannah collected the information I needed from New Register House. It looks like we may have another Hartondee heir." He glanced towards the briefcase. "As soon as we finish talking, I'm driving up to Stonehaven."

"Who have we got?" asked Gaunt. "I thought the family tree had withered."

"I had. But we're talking about other aspects." Falconer hesitated then shook his head. "Leave it there, Jonny. Till I'm sure. All right?"

Gaunt shrugged, puzzled. "Whatever you want."

"I'm trying to be careful," said Falconer grimly. "I don't want to bring any Florian Beck type trouble on anyone else, maybe without reason. We're talking about—well, uncertain things." He paused, cleared his throat, then added blandly, "I'm taking Hannah with me. She might be useful."

"Because of things?" suggested Gaunt helpfully.

"What else?" Falconer treated him to a quick, suspicious glare, then seemed satisfied. "We'll have to overnight up around Stonehaven, one way or another we should be back in the office by tomorrow afternoon at the latest. Then we're maybe into a new chapter with the Hartondee saga." He paused, considered Gaunt again, then asked, "Any progress, home or away?"

"Some. Not all of it solid," said Gaunt.

He told Falconer, starting with Gladstone Baxter, then going on through what he'd learned from John Darnley's secretary, ending up with what he'd just been told by Dieter Vogt. Throughout it all, Henry Falconer sat wooden-faced but listening carefully. To become senior administrative assistant to the Queen's and Lord Treasurer's Remembrancer required both attributes in fairly equal measures. But at the finish, Falconer spent a moment scraping a thumbnail along his chin while the grandfather clock ticked in the background.

"You think John Darnley could be Mr. Smith?" he asked.

"Yes," said Gaunt.

"But you can't prove it, of course." Falconer sighed. "Let's go into an 'if' mode. If that couple you glimpsed at the airport were by chance this William and Mary Hamilton—"

"Which we don't know."

"Then maybe they were going out on one of the Spanish flights. We don't know why they'd be in Edinburgh, we don't know what reason there would be for them meeting Darnley at the airport before he took his London flight, we don't know what names they're using, we would have one hell of a job proving anything about them?"

Gaunt nodded.

"That's what I thought," said Falconer acidly. "You say you didn't tell any of this to your friend Vogt?"

"Would it have helped?"

"Probably not—not on its own." Falconer pointed a forefinger for emphasis. "Keep every part of this notion on Hold until we've something more to back it. You're going to see John Milton this evening?"

"As he invited. With luck, Joan Dennan might be there," said Gaunt.

"Then be careful," warned Falconer. "The woman sounds the kind who could eat you for breakfast." He saw Gaunt grin and flushed. "I mean it."

"I won't forget," said Gaunt, and rose, still grinning. "Good luck at Stonehaven, Henry. But the nights can be cold up there—tell Hannah to pack her thermals."

He left while Falconer was still spluttering. Outside, Hannah North looked up at him from her desk as he appeared. She gave him a slight smile, but there was a glint in her eyes which dared him to open his mouth. Gaunt contented himself with a faint quiver of a wink. Then he retreated back to his own part of the building, to the Hartondee file, to his telephone, to a list of contact names who could sometimes help, and to the kind of slogging afternoon which was the way most things that mattered got themselves sorted out.

Fifteen minutes later one of the typing pool coven looked in on him with an unasked mug of coffee and casually managed to mention that Falconer and Hannah North had left together. Gaunt just as casually told her to mind her own business, knew he'd regret it later, and went back to his telephone again.

Three hours on, he was one of the last few people still in the building. He had a splitting headache and his back was hurting. He did the only sensible thing left. Gaunt gave up, heaved the Hartondee file into his Pending basket, and went home.

He checked the BMW's rear-view mirror a few times to make sure he wasn't being followed through the evening traffic. Satisfied, Gaunt parked the car outside his apartment and went in. The first thing he saw was a note left by the cleaning woman. Something had gone wrong with his washing machine, and could he get it fixed so she could use it on Wednesday? No magic wand was attached. The day's mail amounted to a reminder that his car insurance was due for renewal.

A painkiller with some water dealt with his back. Gaunt took a shower and put on a clean shirt. He loafed in his armchair and sipped a small Glenlivet malt from the duty-free bottle while Thelonious Monk had another hissing romp on the turntable. Then he went out and ate at the small Italian restaurant round the corner. But he kept an eye on the clock and avoided the we-never-close poker game run by the waiters behind plastic curtains in the front kitchen. He was home in time to catch the TV news headlines at nine.

It was dusk when he left again and got into the BMW. By nine-thirty he was in the expense-account suburb of Barnton, where the houses had treble garages and designer gardens. He parked in a side street, then walked from there, through a thickly hedged lane, to the rear of John Milton's home. A small gate led into Milton's back garden and the plump stockbroker had been waiting. The kitchen door opened quickly, Gaunt was beckoned in, then the door closed again the moment the visitor was inside.

"Sorry," said Milton. He gave an embarrassed grin, but he took a last, cautious look out at the garden before he switched his full attention to Gaunt. "Did I ever pretend I was meant to be a hero?"

"Did I ever suggest it?" asked Gaunt. He looked around. "Where's Joan?"

"Joan, who is my wife, went out. She thinks it was her idea. She'll be late back, and she doesn't know about this." Milton didn't elaborate. "But about Joan, who is her cousin, I don't know. The last we heard was that telephone call to say she was back from Bavaria. You haven't—?"

"Not yet."

"Jonny, I—uh—" Milton shuffled his feet and gestured around them. The kitchen was big, modern and airy. "Do you mind if we talk in here? There's a strange car parked near the front of the house, with people sitting in it. I think I've seen it before. I don't know why, I don't particularly want to find out."

Gaunt considered him. "You still think that way?"

"That I'm being watched?" Milton nodded. "Maybe not all the time, but it's like someone wants to know about me."

"Then it's the kitchen and I'll settle for a beer." Gaunt winked to put him at ease, took one of the chairs at the kitchen table, swung it round and used it saddle-style.

"A beer, you get." Milton relaxed a little and brought two cans from the big white refrigerator. He took another of the chairs, they opened the beers, gestured a silent mutual toast, and drank from the cans.

"I'll start," suggested Gaunt.

He deliberately missed out any mention of the three thugs who had tried to attack him, but he gave Milton a fast canter through most of the other things that had happened that day, enough to bring him up to date. At regular intervals, the stockbroker either nodded gloomily or raised a surprised eyebrow.

"Stirred things up, hasn't she?" he said softly at the end. "Wife's Cousin Joan, I mean."

"With some people, it's a gift." Gaunt took another moisten of beer then wiped his mouth with the back of his hand. "Your turn."

"I'll try." Milton was wearing denims that cost money to look ragged. He sat back, hooking his thumbs into the broad leather belt which protected his substantial girth. "I've nosed around, I've asked a little, and I've discussed things with my computer—she's friendly enough if you talk nicely to her. Then I've telephoned some people I won't name—people who matter, the kind who even pay their accounts when I send them. Understand?"

"Real people." Gaunt gave a respectful nod. "Get to it, John."

"I'm trying." Milton opened a drawer in the table and brought out a notebook. He flicked through pages crammed with notes and calculations. "This is background detail—all I've kept. I shredded the computer print-outs." He closed the notebook. "We've one big start-point question. What is Hartondee about? I had a wide enough choice. We were looking at White Knights or Chinese Walls, could we have found ourselves a Poison Pill lying waiting?"

"Meaning we're deep into financial jargon." Gaunt frowned.

"Jungle jargon," Milton corrected him, and wasn't smiling. "Jonny, some of today's financial giants would look at Al Capone and think him a sissy. To be in their league, you've got to combine the moral scruples of an alleycat with the caring touch of Genghis Khan. If the bottom line to a calculation says kill, they kill." He looked at Gaunt over the top of his beer. "You've seen."

"I've seen," agreed Gaunt softly.

"When I started, I wondered about a White Knight set-up. You know about them? That's when a friendship group of companies set up a secret agreement. If any one of them looks like being taken over by an unwelcome predator from outside, the White Knight is ready to gallop in. Meaning there will always be a better takeover offer when required, with friendlier terms." Milton paused. "At least, that's what is supposed to happen. In the last big one I know about, the White Knight was a Robber Baron in disguise. You follow?"

"I'm trying." It wasn't easy.

"Forget any Chinese Wall scenario—not with Hartondee." Milton finished his beer in a long gulp and set the can aside. "There was a spell when I thought about a Poison Pill—that's like when Company A is being attacked by big bandit Company B and knows it can't win. So when it knows that Company B is locked into as expensive a takeover offer as possible, Company A very quickly and quietly sells off its best assets at cut-rate prices to Company C. What happens is that Company B thinks it's buying a bag filled with goodies. It pays a lot of money, but the goodies have already gone. Still with me?"

"I count on my fingers," said Gaunt grimly. "Slow down. What happens to Company A?"

"Finished, taken over. But big bad Company B discovers it's bought itself a self-inflicted, hopefully mortal wound."

"Is it legal?"

"Is anyone left with clean enough hands to take it to court?" Milton grimaced, closed the notebook, and rose to his feet. "I want to check that car outside." He left the kitchen, but was back inside a minute. He looked at Gaunt and shrugged. "It's still there. I'm not happy."

"I'll deal with it," promised Gaunt.

"When?"

"When we're finished. Before Joan comes home."

"I'll trust you on that." Milton went to the refrigerator and returned with two more cans of beer. Once they had opened them, he sat down. "You want to know about Hartondee, I'm going to tell you about Hartondee. Forget the outside face—that's camouflage. In my trade some people would call it a parking garage. You understand?"

"No." Gaunt shook his head.

"With your kind of investment record, that figures." Milton managed to grin at him. "Jonny, all Hartondee really amounts to is a great, big, safe-deposit box, a very private bank. Like a hoard of pirate gold—" He saw Gaunt's expression. "Have I lost you?"

"Yes," said Gaunt bleakly. "Try harder."

"Hartondee." John Milton savoured the sound of the name. "Right, but this time pay attention. A few years ago some very rich people—maybe one in particular—spent time locating the right little company for their needs. It had seen bad times and it had seen good. An existing company that wouldn't attract any particular attention, and where they certainly didn't expect to take out any particular profit. Got it so far?"

Gaunt nodded.

"The new owners knew there were still some minority shareholders around, but they were nothing to worry about. They wanted Hartondee as a garage—a place where they could shelter assets from other places. Maybe dividends, maybe shares, maybe bonds, maybe cash, everything coming back to that one little base. Filtering back through layers of nominee shareholders, through layers of funny-bunny boards of directors—multi-national style."

"Taxes—"

"Everything probably legal, Jonny. We're not talking tax evasion. We're talking investment power. The kind of power that suddenly appears as surprise proxy votes at a crucial time. It explodes—bang!" The plump stockbroker slapped his cupped hands together, loud and hard. "It makes things happen, then it disappears again. But Hartondee, the upfront company, doesn't break any laws. It just ambles along."

"How much are the Peter Church shares really worth?" asked Gaunt in a slow, deliberate voice.

"Five per cent of Hartondee." Milton sighed and shook his head. "Florian Beck was offered four hundred thousand?"

Gaunt nodded.

"That could come out of the Hartondee petty cash," said Milton derisively. "That's—ah—assuming I'm right about the rest."

"Then what could Hartondee be worth?" persisted Gaunt.

"I asked my computer to consider the possibilities." Milton took a long swallow of beer then gave a comic grimace. "She tried for three hours, then she switched herself off."

"Guess."

"Pick a number." Milton shook his head. "We're talking tens of millions."

"Proof?"

"Not from me. You're speaking to a simple little Edinburgh stockbroker who doesn't want to get involved. I like the way things are for me, I can even tolerate having one or two nut-case clients." Milton paused, looked warily at Gaunt, then surrendered a little. "I could maybe give you a non-attributable hint or two—"

"I'll take them."

"Check with any newspaper clippings library, and you'll be surprised how many of our real financial moguls have died over the last twelve months." Milton gave a quick headshake as he saw Gaunt's unspoken question. "Not that way, Jonny. Mostly they were old men, natural causes. But their deaths caused some ripples in the markets—some of them strange ripples. A couple of ripples even started about Hartondee. The suggestion was that some minority shareholdings might have quietly changed hands."

"Which in turn could make the Peter Church sleepers more important?"

"There's a play in bridge called the see-saw squeeze," said Milton obliquely. "Everything in it depends on timing. A five per cent holding in Hartondee could swing a takeover attempt maybe one way, maybe another. Or the Church shares were going to be kept in reserve while the battle shaped."

"Except that Joan Dennan came along?"

"Light blue paper, retire immediately," agreed Milton.

Gaunt gave that a moment, letting it sink in. "Whoever gets Hartondee—?"

"Gets everything," said Milton. "Presuming someone knows how to look."

"Someone like Darnley?"

"He's got my vote." Milton frowned. "Darnley has to know his way around better than anyone else."

"Better than Gladstone Baxter?"

"I'd rate Baxter as high-class hired help."

Gaunt gave a faint grin at the description. "So now tell me about Spain."

"Spain?" Milton said very softly. "How do you know about Spain, damn you?"

"Henry Falconer backtracked one of the feeler offers that came into the Remembrancer. There was a built-in block, but something about it said Spain."

"Off-shore Spain—Majorca in the Balearics," corrected Milton with a degree of pleasure. "Or that's how it looks."

"Who says?" asked Gaunt.

"People," said Milton. "Some people who notice that kind of thing. There's been a pattern of computer chatter which has been coming out of Majorca for a lot of time now—business chatter, heavily coded. Immediately afterwards, some things usually happen in some of the European markets."

"Does this chatter have a label?" asked Gaunt patiently. He tried again as John Milton shook his head. "How about a wild guess?"

"One or two people think it might be a man named Edward Sarr. Have you heard of him?"

"No."

"Edward Sarr spends a lot of money keeping things that way." Milton nursed his beer-can. "He's one of the genuine old financial giants, the real kind, Jonny. Over a decade ago, he built himself some kind of fort in Majorca, got inside, closed the door, and began keeping everyone out. There were noises that he'd retired from business life, and it's stayed that way." He stopped Gaunt's next question. "That's all I know, Jonny. I can try for more—but tomorrow."

"Do that," said Gaunt softly. Getting information out of John Milton could be like pulling teeth. But the Edinburgh stockbroker was always reliable, didn't deal in wisps of fiction. "Give it a try, we'll do the same." He pushed back his chair and rose. "Now suppose we see if this car that worries you is still outside."

They left the kitchen and went through a long, oak-panelled hall to the front of the house. Darkness had arrived, but Gaunt stopped Milton as he made to switch on a light. They went into one of the front rooms and around a black-shadowed obstacle course of furniture, then reached a window. There were street lights, and a clouded moon. Again Gaunt grabbed Milton, keeping him in the shadow of the window.

"It's still there." Milton pointed.

The car was on the other side of the street, not far distant, and parked under a tall hedge which fronted a large two-storey villa. The vehicle was a big, old-model Ford and Gaunt could make out two figures in the front seats.

"Wait," said Milton. He retreated further back into the room, a drawer opened then closed, and he came back with a pair of binoculars. "Try these."

Gaunt did. He adjusted the focus, saw the car suddenly become large and very near, then gave a soft whistle and tightened the focus another fraction. The street lighting was good, the binoculars were good. He could see the faces of the two men aboard the car, and they were two of the trio who had tried to attack him in Queen Street. There might be a third shape behind them. Putting down the binoculars, knowing he hadn't told Milton that part of the story, remembering that Milton's wife was still out, he hesitated.

"Well?" asked Milton.

"I'm thinking." Gaunt looked at the car again, then at the villa beyond the hedge. The villa had lights behind some of its windows. "Who lives over there?"

"You met him once. He's a banker named Macdonald." Milton shook his head. "But he's on a business trip to New York. His wife Rose is over there, on her own with a couple of kids. She can't help."

"You know her?" persisted Gaunt.

"She's friendly with Joan." Milton was puzzled. "Why?"

Gaunt told him. For a few moments the stockbroker stared, then a wide grin spread across his face.

"I like it," he said happily. "Let me back off to reach a phone." He went away. Moments later, Gaunt could hear him using the telephone, then a pause while the voice at the other end made some kind of startled reply. Milton made soothing noises, then said the same thing over again. There was another brief exchange, then the telephone went back down on its rest and Milton returned.

"She'll do it," he confirmed.

They had to wait another full seven minutes by Gaunt's wristwatch. Outside, the old Ford remained parked in the shelter of the hedge, there was no sign of any movement by its occupants.

Then, suddenly, the little world down below seemed to erupt in a glare of headlights as a total of four police cars that had crept into position made their move. Two blocked any chance of escape from the street. The second pair roared in, blue lights flashing and sirens braying. Uniformed men tumbled out, the Ford's doors were pulled open, three struggling figures were dragged into the light.

At last, as the three prisoners were driven away, Milton's telephone rang. He left Gaunt, answered the call, then switched on the room light when he came back.

"She enjoyed doing it," he reported.

Gaunt grinned. A worried telephone call to the police from a woman on her own in a house, reporting that she had a suspicious car outside and possible prowlers, usually got results. When the woman was a banker's wife it helped even more.

John Milton hadn't been directly involved. He certainly wouldn't be worried for the rest of the night. The three men from the car were going to have to do some heavy explaining—if they could.

"Another beer?" suggested Milton.

Gaunt shook his head. "I'll be in touch tomorrow. But I need one more favour."

"I'll listen," said Milton cautiously.

"It's simple enough," Gaunt assured him. "It's for when Wife's Cousin Joan contacts you—"

"I'll tell her a little, but not a lot. Definitely nothing about Majorca or that old devil Edward Sarr," said Milton without having to be prompted. "That way, everybody else stays happy—including her husband."

"She's married?" Gaunt blinked.

"An airline executive, the kind who only gets home at weekends. You'd like him." Milton paused, looked at Gaunt, sighed, and gave a slight grin. "Jonny, I warned you off—remember? I thought you knew or that at least you guessed. Joan Dennan keeps it a very quiet marriage—"

"Female accountants are bad news, married female accountants are worse?" guessed Gaunt.

Milton nodded. "But she seems to love the idiot. That's why she disappears at weekends. They go off to the original log cabin in the hills and hide together."

"This husband," said Gaunt wryly. "What's his name?"

"Dan. We call him Dan, Dan the Flying Machine Man," said Milton. "Why?"

"No reason," said Gaunt.

He clapped Milton on the shoulder, then left by the same back-door way he'd arrived, and headed towards his car.

It was nearly midnight when he got home. His telephone was ringing as he opened his front door. Kicking the door shut behind him, Gaunt strode over and answered the call in time.

It was Henry Falconer, and the Remembrancer's senior administrative assistant sounded impatient yet pleased with himself.

"Where have you been?" he demanded. "I've been trying your number for the last half hour."

"Out," said Gaunt. "Out working, Henry. Talking with John Milton."

"Good." Falconer made it an unimpressed grunt. "Hannah and I are still in Stonehaven. At this hour, we'll—ah—stay overnight. But we've made some progress. So I need you up here, first thing in the morning—you understand?"

"No," admitted Gaunt. "When is first thing?"

"Ten A.M. There's parking space down at the harbour, near the old

Tollbooth. We'll be waiting." Falconer paused, partly to make sure he was understood, partly to draw breath. "Was Milton interesting?"

"Very," said Gaunt.

"Good." There was a background noise at Falconer's end of the line, which could have been the clink of a bottle against glass. "You can tell me in the morning."

"Any messages for anyone?" asked Gaunt.

"Jonny, don't push your luck," said Falconer icily, and hung up.

Stonehaven is one hundred miles north of Edinburgh and fifteen miles south of Aberdeen, a fishing town of about five thousand people on the long, grey Scottish east coast. Inland is some of Scotland's richest farmland where plenty of names go back to Viking times and where carved standing stones tell of a history which was old long before then.

Jonathan Gaunt got there along the inland M90–A94 route, less scenic than the coastal A92 but faster. He timed it well. It was just after 8:15 A.M. when he left an Edinburgh which was misted by rain, three minutes before Falconer's 10 A.M. and bright sunlight when he reached Stonehaven.

He drove the BMW sedately into the little, saltaired town, and headed for the harbour. He saw Falconer's car straight away, parked near the main quay. There was space beside it, and Falconer got out from the passenger side as Gaunt drew in. Hannah North was in the driving seat and stayed there. Gaunt joined Falconer near the edge of the granite quay. The sea lapped below them, gulls were screaming around a newly arrived boat, and the smells of a working harbour were strong in their nostrils.

"You're prompt," said Falconer. His broad face looked unusually pleased, his voice was briskly cheerful. "That's good. And things are going well here—easier than I expected." He rubbed his hands together and beamed. "Yes, we've got our Hartondee heir—in fact, we've found a whole tribe of them. It's strange the way things happen, Jonny."

"Am I supposed to know what you're talking about?" asked Gaunt with a stony patience.

"You will." Falconer grinned. "We only got the last details settled this morning. Until we came up here yesterday, it was partly guesswork. Then, even as late as last night, I was trying to persuade a local lawyer with the splendid name of Hamish MacDonald that there are times when client confidentiality is a nonsense." He gave his forehead a wry massage with one hand. "That wasn't easy. I've the makings of a hangover to prove it."

"When do I get to hear?" asked Gaunt.

"Straight away." Falconer, wearing his city business clothes, looked out of place on the fishing port quay. But he was beaming. He waited as two fishermen in overalls and sweaters got into a rusty Volkswagen pick-up and drove it away in a stink of oily exhaust fumes. "We'll leave Hannah here, with my car. I'll come with you, in your car. I want you as a witness when we meet our new heir—to be more accurate, heiress!"

"Why me? Why not Hannah?" Gaunt raised an eyebrow.

"Hannah has her own things to do. There are statements to be collected, and copy documents from lawyer MacDonald and some other people. Anyway, I'd prefer her in the background." Falconer liked the word. "Yes, in the background."

Gaunt gave a wooden-faced nod, but could understand why. Turning away, Falconer looked over at his own car and at Hannah North. He raised a hand, and she gave a slight smile in reply. Then she turned the smile on Gaunt for a second, and started Falconer's car. Seconds later she drove past them, back towards the town. Falconer took his time about walking back to Gaunt's car. He stopped, his hand resting on the passenger door handle.

"We're not in a rush—not now," he declared. "We'll talk first. Here. I like the view."

They got aboard the BMW. There were several fishing boats tied up around the harbour, but they were outnumbered by pleasure craft of every kind. In the same way as the old Tollbooth building nearby had once been a courthouse and prison, then a storehouse, and was now mostly a museum, Stonehaven's harbour was going through a new time of change.

"I'll keep this to essentials. You'll hear the rest of it soon enough." Falconer sat back in the passenger seat, arms folded, eyes half closed. "James Church, our farmer—and son of Peter, our share-buyer—had an illegitimate daughter. We're going to see her. She's in her late fifties, she's married to a sea captain, and she has grandchildren."

"Dear God," said Gaunt softly.

"That's fair comment." Falconer chuckled to himself. "I'll tell you how we found her, Jonny. When we did the initial research work into the Church family, we had Harry Regan up here for a couple of days. You knew that."

Gaunt nodded. Regan was Companies Branch, young enough to still be eager.

"There was a line in his report about how he talked with a couple of old women who'd worked on James Church's farm as teenagers. They'd cackled about how any female had had to be careful when James Church was around, and that there had been some gossip about why one girl named Gordon left the farm in a hurry."

"You found her?"

"Hannah did, through New Register House's computers. There was a child. The birth certificate said Father Unknown."

"A child, now the lady with the sea captain husband?"

"And with grandchildren of her own." Falconer gently scratched the tip of his nose for a moment. "The rest of it can keep till we get there—that lawyer MacDonald was our real key, despite being so damned stubborn." He paused again. "Now Milton. Tell me."

Gaunt did, keeping his story to essentials, but leaving in the three men in the parked car. That made Falconer chortle. The rest didn't.

"Edward Sarr." He scowled, closed his eyes for a moment, then opened them again, still scowling. "His name used to make headlines —financial and other kinds. Most things he touched turned into gold for him."

"While other people lost out?"

"Usually." Falconer brushed the irrelevance aside. "Edward Sarr has kept a very low profile for years. I had to think to remember if he was still alive. Damn—is there any chance your friend Milton has tapped the wrong grapevine?" He stopped himself. "No, ignore that. We take the other view. Suppose the story is true, what do we do about it?"

Gaunt shrugged. His grey-green eyes were intent on watching a sail-boat manoeuvre its way out of harbour towards the sea. It had a bright blue sail, which was flapping in the wind.

John Darnley, as Hartondee's company secretary, had to know most of the real answers. But with Darnley gone from the scene, perhaps still in London but perhaps a lot further away, who was left? He thought of the limping figure of Gladstone Baxter, but with no real conviction. The accountant had to be someone just hired to fill a particular role. It probably ended there.

"There's an incidental," said Falconer unexpectedly. "Your friend Joan Dennan spent all yesterday prowling Stonehaven." His broad face looked momentarily pleased. "An eager young woman, but asking the wrong questions at the wrong places. Hannah and I managed to dodge her. I gather she ended up staying in a hotel overnight then went back to Edinburgh this morning." He looked at Gaunt. "You—ah—?"

"I haven't heard." Gaunt shook his head moodily. "She's married."

"A lot of people are." Falconer made it a sad commentary. He sat in silence for another moment, then made up his mind. "All right, we finish what we're here to do. We tackle the Edward Sarr theory when we get back to Edinburgh." He took a last look around the harbour. "We're heading inland."

"Far?" asked Gaunt.

"Just a few miles," said Falconer. A small, secret smile showed on his mouth. "A very few miles." He glanced at his wristwatch. "We should be expected, and I was told the way."

They took the main north road out of town, signposted for Aberdeen, but soon left it and turned west on a narrow secondary road which plunged them deep into rich, green farming country where the fields sometimes held cattle and sometimes held crops. The BMW purred past farmhouses and cottages, through a tiny village where half a dozen hens scurried out of their path, and then Falconer told Gaunt to stop. He consulted a slip of paper he took from an inside pocket, then was satisfied.

"Round the next bend, then take a small farm track on your right. A fairly modern house, with a red roof. We stop there." He chuckled. "All will be revealed."

Gaunt set the car moving again. The side road was round the bend, marked by a flame of pink azalea bush, and they made the turn in, then bounced and swayed along the potholed track. In another minute they had reached the house with the red roof. It had white walls and large windows, a neat garden, and a small front porch where a large mongrel dog slept under a baby's pram.

"Here?" asked Gaunt, stopping the car.

Falconer nodded. Gaunt switched off the engine and, like Falconer, got out of the vehicle. An iron gate squeaked as they opened it, then they walked up a gravel path towards the front door. There was a baby in the pram, still sound asleep. But the dog had wakened and was watching them carefully. His teeth bared a little and he gave a soft, warning growl.

"Shut up, Harry," said a firm voice. "It's all right."

The dog fell silent, though those teeth stayed bared. The front door had opened. The woman looking out at them was tall and broad-shouldered, with short, pepper-and-salt hair and a firmly boned face.

She was in her late fifties and was wearing a faded but well-laundered cotton dress which had no particular shape, yet which still looked right for her.

"Mrs. Forrest?" asked Henry Falconer cautiously.

"Sheena Forrest." Though her smile was friendly, her eyes were watchful. "You're the people from Edinburgh?"

"The Queen's and Lord Treasurer's Remembrancer's Office." Falconer took out his identification, and waited while she read it. "My colleague's name is Gaunt. You were told about us."

"Hamish MacDonald telephoned from Stonehaven late last night. He was out here straight after breakfast." She beckoned. "Come in."

They went into the little house and into a bright front-facing living room. It was comfortably furnished, there were family photographs along the top of a bookshelf, and one which had pride of place showed a bald, cheerful man in merchant navy officer's tropical uniform.

"Good morning," said a new voice, and a young woman who had been standing near the window came towards them. She had the same tall, broad-shouldered build as Sheena Forrest, but she had long, red hair and was dressed in a dark green roll-neck sweater and denim trousers. Her eyes were equally careful.

"My daughter Debbie," said Sheena Forrest almost unnecessarily. "We've another Sheena in the pram outside, my new granddaughter." She exchanged a small, slight smile with her daughter. "Debbie's married name is Harris—he's the vet in the next village. I asked her to come over. Hamish MacDonald thought it would be a good idea— he was going to stay too, but I told him we could manage. I'll speak with him later."

"Lawyers always worry me," said Gaunt.

"Hamish wouldn't." Sheena Forrest chuckled. "I've known him since we were teenagers. His father handled everything for my mother since—well, since all this began." She indicated her red-haired daughter. "Don't worry about talking in front of Debbie. I've three children—she's the youngest. They've always known most of the story."

Mother and daughter settled their visitors in two of the living room's big, deep-upholstered armchairs, then sat side by side on a matching couch.

"Your lawyer told you what this is about, Mrs. Forrest?" asked Falconer, probing his way.

"You want to prove that I'm James Church's bastard," she said calmly.

"Illegitimate child sounds better," murmured her daughter, unperturbed.

"You already know it says Father Unknown on my birth certificate." Sheena Forrest looked directly at Gaunt and gave an almost reassuring smile. "It stopped worrying me a long, long time ago, Mr. Gaunt. Did you know it used to be even worse in the old days? That's when they used a different label. The parish register used to say Born in Fornication."

"You'll embarrass them," said the younger woman. She sat with her feet drawn up beneath her, hands clasped around her knees. "Most farming people are realists and always have been. Being illegitimate—"

"A bastard," contributed Sheena Forrest.

"Being illegitimate can be different in the country compared with in the city," said the redhead determinedly.

"Some of the best people qualify," agreed Sheena Forrest. "Why keep it a secret? My husband sails an oil tanker in the Persian Gulf—I told him the first day we met. All my children were told as soon as I thought they could understand. I had only one problem. My mother never really wanted to tell me my father's name."

Falconer nodded slowly. "That was part of the bargain?"

"Yes," said Sheena Forrest.

"Henry," said Gaunt. He waited until he was sure he had Falconer's attention. "It would help if somebody spelled this out for me. Please?"

"I'm sorry." Falconer looked almost uncomfortable. "We have an unusual situation. I want a witness who has had no prior knowledge."

"That's me," agreed Gaunt.

Falconer shrugged and turned back to the older woman.

"Your mother was Ellen Gordon. She died six years ago." He paused long enough for the woman to nod. "Your father—the man not named on the birth certificate—had died ten years before that, hadn't he?"

"Yes."

"So you knew him?" Gaunt was surprised.

"By name. My mother told me just before I married." Her mouth tightened. "After that I saw him once or twice—by accident. He ignored me, I ignored him. That was part of the bargain he'd made with my mother."

"Your lawyer showed me the document," said Falconer softly. "Mrs. Forrest, we'd like to hear it from you—in your own words."

For a moment the tall woman hesitated. She glanced at her daughter, who nodded.

"It's simple enough," said Sheena Forrest. She shut all emotion from her voice. "Ellen Gordon, my mother, was a young farm servant on James Church's farm outside of Stonehaven. She was twenty. James Church was about thirty, already married with two children. They were—"

"A boy, and a daughter named Ann. The boy died young. We know what happened to Ann." Falconer eased the story on.

"My mother had gone into Stonehaven one New Year's Eve to see the fireball festival." She gave a questioning glance towards Gaunt.

"Burn out one year, bring in the new." Gaunt nodded that he understood.

"She met James Church, they spent the night together, and that was how it began." The woman shrugged. "About six months later she was pregnant. James Church did a deal with her. Church's wife didn't know, was never to know. My mother had to leave the farm. She didn't want to go back to her people up north, she wanted to stay in the Stonehaven area. Church got her a job near here, helping on another farm—pregnant farm girls weren't exactly unique."

"And the bargain?" prompted Falconer.

"Ellen Gordon would refuse to name the father of her child. In return, James Church gave her a lump sum down, then she got money every month through a lawyer—Hamish MacDonald's father —until I was sixteen." She ran a hand through that short, pepper-and-salt hair and grimaced. "He was reasonably generous, I suppose. But the real reason was probably that his wife's family had money and could have finished him if they'd found out. Anyway, it was a properly drawn agreement between Church and my mother. They made a bargain, in their own ways they both kept to it."

"And you ignored him even when you knew—"

"The way it was agreed." She nodded.

Her daughter scowled. "I'd have spat in his eye."

"My mother still got the occasional money from him." Sheena Forrest shrugged and gave a wry smile. "The papers they signed didn't in any way acknowledge I was his daughter. James Church didn't take any chances."

"Damn him anyway." Debbie Harris touched her mother's hand, and gave Falconer a puzzled scowl. "How did you find my mother?"

"Old gossip remembered, old records checked, then a degree of luck," admitted Falconer. "The name Ellen Gordon, the registered birth that said Father Unknown—and tracking down your lawyer. If I was right about the rest of it, there had to be a lawyer lurking somewhere."

Sheena Forrest grimaced. "Hamish MacDonald says I may have inherited a chunk of Church family money, and that was why he agreed to help you. But I can't prove that James Church was my father—"

"There are situations where the Remembrancer can be his own judge and jury," mused Gaunt. "Correct, Henry?"

"Don't doubt it, Sheena Forrest," said Falconer. His broad face split in a grin. "We need you. You're going to be reasonably rich."

He told them why and the two women sat open-mouthed for a long moment. That ended when the baby outside gave an attention-seeking cry. Immediately, the dog began barking.

"Debbie, see to that pair," said Sheena Forrest crisply. "Give each of them a bone or something." She got to her feet. "I know what I'm going to do. Where's that bottle of whisky—the special bottle, the one your father was saving?"

She provided her own answer, going out of the room and returning a moment later. She had a bottle in one hand. When Henry Falconer saw the label, he stared in awe.

"You know what this is, Mrs. Forrest?" he blurted.

"Strong drink." She opened the bottle, contemplated the sealing cap, then threw it over her shoulder. "We won't need that again. You'll join us, gentlemen?"

They nodded respectfully. Any bottle of twenty-one-year-old triple-run single malt whisky demanded it.

"There's one thing." Sheena Forrest busied herself pouring stiff measures into glasses. The baby was exempt, but a taste went into a saucer for the dog Harry. "My mother wouldn't admit to anyone else that James Church was my father. But she always told me it made no difference—that an illegitimate child had no legal claim against a father's estate."

"What your mother told you was true—or it used to be." Falconer took the glass he was handed and fondled it carefully. "Under Scottish law, illegitimate children used to have no rights of succession. If this had happened thirty years ago, you probably wouldn't have got anything. But then the law was changed back in the 1960s. There's no problem." He raised his glass. "Your good health, Sheena Forrest."

"Your good health," agreed Gaunt. He sipped the silky-smooth malt and let the liquor glow down his throat, then he waited. "Sheena, just one thing. You said you'd two other children?"

"A married son in Canada, with two children of his own. My other daughter is a doctor in Glasgow. Why?"

"Tell them, but tell no one else for a few days. If any stranger comes near you, contact me or your lawyer."

"But I've not to ask you why?" The woman looked at them seriously for a moment and nodded. "I'll do it that way—I know there must be things you haven't told me. But whatever is happening, I've got family. Isn't there something called safety in numbers?"

"There is," agreed Gaunt, and grinned at the way her eyes sparkled. "We'll make sure you've no problems."

"Good." Sheena Forrest beamed. "How's your glass, Mr. Falconer?"

"Fine," began Falconer. "Still half full—"

"Half full is half empty," said Sheena Forrest firmly. "Bring it here."

Eventually, she made them coffee before they left. Jonathan Gaunt was glad. He had the BMW to drive back to Edinburgh. Henry Falconer, senior administrative assistant to the Queen's and Lord Treasurer's Remembrancer, had fewer worries. In the passenger seat, he sang most of the way.

One part of the Hartondee shares mystery was behind them. All they needed now was the same kind of luck with what was left.

CHAPTER 6

Jonathan Gaunt and Falconer were back in the Remembrancer's Office in Edinburgh by mid-afternoon, after a brief stop for a sandwich at a roadside restaurant on the way back from Stonehaven. Hannah North had arrived at her desk more than an hour ahead of them, and was already busy sorting out the transcribed statements and copy documents she'd collected. She was left alone. When Hannah North was busy, it was safer that way.

But other people had also been busy. There was a package from John Milton waiting to be opened on Gaunt's desk. The stockbroker had sent round a hand-written version of what he had told Gaunt the previous evening. Some old press clippings were attached, each topped by a headline which had shouted about some new exploit of the highly publicized life of Edward Sarr.

Most were about Sarr's financial adventures, from SARR BUYS IN DAWN SWOOP to PROFITS SURGE AS SARR REJECTS TACTICS CHARGES. But not all. Edward Sarr had twice been divorced, messily and expensively the second time. He had lost a son in a horse-riding accident. Another large headline declared FINANCE KING IN DRUGS SCANDAL. Then it had stopped, apart from a couple of brief, short-on-facts gossip column items which claimed that Edward Sarr, the "mystery millionaire," had been seen with friends in the Balearic Islands, mostly in Majorca, where he was now living in seclusion, and that the Sarr business empire was slowly dismantling its involvement in all high-profile activities.

Gaunt cornered one of the junior witches in the typing pool, who promised to get everything photocopied and send a set through to Henry Falconer. Then he tried Milton's private office line.

"I've got your package," he said when Milton answered. "Any problems after last night?"

"Not yet. I checked with the police as a concerned neighbour." Milton said it with a mock solemnity, then chuckled. "They're holding the three characters who were in that car. The car was stolen, then the charges go on through loitering with intent to little extras like assaulting the police."

"Never assault the police," said Gaunt. "They don't like it." He got to the other reason for his call. "Have you heard from Joan Dennan?"

"Not yet." Milton paused. "I could try her office, I suppose. But that might not be clever when Baxter could be sniffing around."

"Better leave it," agreed Gaunt. The chartered accountant might be eavesdropping on any call. "I'll try her at home tonight."

"Let me know if you do. She's still my wife's cousin, I'm supposed to keep her free from all harm." Milton gave a snort at the thought. "I'm scratching a few more odds and ends together on Edward Sarr. The general money market opinion is that the old devil is still out in Majorca, stirring things for the hell of it now and again with his friendly computer terminal." There was a sigh on the line. "Hell, Jonny, by now he's knocking seventy! If you were his age, living out there with his kind of money, would you keep doing it?"

"Only to annoy people like you," said Gaunt.

He said goodbye and hung up.

He had his own paperwork to clear, and his own version of what had happened at Stonehaven to dictate to a tape. When that was finished, he sat back and smiled at the memory of how the tall, broad-shouldered grandmother figure of Sheena Forrest had celebrated good fortune with that bottle of malt whisky.

Hartondee's shares were going to make up for a few of the heartbreaks she must have had as a child with the label Father Unknown. Sheena Forrest was going to enjoy the money coming her way. She was going to spread much of it around her children and grandchildren—a family that gave her what amounted to safety in numbers.

The telephone buzzed and Gaunt answered it. The redhead at the Remembrancer's Office switchboard told him she had a call for him from Germany. Another moment, and Dieter Vogt was on the line.

"Things are happening," said the Bavarian briskly. "Jonny, have you anything planned for the next couple or so days?"

"Why?" Gaunt was suspicious.

"Warum nicht?" countered Vogt cheerfully. "Right now, my boss is speaking to your boss on another line. Will I tell you why?"

"That might help." Gaunt looked round and saw his office door was lying open. At their desks outside, a couple of the typing pool coven were just within earshot. Without rising, he pushed the door shut with his foot. "What's happening?"

"We have ourselves a new witness in the Florian Beck killing." Dieter Vogt made it clear he was having a good day. "She was the fairly steady girlfriend of Heine Norden, who had the Heckler and Koch pistol—the man who drove the Mercedes, *ja?*"

"What about her?"

"A few things," said the Bavarian laconically. "Her name is Anna Horn. The BKA picked her up in Frankfurt and hauled her back to Rottach. Then they showed her Norden's body. They said they needed it identified."

"Playing dirty," said Gaunt softly. Both Norden and Conrad Hass, the second man in the Mercedes, had been formally identified before he'd flown back to Scotland from Munich. "Do they use that one often?"

"It got her talking, more than she'd done up till then." Vogt didn't make it any kind of an apology. "Remember how we had this description of a *Britischer*, tall and well dressed, who called himself Smith? The man who came over and hired Hass and Norden, then targeted them on Florian Beck?"

"Real name probably John Darnley."

"An *Advokat*—"

"An *Advokat* we've temporarily mislaid." Gaunt scowled at the telephone.

"Anna Horn says she only saw him once, and didn't speak with him." Dieter Vogt wasn't perturbed. "But it's different with our tourist couple William and Mary Hamilton. Anna says that she and Norden spent two days with the Hamiltons in Munich. They even met them at the airport when they arrived—and the Hamiltons didn't arrive from London, Jonny. The Hamiltons flew in first class on an Iberia flight from Majorca."

"She's sure?" Gaunt sat upright.

"It gets better," promised the Bavarian. "Some time over the two days, Anna told Mary Hamilton that she'd been to Majorca, that Norden had once taken her out for a week to a hotel in Magaluf. You know Magaluf?"

"Once seen, try to forget it," said Gaunt dryly.

Vogt laughed. "Anyway the Hamilton woman said that she and her husband had come from the other end of the island, up in the north-east, where it was quiet—very different. They had a boat out there, and they'd rented a villa inland. Then the man Hamilton growled at her and she stopped talking. That was all Anna got from her."

"You're certain?"

"I'm certain, the BKA are certain," said Vogt laconically. "Almost everything we get keeps saying Majorca, *nicht wahr?*"

"Almost everything," agreed Gaunt unemotionally. "There's more. There's a man named Edward Sarr, who can wave bags of gold."

He took a moment to sketch the barest outline of what he meant. There was a brief, puzzled silence from Vogt's end of the line. The *Kriminalinspektor* had been given something to worry about.

"Your boss can tell the rest of it to my boss," said Vogt at last. He brightened. "Jonny, I'm being flown out there tomorrow morning. The Spanish authorities have been asked to cooperate, I'll be working for both our own people and the Federal *Bundeskriminalamt*—and the BKA don't let that happen too often."

"It makes sense," said Gaunt.

"That's the same reason we want you out there, Jonny," said Vogt earnestly. "You know more of the background, you know this man Darnley, you've seen the Hamilton couple—"

"I've plenty of gossip and plenty of possibilities. That's about all," warned Gaunt. "I'm low on facts."

"But will you come?"

"I don't make the decisions," said Gaunt.

"I think my boss can sell it to your boss, Jonny." Dieter Vogt was confident. "I think we'll both be on aircraft tomorrow, our people can sort out where we meet." He paused. "I was talking with Bessie King today, out at the Scheckheim test track. She was asking about you."

"How is she?" Gaunt realized he'd almost forgotten the friendly-faced Irishwoman who would have been Florian Beck's bride if he'd lived.

"Getting to accept what happened." Vogt paused again. "Jonny, have you talked or—ah—anything with Joan Dennan since you got back to Scotland?"

"No." Gaunt answered absently. He was thinking about how Henry Falconer might be reacting to the German request.

"She paid Bessie King ten thousand Deutschmarks to sign some papers," said Vogt mildly. "That's enough to buy a few hot dinners, and I'd like to know why."

Gaunt swore aloud. "What does Bessie King say?"

"That it had to do with Florian Beck's death and those Hartondee shares. She's not sure about the rest of it—but she decided she couldn't lose, so she signed and took the money."

"I'll check," said Gaunt. "I'll let you know."

"Tomorrow, in Majorca," suggested Vogt. "Over a drink. Your turn to buy."

The call ended. Replacing his receiver, Gaunt put his hands over his eyes for a moment and took a deep breath while he tried to slot what he'd been told into place. Some things fitted, too many other things didn't, and whatever Joan Dennan thought she was doing, he could have done without it. After another moment, he shoved back his chair and made his way to Henry Falconer's office. The door was open, and Hannah North was at her desk outside.

"He went upstairs to see the Remembrancer, Jonny." She nodded towards the room. "He said if you appeared you were to wait."

"He had a phone call?"

"From Munich, about you," she agreed. "He shouldn't be long." Hannah North sat back and gave him a smile of minimal sympathy. "Today Stonehaven, tomorrow the world—"

"Go to hell, Hannah," he said wearily, and went past her into Falconer's office.

The ponderous tick of the big, old-fashioned grandfather clock in the corner was a soothing sound as he stood at the window and looked down at the busy scene in George Street. It had its usual traffic tangle and the shops were busy. He watched a couple who had to be husband and wife and who were fussing around one of the parked cars. They seemed to be arguing about a package the man had dropped and the woman had retrieved. It was hard to decide whether they were arriving or leaving.

It could be difficult from a distance. Very difficult—and he saw he had it wrong as the couple went away from the car, walking in the late afternoon sunlight, disappearing into a shop, unaware of the way he was staring down at them. Very difficult—easy enough to see something the wrong way round.

He heard Falconer enter the room, and the door close.

"Something interesting?" asked Falconer, coming over. "The other day, I saw a couple of old-age pensioners knocking lumps out of a very large policeman." He rested his hands on the window sill. "I don't know what it was about, but they looked like Granny and Clyde."

Gaunt shook his head. "Not this time, Henry."

"Little things make life worth living." Falconer's face had acquired some red from the sun on his trip north. He left the window, beckoning Gaunt over to his desk, and they settled in chairs. "So—you had a phone call, I had a phone call."

Gaunt nodded.

"The West Germans want our help, the Remembrancer agrees they should get that help. Meaning you." Falconer bared his large teeth in what was meant to be a smile. "Then they'll owe us, which is always useful. You'll fly out tomorrow, Hannah can arrange the details. Any problems about it?"

"None."

"Good." Falconer considered him with a degree of doubt. "I'll be honest. I'm almost glad the West Germans are taking the initiative. I'd come very close to making the same decision—despite how little we've got in the way of real evidence. You understand me?"

"If things go wrong, this time we don't carry all of the blame," suggested Gaunt.

"Yes." Falconer pointed a warning finger. "Remember, Edward Sarr is still a considerable financial figure. You're only going out there because you're the nearest thing we have to an expert on the Hartondee shares situation and because if certain people are out there, then you can identify them."

"If."

"Damn it, what else?" demanded Falconer. "Our best bet is that if Sarr is in Majorca then John Darnley could be doing a London stopover then heading out there. We agree Gladstone Baxter is hired help, nothing more—"

"What about the Hamiltons?"

Falconer blinked. "Well, if they were the couple at the airport yesterday—"

"I say they were. I've had time enough to think about it." Gaunt rose and prowled back to the window again. "Henry, when you came in, I was watching people in a car down there. I didn't know whether they had arrived or were leaving—coming or going."

"So?" Falconer raised a puzzled eyebrow.

"I tried to guess," said Gaunt simply. "I got it wrong. They'd just arrived."

Henry Falconer took a bewildered moment or two longer then understood. He swore softly, under his breath.

"William and Mary Hamilton?" he asked.

"We thought they were leaving. Suppose we had that wrong?" asked Gaunt simply. "Suppose they'd arrived, suppose they were waiting in that airport bar to meet Darnley—"

"Why?"

Gaunt shook his head.

"It's possible." Falconer was reluctant. "They looked harmless—"

"But they're not."

Falconer sighed. "All right, I'll let people know that it's possible. We can run a check on passenger lists on yesterday's incoming flights—"

"If they called themselves Hamilton."

"Unlikely," agreed Falconer. He sucked his teeth for a moment while the grandfather clock sounded its slow rhythm. "All right, get everything for tomorrow sorted out with Hannah. Then—yes, maybe you should say a gentle word to your friend Milton. I think he'll be left alone after last night. But tell him that if anything worries him then we'll provide a couple of large police officers for a few days." He held up his hand as Gaunt nodded and rose. "I've got to attend a meeting at Crown Office, one I can't duck. I'll be late back, so—well, have a good trip."

It took another hour to "sort things out with Hannah." By then it was almost 6 P.M. and, apart from the security men, they were probably the last people in the building. She turned down Gaunt's offer of a drink, saying she had planned to work late anyway, and he made his way back to his own room. He hesitated a moment, then lifted the telephone and tapped out John Milton's office private number. It was a minor surprise that Milton answered, although he didn't sound pleased.

"I was on my way out," complained Milton. "I've got to get home, I've got to get changed, we're going out for the evening—there's a formal as hell reception up at the castle. Medals and things. I thought maybe you'd be there."

"Taking out the garbage?" Gaunt grinned at the telephone.

"So?" Milton was impatient.

"Any word about Wife's Cousin Joan?"

"No." Milton made it a sigh over the line. "I tried at the Gladstone Baxter office number this afternoon. The switchboard said she'd been in, and had talked with Baxter, then had gone again. I didn't ask for Baxter. Sensible?"

"Sure-footed brilliance," agreed Gaunt.

"I've tried her home number a couple times. It's ringing out, but it's like before—no reply."

"Where does she live?"

"Where?" Milton was mildly surprised. "You've got her phone number—"

"But she's ex-directory," reminded Gaunt. "What's the address?"

"Out along the old Dalkeith Road," said Milton. "Keep on until you get to some new housing at Douglas Hart. Second road on the right, Douglas Bank—number 20, third house along. If you go, tell her that my Joan says to answer her damned phone."

"I will," promised Gaunt. "John—"

"What?" Milton's impatience was mounting.

"Call it a postscript to last night." He heard a noise like a grunt and knew he had Milton's full attention again. "I'm not going to be around for a day or two. Nobody expects any more trouble heading your way, but stay out of dark corners. Tell Henry Falconer if you need any kind of help."

"I see." Milton spoke slowly. "This trouble—what could it look like?"

"A man and a woman, young middle-aged, ordinary. We don't expect it."

"Thanks," said Milton bleakly, and hung up.

Gaunt cleared the papers on his desk into the top drawer in one neat sweep, then went past Hannah North's desk on the way out. She looked up, nodded, but kept working. At the main door the duty security man wished him goodnight as he left. Then he walked through the sunlit cool of the evening along George Street to where he had left his car. There were people who claimed that George Street, with its calm dignity, could make the famed Princes Street look like an old tart when the light was right.

It was one of those evenings when he decided they were right.

The old Dalkeith Road began at the far end of Clerk Street in central Edinburgh, then ran due south from there. At that hour, although he was on a main feeder road for the A7 for Galashiels, traffic was light. Edinburgh was mostly indoors, eating, drinking or watching television, and the nearest thing he had to a delay was when approaching traffic began flashing headlights.

He slowed and the BMW drove sedately through a police radar trap, where a queue of unfortunates was being processed.

The Douglas Hart housing development was further out than Gaunt had expected. The gardens were small, some of the houses were still being built, but the second road on the right was clearly marked Douglas Bank and number 20 looked like the modern version of a small, neat ranchhouse. Instead of horses it had a Saab turbo and a Volkswagen GT Golf lying outside. He parked broadside behind them, switched off, then considered the little house for a moment.

A brief movement behind one of the curtained windows showed that he'd already been noticed. He got out slowly, deliberately spent a few seconds looking at what was the early days of a garden, then walked over to the front door and rang the bell.

He waited. Nothing happened, and he made to try again. Suddenly, a hand gripped his shoulder from behind, turning him round.

"Looking for someone, are we?" asked a curly-haired giant of a man who wore a faded khaki work shirt and old denim trousers. His eyes were cold, his voice colder. The massive hand on Gaunt's shoulder stayed there. The giant's other hand stayed at his side, nursing a large metal hammer. "I'm listening."

Gaunt looked at him and took a hopeful breath. "You'd better be Dan, Dan the Flying Machine Man—or I've a problem."

The hand eased its grip. The giant relaxed a little. "I'm Dan. Go on."

"I got your address from John Milton, I met your wife in Bavaria. I'm from the Remembrancer's Office." Gaunt frowned at the hammer. "Fixing something?"

"Sorry." Dan Dennan made an apologetic gesture with the hammer. "You're Gaunt?"

Gaunt nodded and produced his identification card. The curly-haired giant looked at it, then grinned and removed his hand from Gaunt's shoulder.

"Sorry," he said again, and scraped one of his old work shoes on the pathway with some embarrassment. "Look, Joan told me some of the things that have been happening. Right now, I'm wary of strangers."

"That's healthy," murmured Gaunt. "Shouldn't you be running an airline somewhere?"

"I was due some time off. We only moved in here a couple of months ago." Dan Dennan gave a wry glance round. "I'd planned to fix the garden."

"Where's Joan?" asked Gaunt.

"Having a shower." Dennan produced a key and opened the front door. "We—uh—know people have been trying to phone us. We just haven't been answering." He led the way in, gesturing Gaunt to follow. "I don't believe in having an answerphone. Fit one, and people keep leaving you messages about things you'd rather not know."

They went through a neat, narrow lobby. Some closed suitcases were lying outside a bedroom. Dennan saw Gaunt glance at them but only shrugged and took him into a living room at the rear of the house. On closer acquaintance, Dan Dennan looked in his late thirties and had an easygoing smile.

"I'll haul Joan out of the shower." Dennan indicated the drinks cupboard. "Help yourself—I've a beer lying in the kitchen."

"Maybe later," said Gaunt.

The man nodded and left him. Gaunt was alone for a couple of minutes, long enough to look at wedding pictures on the wall and the scatter of silver trophies on a sideboard. Apart from being an airline executive, Dan Dennan seemed to be a championship-class yachtsman—even if the most recent award date was a few years back.

He heard a murmur of quick, low conversation in another room, then new footsteps in the lobby. Another moment, and Joan Dennan came in alone. Her wet hair was caught up in a brightly coloured scarf, she was wearing a man's red bathrobe, and her feet were bare.

"I asked Dan to stay away for a few minutes." She went over to the drinks cupboard and looked back at Gaunt. When he shook his head, she splashed a modest measure of whiskey into a glass, added some ice from a bucket, and sipped the result. She asked, "Why are you here, Jonny?"

"To talk about what's going on. Including why you've stopped answering your phone, and why there are suitcases in the lobby."

Joan Dennan gave a slow, resigned nod. She sat in the nearest armchair, sipped her drink again, and looked up at him.

"I was fired this afternoon—or the next best thing. Gladstone Baxter told me he would totally handle the Hartondee situation from now on, that as far as I was concerned it didn't exist any more. If I wanted to stay working for him, there were some small retail company audits needing done over on the west coast. Travelling audits. If I didn't like the idea, goodbye."

"And?" Gaunt raised an eyebrow.

"He told me that either way, if I'd any sense, I'd keep my mouth shut about anything to do with the Hartondee company." She shrugged. "I told him what to do with his travelling audits and walked out."

"And Dan was conveniently here?" suggested Gaunt dryly. "Making like a large garden-style husband?"

"That was his idea. I told him what had been happening when I got back from Bavaria. Dan decided to take a few days off work. He wasn't happy about things."

"The suitcases?"

"We're leaving in the morning, going up north for a break. "We've a sort of cabin—"

"John Milton told me." Gaunt nodded. "It could be a good idea. Did

Gladstone Baxter or anyone else make any particular threat—or has anything happened, specific or otherwise?"

"No." She nursed the whisky glass, her eyes pensive. "But I may have been followed by someone a couple of times since I got back. Then this afternoon—I've never seen Gladstone Baxter so angry. I thought he'd hit me."

"Before you left Germany, you paid Bessie King ten thousand Deutschmarks to sign some papers." Gaunt saw her give a nod of agreement. "Why?"

"Gladstone Baxter's orders." Joan frowned at the memory. "I'd mentioned Bessie in a report I sent back when Beck was killed. He telephoned from Edinburgh and said we had to cover any chance of the Hartondee shares going to Bessie King—any chance at all."

"How did she react?"

"She's a practical woman. I told her it wasn't likely to happen, that she might as well take the money. So she signed. The agreement's wording was faxed out to me by Baxter, but it seemed fair. If she inherited the Hartondee shares then decided to sell, we acquired the right to match anyone else's price."

"Baxter was pleased when you brought it back?"

Joan nodded and sipped her whisky. Somehow she didn't look totally happy.

"So what was wrong?" demanded Gaunt. He had a sudden idea. "Joan, exactly who acquired this right? Hartondee—or was it Gladstone Baxter?"

"Baxter. He said Hartondee wanted it done that way. But otherwise it was a fair agreement."

From Bessie King's viewpoint, money for nothing, thought Gaunt to himself. Maybe Baxter had decided to increase his chances of a slice of the cake. Maybe Hartondee—meaning John Darnley—had really wanted it that way. It didn't seem to matter.

"Henry Falconer and his secretary were up around Stonehaven yesterday." Joan Dennan had a question of her own to ask. "I went up for the same—one more sniff around the Church family tree—lost cousins or whatever. I didn't find anything. Did they have any luck?"

"No," lied Gaunt. "It was a waste of time."

A grandmother at Stonehaven would probably have thanked him for that lie. He could explain it to Joan later. It might even be safer for her that she didn't know.

Gaunt made a throat-clearing noise that meant he was leaving, and she rose to see him out.

"I'll manage." He smiled at her. "You've things to do. Enjoy your trip, forget about Hartondee for a few days."

She still came part of the way through the little lobby with him, then said goodbye and went into a bedroom. Gaunt walked on, opened the front door of the little house, and found Dan Dennan making a half-hearted attempt at pulling weeds in the garden. The curly-haired giant straightened.

"Finished?" he asked.

Gaunt nodded. "Joan says you're driving up to your cabin tomorrow. How long does the drive take?"

Dennan shrugged. "About three hours—it's north of Inverness."

"About three hours." Gaunt glanced deliberately at his wristwatch. "Leaving now, that would get you there before midnight?"

"It would." Dennan considered him carefully. "Yes, it could. Thank you."

He turned quickly and went into the little house while Gaunt returned to his car and set it moving.

On the way back, Jonathan Gaunt passed a string of large, glinting limousines making their way up towards Edinburgh Castle. He remembered the castle reception that John Milton had talked about, glanced briefly in that direction, and smiled to himself.

The castle was hard to beat for ceremonial settings. He had been there twice, officially, as Parachute Regiment. Occasions to remember for anyone.

Once it had been as guest at a special evening hosted by the Royal Scots, the proud First of Foot, the oldest regiment in the British Army —who never let anyone forget it. The other had been even more elaborate, run by Scottish Command. Every army world-wide who could claim a unit with a Scottish connection had been represented. Corps and regimental silver had gleamed, bagpipes had skirled, old soldiers had marched around with clinking medals.

It had been a night for forgetting what soldiering was really all about.

The evening was still bright and cool. Gaunt parked in a lane off Frederick Street then ate at a basement restaurant around the corner where the attraction wasn't the food but the Tuesday evening live jazz sessions that began at around 10 P.M.

Before he ate, he used a phone to call the Remembrancer's Office and leave an answer-tape message for Henry Falconer, telling what Joan Dennan had said about the Bessie King agreement. Then he let the music take over. It came from a trio who thought that the world began and ended with the alto saxophone style of Charlie Parker. There were people around who were the same way, most of them faces he knew.

He left around midnight, and was home and asleep by 1 A.M. The falling nightmare brought him awake once, sweating as usual, then he slept soundly. But by 5 A.M. he was up, dressed, and boiling water for coffee. By six-thirty he was at Edinburgh Airport, where most people still looked grey as they crawled in from the dawn.

Hannah had booked him on the early Air UK flight to Gatwick, London's second airport. Air UK flew HS 146 jets, slower than the regular shuttle jets going into Heathrow, but there was method in her thinking. She had him booked out of Gatwick on a Boeing 737–300 Monarch flight to Majorca, a tight transfer but the kind that would save a lot of time. The Monarch flight would land at Palma at about the same time as Dieter Vogt's Lufthansa jet arrived from Munich.

His ticket was waiting at the Air UK desk, where they also had a thick envelope. By the time he had gone through security, the flight was being called.

Gaunt settled back once the jet was airborne, sipped a cup of coffee, and opened the envelope. It had been hand-delivered and, as usual, Hannah North had been thorough. He had copies of telex messages exchanged between Henry Falconer and a small flock of Spanish officials. He had a thin bundle of Spanish peseta banknotes clipped to a receipt he was to sign and return. Among the rest, a biographical sketch of Edward Sarr filled two close-typed sheets of paper. All that was available on John Darnley filled part of a third sheet.

Somehow, Hannah had found time to acquire an old head-and-shoulders newspaper photograph of Edward Sarr. It showed a bald man with sharp, deep-set eyes and a large mouth. Sarr had been trying to smile at the camera, but the result simply showed he had large teeth.

Gaunt tucked the photograph away as the man who had been dozing in the next seat stirred and wakened. But Edward Sarr's face stayed in his mind. It was hard to forget.

They landed at Gatwick on schedule. Gaunt was one of the first passengers to disembark, but as he made to leave the aircraft, a stewardess stopped him.

"Mr. Gaunt?" she asked.

"Yes."

She looked past him. Two men in maintenance overalls were standing outside, watching her, and she nodded. Gaunt went over, and one of the men showed a warrant card.

"Airport police—we were told to collect you." He gave Gaunt a friendly grin. "Whatever you've done, mate, we've got your boss hanging on a phone. It's urgent." He saw Gaunt glance at his wristwatch. "And we know about the Palma flight. You'll make it."

Puzzled, Gaunt followed them along an airport corridor and into a small office which hid behind a door marked Private. A sergeant in uniform looked up from his desk, lifted a telephone, punched a button, and spoke briefly. Then he looked at Gaunt again.

"Yours." He handed over the receiver.

Henry Falconer was at the other end, a Falconer who sounded tight-voiced and shaken.

"We've a new problem," said Falconer without preliminaries. "It's called Gladstone Baxter. He was found dead at dawn this morning. Someone seems to have thrown him off the battlements at Edinburgh Castle. It was a long way down."

With rocks at the bottom. Gaunt moistened his lips. "When?"

"According to the police, the medical estimate is around midnight," said Falconer wearily. "It fits. One of the merchant banks organized a reception at the castle last night, Gladstone Baxter was there as a guest, and the party broke up around midnight."

The three airport police in the room were listening. One of them took a first, crunching bite from an apple then leaned nearer.

"When was he missed?" asked Gaunt.

"He wasn't. He went alone, he had a wife who didn't expect him home at night." Falconer went straight on. "When word reached the Fraud Squad, they knew our interest. I heard that he was dead at about the time your flight left Edinburgh. They say there are signs he made—ah—an assisted take-off. They're asking if we've any specific idea why."

"I phoned the department and left a message for you last night," said Gaunt. "Baxter may have annoyed people."

He took three short sentences to explain Joan Dennan's story—and left Falconer to understand what it could mean. The three airport police officers listened intently. The man with the apple even stopped crunching. At his end of the line, Falconer stayed silent for a moment then made a noise like a snarl.

"Maybe now we know why William and Mary Hamilton were brought over," he said bitterly. "John Darnley arranges to fly out, and arranges them to arrive, with Baxter as their target. It helps if they're properly introduced as just friendly, visiting Hartondee back-up."

Again it fitted. Gaunt glanced at his watch again. The minutes were ticking past, he thought of the Majorca flight.

"Tell people when you get to Majorca," snapped Falconer. "The police will watch airports and seaports here—but the Hamiltons could be long gone by now. They've had since midnight."

"If they did it," said Gaunt carefully.

"They'll do until we find someone better," snarled Falconer. His voice was loud enough over the line to reach Gaunt's audience. The sergeant raised an eyebrow. Then, just as quickly, Falconer's mood changed. "Go carefully. Hannah would be upset if anything happened to you."

"That would worry me," said Gaunt.

He heard Falconer hang up, and did the same.

"Having problems?" asked one of the airport police sympathetically. He beckoned, without waiting for an answer. "You've an aircraft to catch. Let's go."

Jonathan Gaunt tumbled aboard the Monarch flight at the end of a rush which included collecting his travel bag then being propelled past check-in desks and security. As soon as he was aboard, the aircraft's door closed. By the time he was in his aisle seat, the Boeing was rolling. A passing stewardess grinned at him and shook her head.

"You were lucky," declared the woman in the seat beside him, then laughed. She was middle-aged, blonde, and from the liquor on her breath she'd already fortified herself for the flight. "Now relax! Enjoy it!"

Gaunt nodded. He had a feeling he wasn't going to have much choice.

Two hours and fifteen minutes later, on schedule, the glinting Boeing with distinctive black-and-yellow Monarch tail markings eased down towards the blue sparkle of the Mediterranean. It came in over the rocks of the Majorcan coastline, made a routine approach circuit over the sea and sand of the great hotel-fringed curve of Palma Bay, then touched down in a scream of reverse thrust.

Palma de Majorca airport was busy as usual. The Monarch arrival taxied in past lines of parked jets and surrounding swarms of shuttle buses and servicing units. They had drawn a slot close to the terminal, within walking distance, and the passengers disembarked into a blend of hot sun, the reek of aviation fuel, and the scents of flowering shrubs and cactus.

The smell changed to strong pine disinfectant inside the terminal building. As Monarch passengers tailed a Swedish flight at the passport control booths, the first arrivals from a Dutch flight were already beginning to slot in behind them. Mostly it was a perfunctory wave-on check by the immigration staff, but the sleepy-eyed official who flickered a glance at Gaunt's passport shifted slightly on his stool and nodded.

Another figure who had been lurking in the background came forward. He was in the blue uniform of a police lieutenant, with *Policía Nacional* shoulder patches.

"Señor Gaunt." A hand came up in the start on a salute that didn't quite finish. Instead, there was a hopeful twist of a smile of greeting. "I am Teniente Jaime Vicente. I was sent to collect you."

They were about the same age. The *Policía Nacional* lieutenant was tall, thin in a stringy, muscular way, and was tanned the colour of teak. He had fair, sun-bleached hair. A black harness belt was hung with a holstered automatic pistol on one hip and a small personal radio on the other.

"I have transport waiting, Señor Gaunt." Vicente took charge. Somehow, Gaunt's travel bag appeared like magic, then they carved a way through the crowded arrivals hall and past Customs. Outside, in the terminal's main concourse, tour firm couriers were shouting and waving clipboards while they herded the latest flocks of arrivals. The fair-haired *teniente* flashed a grin at two of the couriers, both female and in their twenties, who made it very clear they knew him. Then he beckoned to Gaunt again. "Through here."

They passed through a doorway marked *Prohibido,* emerged in a large bus park filled with buses and coaches, and crossed to a white Seat personnel wagon with blue police lights on the roof. The rear door was open, waiting on them. Already in his shirt sleeves and carrying his jacket, Dieter Vogt grinned as Gaunt arrived.

"What took you so long?" he asked cheerfully. "Did your pilot get lost?"

Gaunt returned the grin and got aboard while Vicente heaved his passenger's travel bag into the rear of the Seat. A woman officer was at the vehicle's controls, and the passenger beside her smiled round.

"Hello, Jonny."

He stared. Like her brother, Sergeant Krissa Vogt was out of uniform. Her choice was a pastel-green silk shirt-blouse, worn with a figure-fitting denim jacket and trousers. She had a dark green silk scarf tied loosely at her throat. Her copper hair glinted in the strong sunlight.

"I had to bring the woman," said Dieter Vogt with an attempt at a scowl. "It was the only *verdammt* way I was going to get any peace!"

Their driver followed enough of it to look away. A badge pinned to her shirt said her name was Anita Lopez, and she was grinning.

"It's called blackmail." Gaunt settled in the seat beside Vogt. "All right, now what's the real reason?"

"She remembers seeing the Hamiltons at Rottach," said Vogt grimly. "I know Krissa. If she says she'd know them again, she means it. My bosses think the same way—we've no one better."

"Danke," said his sister with a dry politeness.

Vogt ignored her. "Jonny, you're shaky on the Hamiltons, but you know John Darnley. We don't know Darnley, but Krissa can be positive on the Hamiltons. It makes sense." He paused and grimaced. "I got a telex about Baxter, the accountant—that he was killed. Did that come as a total surprise?"

"At first. Not when I'd time to think about it." The signs were there, the pressures had been growing.

Dieter Vogt grunted. Then the Seat's side door had squealed shut and Jaime Vicente had dropped into a seat. Their driver set the vehicle moving.

"Where now, *teniente?"* asked Gaunt.

"Into Palma." Vicente glanced at his wristwatch and winced as the Seat lurched on a pothole as it weaved through the parked buses. "Major Juan Ruiz, who is *Guardia Civil,* not *Policía Nacional,* will be senior Spanish liaison officer for what you are here to do. Our forces have a joint office near the harbour—we get a lot of trade around there."

Even using an occasional impatient rasp of its police siren, the Seat had to battle with traffic all the way along the main route from the airport into the city. Palma was big, Palma was a blend of everything new and everything old. Avenues of sleek, expensive shops and office blocks told of the sophistication of the accumulated riches from tourists. The white, circular battlements of Bellver Castle and the Gothic bulk of Palma Cathedral were just two reminders of a different past. Large cruise yachts lay berthed side by side marina style and the main commercial harbour looked clogged with shipping.

Their destination was a plain-fronted office block on the Pasco

Maritimo. The Seat swung under an archway, stopped in a yard filled with other police vehicles, and they got out.

"Anita." Vicente glanced at his policewoman. *"Por favor."*

She nodded, smiled, and guided Krissa Vogt away. Looking at his watch again in the same worried way, the tall police lieutenant turned to Gaunt and Dieter Vogt.

"Major Ruiz is—ah—" He searched for the word.

"Like we'd better get there?" suggested Gaunt helpfully.

"We have them too," said Vogt.

Vicente grinned and led the way. They went into the building, rode an elevator up several floors, then emerged in a plain, brightly lit corridor. Jaime Vicente knocked on a door, there was a bellow from inside, and he ushered them into a big, simply furnished office. Sunlight flooded from a large balcony where the window was open, allowing the traffic noise in.

"Buenas tardes." The brisk greeting came from a grey-haired stockily built man who prowled across the room to greet them. Major Juan Ruiz wore a well-tailored grey pinstripe suit with a Rotary Club badge. He looked more like a prosperous business executive than any kind of policeman. "Welcome to Majorca, gentlemen."

Jaime Vicente made the introductions, they shook hands, then the *Guardia Civil* major led them over to where three chairs were arranged around a marble-topped coffee table. Gaunt and Vogt were each waved into a seat, Major Ruiz took the third, and Jaime Vicente stayed resignedly in the background.

"We'll speak English," said Ruiz. He gave an apologetic shrug and indicated Vicente. "The *teniente* doesn't speak German. You don't mind, Inspektor Vogt?"

Vogt shook his head.

"Then to explain." Ruiz settled back, took out a gold cigarette case, opened it, and lit a thin filter-tipped cigarette with a matching lighter. He took a gentle first draw of the smoke. "I am *Guardia Civil*—the black leather hats, the grey-green uniforms, a certain amount of military hardware and political responsibility. We work under the direct authority of Central Government in Spain." He indicated Vicente again. "The *Policía Nacional* are less political—an easier life, though they have a good anti-terrorist capability. We also have local, municipal police in some areas—but they don't concern us. You follow me?"

They nodded. Satisfied, Ruiz drew on his cigarette again.

"I have direct orders to cooperate and assist. The *Policía Nacional* has similar instructions, I will run the operation." He tapped a file of telex messages lying in front of him. "I have one clear instruction from Madrid, one I can totally understand. As there is no real evidence that Edward Sarr is guilty of anything, the whole matter must be treated with great care."

"It will be," promised Dieter Vogt.

"*Bueno.* You will also remember that neither you nor Señor Gaunt has any official status on Majorca. Spain is offering assistance as an enthusiastic member of the European Union." The grey-haired *Guardia Civil* officer frowned at the tip of his cigarette and blew on it for a moment, until it glowed. "Vicente and one of my own people, Raimon Alberti, will be with you and will report back to me. There are many people like Señor Sarr on Majorca—rich people who live in semi-retirement but who still have important friends."

"Suppose he's guilty?" asked Gaunt.

"Prove it, and we arrest him," said Ruiz curtly. Suddenly he stubbed out his cigarette and rose. "How many people have been killed in this so far?"

Dieter Vogt shrugged. "Five we know about."

"Five." Ruiz nodded. "Edward Sarr built himself a small *castillo* in the north of the island, near a village called Larca." He glanced at Vicente.

"Everything is barbed wire and *privado* signs. Maybe electronics too," agreed Vicente. "As far as we know, he's there now."

"As far as we know," emphasized Ruiz.

Dieter Vogt leaned forward. "A man called John Darnley may have joined him—"

"That we don't know," said Ruiz bluntly.

Vogt tried again. "An English couple named Hamilton may be on their way to the island—"

"And you want us to watch for them at the airport?" asked Ruiz. "*Sí*, we know about the Hamiltons. We are trying right now. But don't expect any results, Inspektor. Will I tell you why?"

"They could matter, Major," began Vogt warily. He was cut short.

"This island is small, only sixty miles long. Maybe the size of Cornwall in England, or America's Long Island. It is home for half a million people." The grey-haired man paused, drew a deep breath, then exploded. "But how many *turistas* do you think go through Palma airport in a year? More than ten million! Last weekend alone? Two hundred thousand, on nearly thirteen hundred flights! They come from all over the world, they go back to all over the world—armies of people, all day and every day. We just keep them moving."

"Tell us that someone will be on a certain flight, fine," said Jaime Vicente. "We'll collect them—you've seen that."

"But any general watch is a public relations exercise," said Ruiz acidly.

He turned on his heel, prowled over to the balcony window, and slammed it shut. The traffic noise from the Pasco Maritimo ended. Still moving around the room in that same impatient, prowling way, he stopped beside a small olive-wood display pedestal which stood near his desk. On the pedestal was a striking bronze figure of a naked man, quarter life size. Poised like a hunter, the man was wielding a primitive sling. Superbly, the bronze had captured in metal all the energy being used as the sling let its missile fly.

"That's a beautiful work," said Gaunt softly, meaning it.

"It's a cheap miniature of the original," replied Ruiz. But his face softened for a moment and he rested a hand lightly on the figure's shoulders. "I just happen to like it, even though I am from the mainland." His mood had changed. "People in the Balearics are a separate race." His hand moved along the figure's arm. "This sling was their weapon—and they were deadly, stubborn, unconquerable with it for centuries. That's how the islands got their name, from an old Greek word meaning 'to throw.' Today—" he scowled at Vicente—"they're still stubborn. True, *teniente?*"

Jaime Vicente gave an awkward grin. Suddenly, looking at Vicente, then at the slim, muscular bronze from the past, Gaunt and Vogt understood.

"Vicente is Majorcan, from the north of the island," confirmed Ruiz sourly. "That's why he'll be with you. That's also why he has fair hair —he claims." He snorted. "More likely some island woman a few generations back had a night's fun with a sailor."

Jaime Vicente didn't protest. He had obviously heard it all before.

"You'll need him," said Ruiz shortly. "These people keep their own style of dialect, their own language—some of them even want independence from Spain. There was a time when a squad of *Guardia Civil* would quickly have ended that!" He stopped, sucked his lips with some annoyance, then seemed to feel an explanation was due. "Ignore me. I am a relic from yesterday's Spain. This time next year, I will have left this job and be drawing my pension. My sister lives in Barcelona, and wants me to join her there. What I am trying to say is that since we gained democracy here, policing has lost its old role. Things are more difficult."

"New rules?" Dieter Vogt tried to be helpful.

"New rules," said Ruiz, nodding. "Old rules relaxed—no more knowing everything about everyone, everywhere. That's why we can't tell you much about Edward Sarr or his people. Foreign visitors, even visitors who decide to live here most of the year, don't particularly interest us." Then he paused and gave a sudden bear-like growl. "But if you find the people you want and the proof you want, bring them here. I'll have the cells waiting."

The interview was over. Jaime Vicente ushered Gaunt and Vogt out of Major Ruiz's office and along to the elevator.

"I think he liked you," he said seriously.

"Gott," said Vogt softly. "What happens to the other ones?"

Jaime Vicente took charge again. They left the building and walked a short distance through the heat of the early afternoon to a small, quiet hotel where there were rooms booked and their baggage was waiting. Krissa was there, and Anita Lopez was with her, changed out of uniform. There was a light buffet lunch of thin-sliced ham and crisply fresh salad, backed by a choice of chilled wine or beer.

Briefly, Vicente disappeared. When he returned he was out of uniform and wearing a faded corduroy jacket over a grey roll-neck shirt and dark trousers. The man who came with him, a dark, thick-set Spaniard who wore denims and a sports shirt, was the *Guardia Civil* lieutenant they'd been promised. Raimon Alberti showed strong white teeth when he smiled, but didn't say much. When he did speak, it was usually in Spanish to Vicente or to Anita Lopez.

"Will we get started?" asked Vicente. He cleared a space on the lunch table, produced a large-scale road map of the island, spread it out, and gave a murmur of thanks as Krissa Vogt used a plate and an empty wine bottle to help anchor it down. Then he waited until he had his audience gathered round. "First, where we are going. Okay?"

The fair-haired Majorcan used a fork as a pointer, stabbing at the map when he wanted to emphasize anything.

"Palma is here, to the south, your Edward Sarr is in the north at Larca, not far from the town of Pollensa—here." The fork stabbed. "The geography is simple. Larca is on the edge of the Sa Muntanya mountains—they run all the way to the west, like a chain almost five miles wide."

"We know about mountains," murmured Dieter Vogt.

"Sí." Vicente gave an apologetic nod. "These aren't as big as your Alps. But they are enough for us—the largest is Puig Mayor, over fourteen hundred metres and with mist." The fork moved again.

"There are a few mountains to the east, but they don't concern us. Most of the rest of the island is tourist coast or farmland."

Alberti nudged him, made a soft, throat-clearing noise, and murmured in Spanish. Vicente hesitated, then nodded agreement.

"Maybe we should tell you that things aren't totally bad," he said warily. "Major Ruiz is cautious by nature, we knew nothing of any of this until late yesterday—"

Alberti prompted again.

"We have had very little time," said Vicente. "Only since late yesterday, and we have orders—"

"To go carefully," agreed Gaunt.

Vicente gave him a grateful nod. "Very carefully, and Larca is not a place where any kind of visiting policemen can go unnoticed. But I have a contact, a relative of sorts, near there. Edward Sarr has had several visitors over the last few months. This English couple Hamilton—how would you describe them?"

"Krissa?" Gaunt left it to her.

"Middle-aged, very ordinary." She shrugged. "Except I'd know them if I saw them. Anywhere."

Gaunt nodded. It was as far as he would have gone—maybe further.

"And the man John Darnley?" asked Vicente.

"Jonny?" Krissa passed it back to Gaunt. "He's yours."

"Tall, thirties, narrow face, a beak nose, prematurely grey hair—a neat dresser."

Vicente and Alberti exchanged an apparently satisfied glance.

"An English couple, early middle age, very quiet, very ordinary, sometimes visit at Larca. Their name isn't known." Vicente shrugged. "Your John Darnley matches someone who visits there even more often—a Señor Smith."

"Simple names are best," said Gaunt wryly. "He used it before. When do we go?"

They set off twenty minutes later, a convoy of three unmarked, apparently nondescript cars. Dieter Vogt travelled in the first, with Vicente and Alberti. The two Spanish officers seemed to find it easier to relate to him. Gaunt, as the next best thing to a civilian witness, was in the second car with Krissa Vogt. Their driver once more was the dark-haired Anita. Behind them, the third car was occupied by four plain-clothes men who were a matched set in terms of size and appearance.

From Palma the route was straight and simple, north along the main Route 713. They left the city's outskirts behind, and met farmland where irrigation sprays drenched fields and where other crops grew under great stretches of black plastic. They bounced and shuddered over potholed, broken road at Santa María, then on through Binisalem, and by-passed the town of Inca and its leather factories.

All the time the mountains to the west and north seemed to grow nearer. They were bald and grey, grotesque in their shapes, sometimes savage in their silhouettes. A rainstorm whipped briefly out of nowhere at one point, drenched the road, then vanished. Within moments the tarmac had steamed dry again in the heat. They passed olive groves and fields of almond trees. Oranges grew in profusion— and every so often they would pass a tumbledown line of peasant cottages that might have come out of another age.

"Anita." Up front, Krissa Vogt had established a good relationship with their driver. "Teniente Vicente says he has a contact at Larca— do you know who it is?"

"*Sí.*" Their driver frowned in concentration while she overtook a Pegaso truck laden with gas cylinders and which was travelling as if on a count-down. "His sister. He drove there late last night. He got back about three this morning."

"A relative of sorts," said Krissa Vogt. "Just like he said." She glared at the car ahead. "Brothers—they're all the same."

The mountains grew nearer, the countryside became more wooded, and some of the small fields held sheep grazing under the shade of gnarled olive trees. They reached a main junction, where they forked left for Pollensa. The sea was somewhere not too far away, but those nearing raw peaks of rock dominated everything.

Pollensa was small, Pollensa was neat. It was built under a medieval hilltop monastery, it had a bridge that had been built in Roman times. It had green shutters on windows along streets that were so narrow it seemed crazy that cars could get through. Then it was behind them. The little convoy of cars was one minute driving past neat gardens and expensive housing, the next minute in low gear and climbing. It was a narrow country road, winding and clinging to the rock, peppered with warning signs and occasional crude crash barriers. They steered on the dust of the car ahead while Krissa glanced round at Gaunt, her eyes startled, and a new sound rose above the noise of the car.

Anita was singing to herself, one hand tapping the steering wheel in rhythm.

Suddenly there was a gash where the road had been blasted through raw rock. On the other side, down a gentle slope, everything was green in a broadening funnel of land. There was the blue of the sea in the distance, and the car ahead was slowing, then stopped outside a substantial old house built of mellow golden-brown stone.

Their car and the third vehicle halted in turn. Vicente left his car, glanced back at them, then walked over to the house. A door opened and he went in.

"His sister?" asked Gaunt.

"*Sí.*" Anita Lopez leaned in front of Krissa Vogt, opened the car's glove compartment, moved the holstered automatic she'd stowed there, then rummaged. She produced a comb and lipstick. Squinting into the rear-view mirror, she used them.

"*Bitte.*" Krissa Vogt grinned at her, borrowed the comb, and did the same. "How far now?"

"To Larca?" Their driver shook her head. "Maybe three kilometres. No more." Then she stopped. Vicente was coming out of the house. They had a glimpse of a young, very pregnant woman standing in the doorway before it closed again.

Jaime Vicente strode rapidly to his own car, spoke briefly to his companions, then came hurrying back. He stuck his head in at the open window on Gaunt's side.

"Maybe we are late," he said tightly. "Every dam' *teléfono* in this valley was dead first thing this morning. Nobody knows why. So we go straight on, straight in. *Comprende?*"

Then he had spun on his heel and was almost running back to his car. A moment later he was aboard and it was moving.

The road was wider and ran straight now they were past the spur of mountain. The three-car convoy raced along it, passing a clattering farm tractor and horn-blasting a meandering local who had to yank his donkey and cart out of the way. They were back among neat fields, they had lost sight of the sea. Then they were through Larca, a small huddle of houses built of that same golden-brown stone. Only a child and a dog watched them pass in a scatter of gravel.

Less than two kilometres on, a narrow track of tarmac led off to the right. Vicente's turn indicators flashed and the two other cars followed. The track took them through a strip of lemon trees laden with fruit. Ahead was a broad wooden gate, closed by a chain and padlock. Behind it was a small concrete lodge house with a corrugated iron roof. The track went on through more trees and grass fronting a large modern villa which had mock turret windows.

Jaime Vicente's car didn't slow but hit the wooden gate head-on, smashing it aside like matchwood. Going through, the vehicle braked and skidded to a halt outside the little lodge, then the fair-haired Majorcan was out and heading for it with Dieter Vogt and Alberti at his heels.

Anita took her car through the gate, braked hard, stopped—and Gaunt was also out and following. He sensed Krissa Vogt close behind him and saw the other police vehicle had halted broadside across the track, the plain-clothes men tumbling out with guns drawn, forming a defensive fan. By then, Vicente had kicked the lodge door open and gone inside, Vogt and Alberti still with him.

There was a frightened yelp and the brief sounds of a scuffle, then Alberti emerged first, carrying an old shotgun. He drew the cartridges, then propped the weapon against the splintered door frame. Krissa Vogt made to push past him, but he shook his head and stopped her. They could hear Vicente questioning someone inside. There was another yelp and something smashed.

At last, pushing a scrawny figure ahead of him, Vicente emerged again. The stranger was unkempt, unshaven, barefoot, and was still buttoning up his overalls. They were followed by a grim-faced Dieter Vogt, who came straight over to Gaunt. "That's the gardener." He shook his head in answer to Gaunt's silent question. "They left first thing this morning—*schnell*, no warning. The domestics were paid off, he was told to stay and look after things."

"But Sarr was here till this morning?"

"Sarr and some other people. They left in a car and a yellow Seat pick-up." Vogt shrugged. "He's just a gardener, Jonny. He doesn't know much about anything unless it grows."

Gaunt swore under his breath. Over at the track, Vicente had left the unshaven gardener answering questions from Alberti. The other men had got back aboard their car and it was on its way up towards the main house.

"You've heard?" asked Vicente as he joined them.

Gaunt nodded.

"Forget that one." Vicente thumbed in the gardener's direction. "He doesn't know why they've gone, he doesn't know where they've gone."

"Sarr and how many others?" asked Gaunt.

"Maybe three, maybe four—he's not even sure of that." Vicente gave a resigned shrug, then brightened a little. "But he knows one of them arrived two days ago. He has seen him before, he's the one who told him what to do this morning. The description could match your John Darnley."

"No Hamiltons?"

Vicente shook his head. Some tiny beads of sweat had formed on his upper lip. For a moment he scowled at the shattered gate while he scuffed a foot along the ground. Then he turned and looked towards the house.

"So I was supposed to do this with discretion, with care," he said deliberately. "So now Madrid will probably want me roasted over a slow fire. *Es igual*"— he gave a wry grin—"things happen." He looked at Gaunt and Vogt. "We can search the house—break a few more regulations. Do you know what we're looking for?"

"No," said Krissa flatly. "They don't. Not yet."

Vicente nodded, beckoned, and they started walking.

CHAPTER 7

The harsh mountain light was fading by the time they drove back down from the Larca valley towards Pollensa. They had spent three hours searching in and around Edward Sarr's luxury hideaway. They had come across several signs that the people who had abandoned it had left quickly, yet methodically.

But Jonathan Gaunt felt a sense of total, angry frustration as the little convoy, now reduced to two police cars, made the return journey over that frightening road.

In practical terms, they were still coming back empty-handed.

The evening was beginning to cool, new pockets of mist were beginning to form. He saw a goat scramble out of their way and disappear among the rocks, then the rocks themselves disappeared as an eddy of mist swept in. Their driver didn't sing. She nursed the car's steering wheel and kept her eyes on that ribbon of tarmac and the red tail lights of the car ahead.

"It's still progress," suggested Krissa Vogt from in front. "We're in the right place, looking for the right people—"

"But we don't know why," said Gaunt moodily. He winced as they rounded another tight and narrow hairpin, where some road gang with a sense of humour had painted a white centre line. "Why would help."

"So would a drink." Krissa looked round. "A long, cold beer—the kind that when you hold the mug, you see your fingerprints on the glass." She glanced at their driver. "How about you, Anita?"

Anita grinned a little and nodded.

"I'll buy," said Gaunt.

They'd left the third car with Alberti and two of the plain-clothes men back at the empty villa. The *Guardia Civil* lieutenant had the task of searching it yet again, then keeping it secure. The telephones in the area were still dead—they'd found where the junction box for the

Larca valley had been smashed by a sledgehammer. Having it repaired was a priority. The mountains reduced any signals from the cars' radios to a pathetic, broken, static-laced hiss.

The room Edward Sarr used as a study—a room dominated by a computer—was still crammed with files and documents. But the computer's storage discs were gone. Only an empty cabinet remained.

What had been left wasn't likely to yield many secrets. Neither Edward Sarr nor John Darnley—whoever they were dealing with—was the kind to overlook anything that might matter.

Gaunt suddenly stiffened.

Like a summoned ghost out of the mist, a battered local bus filled with passengers was snarling up the mountain road towards the two police cars. Headlights glaring, it shaved past without slowing. Two nuns were in the first row of seats behind the driver. One was reading a newspaper.

Then it had gone again, like it had never been. Anita swallowed, then gave what was meant to be a reassuring smile.

Twenty seconds later both cars broke out of low cloud and back to a world of crystal-clear visibility and the light of the setting sun. Far below, the town of Pollensa lay tiny and doll-sized. In the distance the sea sparkled and glistened around the twin bays of Pollensa and Alcudia and their tourist resorts. A large yacht under full sail was a small speck that had just rounded the long cliffs of Cape Formentor.

Down there were tens of thousands of people who had never heard of Edward Sarr or John Darnley, or of a strange little firm called Hartondee. If they were told, they probably wouldn't care.

The lead car setting the pace, they coasted down the rest of the way.

The *Policía Municipal* post in Pollensa is a long, cool, two-storey building with a rough stone finish, a clay tile roof, and brown wooden shutters at all of its tall, narrow windows. It is on the east side of town, not far from Pollensa's market square, yet close to the main road and a stone's throw away from a patch of level waste ground which gives extra parking space or where a helicopter could land.

When they arrived they found the senior local police office was a neat, greying, thick-set *teniente* named Palacin. He knew Vicente, and reacted with surprising calm to the *Policía Nacional* invasion, and the people who came with it. He gave Vicente a glimmer of a smile, shook hands with Gaunt and both Vogts, then hooked his thumbs into his black leather waist belt.

"Bones tardes," he said dryly, greeting them Mallorcan style then switching to Vicente again. "Jaime?"

They spoke together, fast and low-voiced, for a couple of minutes. Then the local man shrugged and nodded.

"Es igual, Teniente Vicente," he said with a deliberate formality. Then he turned to Gaunt and explained in careful English, "If we can help, then the *Policía Nacional* and their friends are welcome." He gave Vicente a sideways glance, fired another question at him, received a nod in reply, and turned back to look first at Dieter Vogt then at Gaunt again. "Jaime has told me enough of what is happening. I don't like it, but I'll do what I can."

"You know Edward Sarr?" asked Dieter Vogt.

The local policeman nodded sadly. "One of our very rich foreigners. The quiet kind, who doesn't make trouble."

Turning on his heel, he began shouting orders to some of his men.

There were priorities as the *Policía Nacional* squad's move-in got under way and they had full communications again. The search was on for two cars and a yellow Seat pick-up truck which had been taken from Sarr's villa compound. Sarr was listed as owning a large motor cruiser berthed at the marina piers at Puerto de Pollensa. That was one for the local police to check. The plain-clothes men who had arrived with Vicente tackled a list which began with tracing two of the paid-off domestic staff who lived in Pollensa and went on from there to the local garages, the post office supervisor, the president of the English-speaking community club—anyone who might know anything about the people who inhabited the villa at Larca.

Behind one closed door, Vicente made a long telephone call to Major Ruiz in Palma. Behind another, Dieter Vogt called the *Bayers Landes Kriminalamt* several hundred miles away in Munich. Neither of them looked happy when they emerged.

Gaunt tried. He put in a call to Henry Falconer's home, and Falconer's wife answered.

"Henry's out. I don't know when he'll be back," she said curtly, and hung up on him.

When Gaunt put down the receiver, Jaime Vicente gave him a sympathetic grimace.

"Your boss trusts you," suggested Vicente.

"Nice for him," said Gaunt sarcastically. "His wife doesn't."

Vicente allowed himself a mild laugh. "Have you a wife, Jonny?"

"No." He left it there.

"I'm married. Our first child is due soon." Vicente's face softened.

"So why the hell am I here, chasing after some rich old man? I have better things to do."

Gaunt nodded. The telephone beside them rang and Vicente answered. He listened, murmured his thanks, and hung up.

"The phones on Larca are working again. That was Alberti, at the villa—nothing new." The fair-haired lieutenant nodded a greeting as two blue-uniformed local police went past. They smiled at him and one gave a half-salute. Leaning his hands on the desk, he looked down. "Jonny, can I ask you a dam' fool question?"

"Go ahead," invited Gaunt.

"I've read the telexes, I've heard you talk with Dieter Vogt, I've been snarled at by Major Ruiz. I know that people have been killed, I know that a lot of money is involved. But"—Vicente stopped and drew a deep breath—" suppose your Edward Sarr walks into this police station right now, what do we charge him with?"

"You'll think of something."

"Gracias," said Vicente sourly. "I've seen his photograph, I know he has money, but how much else do we know about him—the real man?"

"Not a lot," admitted Gaunt. "Some divorced wives—he began by being nobody. He started off running a corner shop somewhere."

"Like any other millionaire." Vicente shook his head. "Jonny, I'm not totally sure I even understand what has been going on—"

"People like you and me are not supposed to have minds that work that way," said Gaunt sadly. "I've a stockbroker friend back in Scotland who spent a lot of time trying to explain it for me." He rubbed a thumbnail along his chin, remembering. "His name is Milton. It's clever, it's complicated—part of it is money being moved around and around in different ways by different people using different names. You think you've cracked it, but then you're either at a dead end or you should have gone another way."

"Has it a name?"

"Milton gave it one." Gaunt nodded. "He christened it The Spanish Maze Game."

"Thank your friend very much." Vicente scowled, then glanced at his wristwatch. "I have a lot to do. Anita will take you and the Vogts to a place where the food is usually good." He saw the doubt in Gaunt's eyes. "If anything happens, you'll hear. That's a promise."

The grey-haired Teniente Palacin was coming towards them.

Leaving the two lieutenants, Gaunt went through to the police station's front office where more telephones were ringing and an arthritic telex machine was clattering. He saw a glint of copper beside a gleam of raven-gloss black, and went over to where Krissa Vogt was perched on the edge of a desk beside Anita. The young *Policía Nacional* officer was sitting saddle-style on a wooden chair, and they smiled at him. But there was no sign of Dieter Vogt.

"What have you done with him?" he asked Krissa.

"He'll be along later." She came down from the desk, smoothing down the front of her denims with her hands. "There's another call due in from Munich."

"Anything that matters?" he asked.

"Some *Bundeskriminalamt* heavy." She wasn't impressed. "The BKA either has a finger up its nose, or is trying to steal someone else's pie."

"Can I quote you?" he asked.

"They wouldn't agree." For a moment, her tanned, attractive face changed expression and her green eyes met his squarely. "Dieter isn't good at being patient, Jonny. Neither am I —and suddenly there just doesn't seem to be anything happening."

"It's slow," he admitted.

There was still no sighting of the men or vehicles from Larca. The check on the boat owned by Sarr had been a waste of time. Majorca was an island, a not particularly big island. But in terms of sheer geography of mountains and rocks, of valleys and coastline, a small army of men could have found ways to stay hidden.

If that was what they had in mind.

Anita was over at the police station door, holding it open, waiting for them. Krissa picked up her leather purse, and they joined her.

It was late evening and there was a huge cream-coloured moon sitting over the little town. The narrow, shadowed streets were pleasantly cool after the heat of the day and the shops were still open, busy with customers. No one seemed to be hurrying.

They let Anita lead the way, past the children playing games at the town square and the old men sipping drinks at pavement tables outside some of the small bars. Every street had its flow of cars and small, noisy motor scooters weaving and hooting at unhurried pedestrians.

"Teniente Vicente said you should see this." Anita stopped. To their right, leading directly from the street, a long, broad flight of stone steps lined with cypress trees climbed on and on up the side of a hill. In the moonlight they could see that the steps led to a tiny church high above the town. The young woman officer pointed. "These are the Calvario steps—one for each day of the year. Many *religiosos* come to see them."

There were still plenty of people using the steps in both directions, despite the hour. Gaunt guessed at a spectacular view from the top, across the rooftops of Pollensa. But it looked a long climb.

"Do we—uh—go that way?" he asked warily.

Anita chuckled at the equal dismay on Krissa's face. "No. Another time, if you want—and there is a way you can drive round to the top. But Teniente Vicente wants you to try a little restaurant further along the street."

"Another time and a car will do," decided Krissa Vogt. She had slowed and was taking a second glance at a brightly lit shop doorway. "What the name of this restaurant, Anita?"

"El Peca—we're not far from it now."

"Then you go on"—Krissa indicated the shop—"I want to look in here, on my own. I'll catch up."

She headed for the shop, and Gaunt and Anita walked on.

A few moments along the narrow, crowded street brought them to where it took a sharp left turn at the same time as it was joined by another street. Two teenagers on motor scooters racketed past, then, rounding the bend, Gaunt saw a modest restaurant ahead and a neon sign which said El Peca.

He took a few more steps, then saw something which made him forget food.

"Cross over, Anita." He had taken her arm, his voice was quietly grim. "I'll explain—but do it."

Puzzled, but knowing something was wrong, she went with him. They crossed to the other side of the street and tucked in behind a group of strolling shoppers.

Outside a small supermarket two doors along from El Peca a yellow Seat pick-up truck was parked, with a figure waiting in the driving seat. The supermarket had a small queue of customers at its single check-out point. From the other side of the street, Anita still holding his arm, Gaunt stared for a moment as they passed. The next customer in line at the check-out was a plain-looking woman in her late thirties, a woman with dyed blonde hair, heavy-rimmed spectacles, a wrap-round cotton skirt, and a red top.

The Seat matched the description of the pick-up taken from Edward Sarr's villa compound, even if there had to be several score of others like it on the island and the registration plates had been altered. Change the spectacles, change the hair, and the woman now starting through the supermarket check-out with a trolley-load of food was Mary Hamilton.

"Anita." He hauled her into the shelter of the first doorway they reached. The young officer didn't have a radio, didn't have her gun, and was only clutching a small leather wallet. "We do this my way, we don't try anything foolish—you understand me?"

"*Sí.*" She frowned up at him.

"You walk away from here, slowly. You get to a telephone, you call Jaime Vicente, and you tell him that we've just seen Mary Hamilton. Easy"—he stopped her pushing out of the doorway—"stay easy. She's in the supermarket. That's maybe her husband in the pick-up."

She moistened her lips, took a careful glance from the doorway, and nodded.

"Tell him I'm staying here. Watching—nothing else. Then get back to Krissa Vogt, stop her, and tell her."

Anita made a quick intake of breath, a glint of excitement in her eyes, and for a moment Gaunt thought she was going to argue. Then she seemed to change her mind. She nodded and slipped out of the doorway. Gaunt watched her for a moment, then she had gone—just another girl blending among the people on the street.

He switched his attention back to the supermarket. Mary Hamilton looked nervous as she waited, constantly glancing around while the girl at the checkout tapped out her purchases. Then she was packing them into thin white plastic carrier bags, paying the girl, taking her change—and there was still no sign of the man in the truck emerging to help.

Determined to get closer, Gaunt moved from his doorway as another swirl of people passed by. A figure collided with him. He muttered an apology—and ended it as he felt a pistol jam into the small of his back.

"Don't even think of trying anything," whispered a hoarse voice. The gun jabbed more fiercely. "You can look round, Mr. Gaunt— nothing else."

He turned his head. William Hamilton needed a shave and was wearing a grubby shirt and grubbier white trousers. He had a jacket draped over his right arm, concealing the pistol.

"I know you, you know me, why the hell you're here can wait," said the Englishman softly. He nodded towards the supermarket. Mary Hamilton was emerging, laden with plastic bags. "It wasn't our idea to come here, Gaunt. But I look after Mary, Mary looks after me." There was liquor on his breath. "I've had you spotted for the last couple of minutes. What we're going to do is walk over to the pick-up once Mary gets there. That cab can squeeze four in up front, right? We tell our driver friend Alejandro to move over. Then we all get in. Still with me?"

Gaunt nodded and let the man push him towards the parked vehicle. They got there at the same time as Mary Hamilton, and she stared at him in a blend of surprise and horror.

"Company," said Hamilton simply, bitterly.

"You." The woman swallowed then turned to Hamilton, the plastic bags in her hands swinging. "If this one is here—"

The Englishman nodded bleakly. "It's not good. We've no choice. We take him along."

"Where?" asked Gaunt. He managed to grin at the woman, while the pistol kept grinding into his back. "I've had a long day."

He couldn't try anything. A very good reason was walking unsuspectingly along the street towards them. Krissa Vogt was carrying a small package. Anita hadn't managed to stop her.

"In," ordered Hamilton, opening the passenger door. Mary Hamilton climbed up first, still laden with her plastic bags. Another prod, and Gaunt followed her while the driver, a small man wearing bib overalls and no shirt, stared. Hamilton crowded in last and closed the door. The Seat's engine fired crankily and, as the vehicle began moving, the headlamps glared.

They picked out Krissa. She had seen them, was running out in front of the vehicle with one hand raised to stop them, then was trying to jump clear as it still came on. The pick-up seemed to brush her aside and kept accelerating, knocking over a magazine display stand at the bend, swerving to avoid some startled, screaming woman, sending crates of vegetables scattering outside another shop.

Seconds later they had left the centre of the town behind and there was no sign of pursuit. Hamilton signalled their driver, and they coasted to a halt in a dark, deserted street of warehouse buildings.

"So what happens now?" asked Gaunt. In his mind he could still see Krissa being brushed aside. He held on to the chance she hadn't been badly hurt.

"Someone else decides," said Mary Hamilton uneasily. She turned on her husband. "I told you. I told you we were taking a risk—"

"Now you've told me again," snapped Hamilton. "Leave it, Mary. Watch him."

Tight-lipped, she nodded. She had put down the supermarket bags and had produced a small chrome-barrelled automatic pistol. Hamilton tucked his own pistol away, and roughly frisked Gaunt's pockets. Then he fumbled in the narrow gap behind the cab's seating, gave a satisfied grunt as he found what he wanted, and straightened again.

"When did you get back?" asked Gaunt unemotionally. "Was it this afternoon?"

"Back from where?" demanded Mary Hamilton, startled.

"Edinburgh," said Gaunt deliberately.

A croaking noise came from Hamilton. Mary Hamilton moistened her lips.

"You were seen," said Gaunt. He knew the gamble he was taking, but shaking what little remained of their confidence might help. "You met an accountant named Baxter. Then someone heaved him off a roof last night."

"Why should we know anything about it?" asked Hamilton hoarsely.

"Shut your mouth, you fool. Say nothing," said his wife urgently. Her hand holding the pistol quivered a little and she switched to a two-handed grip. Her eyes were narrowed with worry as they turned on Gaunt again. "You too. Nothing."

"Save it until we get to the people who matter?" asked Gaunt.

Her left hand came off the pistol and she hit him backhanded across the mouth. Gaunt felt a cut from the chunky ring she was wearing, and the salt taste of blood was on his lips.

"Enough, Mary," said Hamilton in a weary voice. "Do it my way."

He used a length of thin cord to lash Gaunt's wrists together behind his back. Then an old sack was pulled over Gaunt's head and down over his shoulders. It stank of fertilizer and plunged him into darkness except where there were small rips or holes. But he could still breathe.

"Down," he heard Hamilton's muffled voice order. "Get down and stay down. I'll have a gun two inches from the back of your head."

He was forced down to the floor of the cab and was kicked when he tried to move, then felt Mary Hamilton's heels dig into his back as she used him as a footrest. The engine started up again and idled for a minute or so. He could hear the driver arguing with Hamilton in Spanish.

The argument ended, the vehicle grated into gear, and they were moving. Each pitch and judder seemed to be coming straight at him through the metal floor. The pick-up's speed increased, the movement changed to a bouncing and lurching, and Mary Hamilton's feet were now braced against his back in a way that made some of the nerves along his spine protest in waves of pain he had to fight down.

It seemed a long time, though it probably hadn't been that way. Then the pick-up slowed to a crawl, shuddered its way over a series of what felt like gigantic ruts, and finally stopped. The engine was cut, doors opened, he heard Hamilton shouting then getting out.

He tried to move a little.

"Stay still," hissed Mary Hamilton close to his ear.

There were other voices outside. Then hands were dragging him out of the cab, pulling him to his feet. He was stiff with cramp, the stabbing pain in his back had become constant. The other voices suddenly stopped.

"So let's see him," said a new laconic voice, but one he knew. As the sack was pulled away from his head a blinding torch beam shone into his face. He heard a soft curse and the torch lowered a fraction. The man behind the torch became a tall figure he could recognize. John Darnley pursed his lips a little, his narrow face a harsh silhouette in the reflected torchlight. "You're a surprise, Mr. Gaunt."

"Not planned," said Gaunt unemotionally.

The lawyer nodded. He was in an open-necked sports shirt which flapped loose over dark trousers. A ballpoint pen was clipped into one of the shirt pockets with a small notebook tucked behind it. He looked calm, unruffled.

"I warned you," began Mary Hamilton in the background. "It's like I said—"

"Be quiet," said Darnley. As she scowled but stopped, he looked at Gaunt again. "I think we have to talk, Mr. Gaunt. But I need a few minutes first." He paused, looking around, then beckoned towards a man who was standing near the tail of the pick-up.

It gave Gaunt a brief chance to glance around. The pick-up had stopped in what looked like an open yard. A two-storey farmhouse was not far away, silhouetted in the moonlight. He had a glimpse of low walls and fencing and a background ridge of mountain. Then the other man had arrived. He was bearded and fat, and he was nursing a shotgun. Darnley greeted him with a nod then turned to Hamilton.

"The storehouse will do," he told Hamilton. His mouth tightened. "Come straight back."

Without waiting to see his order carried out, he turned and strode towards the farmhouse. Mary Hamilton went trailing behind him, carrying her plastic supermarket bags. Then the shotgun prodded Gaunt's side.

"This is Benito," said Hamilton, while the bearded man stood silent. "He doesn't like people. Move."

He was shoved away from the pick-up and stumbled his way over a short stretch of rutted, potholed ground towards a small building with a flat roof, a high, narrow window and a stout wooden door. Light showed at the window and round the edges of the door. The bearded man produced a large key, unlocked the door, and it opened outward as he pulled a handle.

"Get in," said Hamilton curtly.

Gaunt was pushed forward. The door immediately slammed and was locked again behind him. He blinked in the bright light of a kerosene pressure lamp which was hanging from a hook over his head.

"So who the hell are you, son?" asked a mildly surprised voice.

Gaunt stared at a face he instantly recognized, although the only time he'd seen it before had been in a newspaper photograph. It belonged to an elderly thick-set gnome of a man with a bald head and large face.

"Well, son?" asked the gnome patiently. *"Habla inglés?"*

"Edward Sarr?" asked Gaunt wearily.

The elderly man nodded. There were tired lines around his deep-set eyes, but he inspected Gaunt with deliberate care.

"I'm no one you know, Mr. Sarr." Jonathan Gaunt sighed. Several things were rapidly falling into place, several things he had wondered about, had thought about. Some others were being shaken loose from the wrong places where they hadn't totally fitted. "My name is Jonathan Gaunt, I work for a funny Scottish civil servant called the Remembrancer—"

"The what?" Sarr stared at him. "Son, this is a damned stupid time to make jokes."

"He's interested in Hartondee," said Gaunt simply. "He's interested in why at least five people that we know about have died because of Hartondee. Maybe we had some of it wrong."

"I know Hartondee." Edward Sarr closed his eyes for a moment, took a deep breath, then looked at Gaunt again. The small, thick-set financier needed a shave. He wore a crumpled white shirt and blue denim trousers which were grubby at the knees. A locket hung on a thin gold chain around his neck and he had a mat of white hair on his chest. "Five people?"

Gaunt nodded.

"Any identification, son?"

Gaunt nodded at his inside jacket pocket. Sarr reached in, brought out the small Q and LTR warrant card, frowned over it, then tucked it back into the pocket again. "If we're going to be sharing, let's get you more comfortable." Going behind him, Sarr swore under his breath a little as he untied Gaunt's wrists.

"Thanks." Gaunt spent some time trying to rub life back into his wrists while he looked around. The storehouse had rough stone walls and a bare earth floor. There were dusty shelves holding a variety of farming oddments, a heap of empty sacks, and a cobwebbed pile of empty liquor bottles. He saw the way that Edward Sarr had placed some of the sacks to make a seat close to where the lamp hung. There was a jug of water and a bucket. Nothing else. He looked up at the slit of a window.

"Not people-size," said Sarr acidly, as if reading his mind. "Forget it."

"Up there?" Gaunt indicated above them. "What's there?"

"The roof," said Sarr acidly. "What the hell else?"

"Sorry." Gaunt leaned against one of the rough stone walls, easing his back a little. "When did they bring you here, Mr. Sarr?"

"This morning. I was told the new facts of life yesterday afternoon." The small figure prowled the confined space a little. "We're at a rocks-and-sheep farm called Colmena—the Beehive. There's a cove called Cala Colmena. We're only about two miles from my house at Larca, and no neighbours. Clever, isn't it? We're so damned near Larca, who'd think of looking for us here?"

"You know the place?" asked Gaunt.

"I think I own it," snarled Edward Sarr. "It's been lying empty for years. It was a bargain, I thought it might be an investment."

They heard a noise outside, then the heavy click of the lock on the storehouse door, and Gaunt stiffened. Laying a warning hand on his arm, Edward Sarr shook his head. "Don't try, son. Behave."

Slowly, the door opened outwards. The twin muzzles of the shotgun poked in from the night, followed by Benito. He took post beside the opened door, easing to one side as John Darnley entered.

"You should knock," said Sarr coldly. He indicated the fat, bearded man. "And he smells."

"He sweats a lot." Darnley ignored Sarr and frowned at Gaunt. "You being here says most of it, doesn't it?"

"I suppose it does," agreed Gaunt softly.

"Damn that old man Church and his shares." Bleakly, Darnley considered Gaunt. "Your people seem to have been busy."

"So have a lot of others," murmured Gaunt. "It went multi-national."

"Congratulations." Darnley grimaced. "But did you have to upset the Hamiltons by mentioning Edinburgh?"

"If they're so sensitive, they shouldn't throw people off battlements," Gaunt told him.

"We had to be practical about Gladstone Baxter. He was a problem." Darnley moved his shoulders to free his sweat-damp shirt, then brushed away one of the flies buzzing around the doorway. "He'd been useful, yes—for a long time. But he was becoming greedy and frightened, incompetent too."

"And could see things starting to crumble?" asked Gaunt.

"No." Darnley fell silent again. For long seconds the only real sound in the storehouse was the hiss of the dangling pressure lamp. He seemed to have to clear his throat before he did speak. "Maybe a few details have gone wrong—that much, I'll agree. But the rest is coming together. There's only been a percentage loss—it's acceptable."

"Acceptable?" Edward Sarr made the word a jeer. "The whole thing has gone wrong—admit it. If you manage to steal as much as a quarter of what's lying in Hartondee you're going to be lucky."

Darnley shrugged.

"You're running out of time," said Sarr.

"Things may be tight." Darnley stopped it there.

Gaunt had made a small movement. Over by the door, the shotgun had moved.

"Cramp," soothed Gaunt. He leaned on the stonework again. "Once it all happens, what about us?"

"Then we're disposable," said Edward Sarr bluntly. "That's what my faithful executive secretary really means. Isn't that true, John?"

"I'm still trying to decide." Darnley was honest. "Things have happened."

"But you'll let us know?" asked Sarr.

"I will." Darnley almost smiled, but his mouth tightened as he turned to Gaunt again. "You see, this is the part that wasn't planned, Gaunt. What was intended would have been sweet and smooth, only needed another year—then I could have cleaned out the Hartondee moneybox. Even after that damned female at Baxter's office started stirring things, most of it could still have happened. No one needed to die—"

"Until Bavaria?" asked Gaunt.

"Until Bavaria."

"When Beck was meant to be frightened, but your hired muscle made a mess of it?" guessed Gaunt. "What were the Hamiltons supposed to do out there? Move in once Beck was sufficiently persuaded, get him to assign the shares to you direct?"

Darnley looked down at his hands and nodded. "That's what was meant to happen."

"And Baxter knew about it? Anything he got back from Joan Dennan he was feeding to your people?"

"Then he got greedy," said Darnley, with a sign of impatience.

"Good help is hard to find," said Gaunt sympathetically. He eased from the wall, ignoring the way the shotgun followed him again. "You did a good vanishing act from Larca. But what idiot allowed the Hamiltons to go shopping in Pollensa this evening?"

"He did," said Sarr. "Ask him why! This place has no food—not as much as a can of beans!"

Suddenly, Darnley moved. Two quick, long strides took him to the grinning little man. His right arm pistoned out, the flat of his hand taking Sarr high and hard on the chest, with a noise like a muffled drumbeat. Thrown back, Sarr collapsed on the piled sacking and lay groaning.

"You've stopped being boss," said Darnley softly. "Remember it." He turned to Gaunt and his face was flushed. It was the first time Gaunt had seen any real anger from the man. "Yes, we needed food. I gave orders days ago—nothing was done. I thought a woman would look more natural at a supermarket."

"Good thinking," agreed Gaunt carefully. "But bad luck."

"Maybe." The tall, grey-haired lawyer ignored the way Sarr was still gasping for breath in the background. He glanced at his wristwatch. "I've things to do. There are house rules. The door is locked, there is an armed guard outside, there's no other way out. You'll get some food and water. But room service is limited."

"Understood," said Gaunt mildly.

Darnley looked at him closely for another few seconds then turned and went out. Silently, Benito backed after him with the shotgun tracing a nervous arc. The door closed, Gaunt heard the lock click.

"All lawyers are bastards," said Edward Sarr hoarsely, laboriously hauling himself to his feet again. "But that one could win prizes."

"So humour him," advised Gaunt.

After a few minutes of painful breathing and quiet cursing, Edward Sarr recovered enough to produce a grubby prize he'd found on one of the dust-covered shelves. It was an abandoned, hall-full bottle of rotgut brandy. One sniff was enough for Gaunt, and he shook his head. But Sarr took a gulp, used it as a mouthwash for a moment, then happily swallowed it. Seated on the sacks again, Sarr set down the bottle and wiped a hand across his lips.

"Son, humour me," he said unexpectedly. "How much do your people really know about my Hartondee?"

"That you use it as a private, personal bank." Gaunt paused, picked up the brandy bottle, and held it nearer to the glare of the pressure lamp. He'd been right. A large and dead black beetle was floating on its back on the surface of the liquor. "Your private bank—and your private power base. Both well hidden."

"But you found it." Sarr pursed his lips thoughtfully. "Does that mean you know how it works?"

"No. We couldn't find the instruction book." Gaunt grinned at him. "Somebody decided we should call it The Spanish Maze Game— maybe we get in, but after that we're lost!"

"That was always the idea." Sarr was pleased.

"So when did it begin?"

"A lot of years ago, son." Sarr picked up the bottle and swirled the brandy a little so that the dead beetle drifted to one side. He took another swallow. "It wasn't a brand-new idea, I just freshened it up a little—and I'm not unique. I know a few similar operations."

"Hartondee." Gaunt stopped him drifting.

"Hartondee." Sarr grimaced. "There I was, the original rags to riches financial wonder—and all the rest of that newspaper garbage. But nobody asked where the real money was going."

"Why choose Hartondee?"

"It was cheap, it was in the backwoods." Sarr grinned. "Hell, son, I've never even visited Scotland. You know the only piece of bad luck I had with it? The damned company suddenly began making money again! I didn't want that—I wanted a nice, low-profile operation, I had to make sure it was damped down."

Gaunt nodded. "What about share capital?"

"One way or another, I control the majority." The smile suddenly wiped from the man's face. "I could count the people who know the real truth about Hartondee on the fingers of one hand. That includes family. I needed someone in Scotland, I picked Darnley. He ran his own people—in more ways than I realized."

"Doing what?" asked Gaunt quietly. "Taking over?"

Edward Sarr nodded. For a moment the little man, who in his time had made financial giants shiver, didn't speak. He fingered the edge of one of the sacks he was sitting on. When he looked at Gaunt, his eyes held an icy anger.

"For three years, son. Buying up any spare parcels of Hartondee shares that oozed on to the market. Softening up some of my nominees, even the trust set-ups. He needed time, but it was happening."

Gaunt was puzzled. "And the Peter Church shares?"

"I always knew about them," said Sarr patiently. "They weren't doing any harm, I didn't want to touch them—low profile, remember? Our snake-lawyer Darnley was doing exactly the same—until this young accountant woman stirred the pot. Then, when things started going wrong, when your Queen's Remembrancer began sniffing around, Darnley couldn't afford to wait. Everything would have come out into the open." He paused. "When I came to live out here, I had a computer link installed at Larca—"

"We found it." Gaunt nodded.

"Well done," said Sarr dryly. "I'm semi-retired, but I still play the markets for fun. The terminal is my link. The brokers get my orders, check the source is genuine, then act as instructed." He considered Gaunt doubtfully. "Am I keeping this simple enough?"

"So far."

"Good." Sarr was amused. "Well, this is simple too. If someone stuck a gun in your ear and told you to do something, would you do it?"

"Probably."

"I did." Sarr swirled the brandy bottle again but didn't drink. "I used the computer link exactly as Darnley ordered. Over the next couple of days, different people will sell different stocks—dump them if necessary, for immediate cash. Price won't matter. Darnley knows the people, knows the holdings."

"And the money?"

"Numbered accounts in different countries. Filters. Double filters. Darnley will have it all within a few days. If anyone felt like checking back this morning, the line to Larca was down. A technical fault."

"Called a sledgehammer."

Sarr nodded. "My snake-lawyer is taking what he can, while he can. If he's lucky, like I told him, he'll maybe get a quarter of what Hartondee is worth."

"How much?" asked Gaunt.

Sarr lifted the brandy bottle again. This time he drank, using his teeth as a filter.

"Around thirty million sterling. Before expenses."

Gaunt couldn't think of anything else to say.

Half an hour later they heard noises outside and a torch beam danced on the window-slit. The door was unlocked, Benito appeared with his shotgun, then a tight-mouthed Mary Hamilton brought in some hunks of bread and cheese and another jug of water. She left without speaking, Benito backed out, and the door was locked again.

They shared the bread and cheese and drank some of the water while the inevitable flies buzzed and crawled around. Sarr produced a stub of half-smoked cigar and some matches, lit the cigar slowly and carefully, and took another sip of his brandy.

"What was the name of that accountant who was killed?" he asked suddenly. "I can't remember."

"Gladstone Baxter."

"If I'd to choose between the Hamiltons, I'd pick the woman," decided Sarr. "She'd enjoy pushing people off battlements. To him, it would be a chore." He shrugged. "Darnley talked me into giving them jobs out here—told me I needed an English-speaking couple to housekeep at Larca." He paused. "Are you married, Gaunt?"

"I was."

"Divorced?" Sarr nodded his understanding. "I parted from two wives that way—didn't like either of them very much." His eyes softened. "Then I married again. Her name was Elizabeth—we were happy together and we stayed that way. Except I woke up one morning and she was dead in bed beside me. She'd had a heart attack during the night." He fingered the little gold locket at his throat. "So I came out here afterwards."

Silently, Gaunt nodded. He watched as Sarr removed the gold chain and locket from around his thick neck and opened the locket with a thumbnail. He showed the tiny photograph inside. It was of a woman who had striking eyes and laughter on her lips.

"Elizabeth," said Sarr softly. "We have a daughter—she's about your age." Closing the locket, he put the chain round his neck again. "If things go wrong for me here, but you're still around, make sure she gets my locket. Will you?"

Another half hour passed, then the door was unlocked again. Benito came first with the shotgun, and John Darnley was with him again.

"I'm doing evening rounds," said the tall lawyer cheerfully, staying where the shotgun would have a clear field of fire. "Settled for the night, or any complaints?"

"A smell just came in," said Sarr.

Darnley gave a tolerant grimace. "Gaunt?"

"I'm curious by nature," said Gaunt. "What's happening outside this place?"

"I sent one of our people back into Pollensa. It seems your friends miss you—the town is buzzing with *Policía Nacional.*" Darnley frowned a little. "It seems the pick-up hit a policewoman on the way out."

"How is she?" Gaunt tried to keep his voice calm.

"She'll mend," said Darnley laconically, and dismissed the matter. "Here, things are like I told you before. I don't particularly want to harm either of you." His eyes flickered lazily to Sarr and back again. "I need Sarr until I know the Hartondee money has moved. I need you, Gaunt, because you could be useful hostage material—though I don't expect anyone to come looking this way. Two more days should be enough—and there's a bonus. By then, the police will believe we've left the island." He paused, and his smile was back. "Maybe you'll just suddenly realize we've gone. So behave, right?"

He turned on his heel and Benito followed him out. The door closed and locked.

"We could have rushed them," complained Sarr petulantly.

"Fun," agreed Gaunt. "Then we could have had our heads shot off too."

"We have to try something." Sarr scowled and brushed away a fly. "Haven't we?"

Gaunt sucked his lips for a moment. At least he now knew that Krissa Vogt hadn't been seriously injured. But maybe, unwittingly, Darnley had told them something else.

"Will this place have a phone?" he asked.

"Here?" Sarr gave a grunt. "Hell, Cala Colmena doesn't know the telephone has been invented!"

"So how will Darnley know when the Hartondee money moves, why is he so sure he can move after that?"

"Radio," suggested Sarr. He paused and suddenly looked unhappy. "He could have a pal on a boat lying off-shore."

"What kind of boat could come into the Colmena inlet—suppose it was after dark?"

"Any damned size." Edward Sarr was avoiding his eyes. "But

maybe your *policía* friends will get here first. Or we'll think of something, right?"

"Before the two days are up?"

Sarr nodded warily.

"Is Darnley going to get that money?" Gaunt had a sudden suspicion, one he cursed himself for not thinking of before.

"Maybe." Sarr gave an uncertain, uneasy grin.

Gaunt eyed him grimly. "John Darnley watched you send the Hartondee instructions. He saw your people check back."

Sarr nodded in that same uneasy way. "But they must have thought I'd gone mad."

"Which maybe you didn't discourage?" suggested Gaunt.

"I just think we'd better try something," said Sarr gloomily.

Turning away, the older man dumped a bundle of sacks in front of Gaunt, then took a second bundle over to a corner and spread them out as a bed. As an afterthought, he returned for his brandy bottle and clutched it close as he settled down.

"Get some sleep, young friend," he advised, using one of the sacks as a blanket. "It clears the mind." He yawned. "Or it does at my age. Goodnight."

In what seemed like under a minute, the financial wizard was asleep and snoring.

Much later, after he'd swallowed two painkillers with a mouthful of water, Jonathan Gaunt finally slept.

It was one of his bad nights. The familiar nightmare that he was falling came twice and he woke each time to find himself shaking and sweating. The second time, he knew he had cried aloud. On his elbows, Gaunt looked through the gloom towards the sack covering Edward Sarr. Although there was no movement, the older man had stopped snoring and was probably awake.

After that, however, came deep sleep. When he woke there was pale daylight coming in through the narrow window-slit high above him. The pain had gone from his back, his mind felt rested. Over in the corner, Edward Sarr was snoring again. But there was another puzzling sound, like a tinkling bell, coming from somewhere outside.

Rising, yawning, combing his hair back with his hands, Gaunt looked around the storehouse then dragged an old bench over to the window. He heard Sarr come awake and ask what he was doing, but didn't answer and climbed up on the bench. That brought his head level with the narrow window, where the glass was broken.

The morning sun had topped a mountain ridge and was flooding down on the sparse, dry greenery that made up most of Cala Colmena.

Geographically, Colmena was a much smaller version of the valley at Larca. High walls of raw, grey rock flanked it on either side, going down to where the sea lapped along the rock and shingle of the beach. There were a handful of sheep feeding around the green weed and dried scrub of the shoreline, and the tinkling bell belonged to one of the sheep. He could see no other life along the shore, or along the grey rock and sparse green of the sun-dappled valley sides. But what mattered more was the much nearer Colmena farmhouse and its outbuildings. It was big, it was old, and it had once been impressive. Two storeys high, the main house was built of a dusky pink stone. One part of the low-peaked roof of faded green tiles had fallen in, but the rest stood proud despite its cracks.

"What are you doing?" demanded Sarr peevishly.

"Admiring the view," said Gaunt without looking round. "Don't interrupt."

He could see a cool courtyard with a dried-up marble fountain. A goat was nibbling among a choked, overgrown ornamental garden. There were broken dry-stone walls and cactus, a couple of dead palm trees, and a gnarled, solitary olive tree. The morning sun was just finding its way into the courtyard—and some birds exploded out in a loud flutter of wings.

The cause emerged a moment later. He was someone Gaunt hadn't seen before, a burly, ginger-haired man who carried a rifle. The stranger came out into the open, yawned, and ambled to the left. Where he scuffed his feet, he raised little clouds of reddish dust. Then he vanished behind the building, but reappeared a moment later. With him came Alejandro, the slight man who had driven the pick-up at Pollensa. They stopped at the courtyard, talked, then Alejandro went into the farmhouse. His companion ambled off. Gaunt had a feeling he had just witnessed a change of guard-duties.

"Anything happening?" asked Sarr from below, tugging at Gaunt's trouser leg. "Anything interesting?"

"A ginger-haired man, broad-shouldered, either going on watch or off. Do you know him?"

"His name is Paul Marran," said Sarr. "Says he's French, he was on the payroll as our maintenance man. Sour by nature."

Gaunt shifted his feet on the bench and looked out again. Then after a moment he closed his eyes tightly but still tried to picture everything as it had been in terms of distance and location. When he opened his eyes again, he checked that what he saw matched the mental picture. It was a paratroop patrol basic, when a quick observation might be all that could be managed before you had to act.

Not that he knew what he was going to do about anything. Not yet. The farmhouse was a good sixty feet away from the storehouse, the ground in between was a rough pebbled surface. Wherever Alejandro was stationed, there was no sign of him. To the left, a track ran out past the two dead palm trees, then divided. One arm led inland, the other linked with some dilapidated barns. To the right, slightly nearer to them than the farm building, some rusted sheets of corrugated iron roofed a simple, open-sided woodshed. It was still partly filled with a litter of dry branches and thin logs.

There was nothing else.

Any vehicles had to be hidden over by the barns. He had a side view of the Colmena farmhouse, with any windows that looked towards the storehouse both closed and heavily shuttered. There was the shape of a dried-up pool beside what had been ornamental gardens. Out beyond, the world seemed made up of dry-stone walls dividing rock and scrub from more rock and scrub.

It was sad, it was desolate, it had been beautiful once. Maybe some day it could be beautiful again, not just a place where flies were beginning to buzz in the first heat of the morning.

The buzzing grew. Then his mouth felt dry as the buzzing became a gradually growing, approaching beat. He stared up at the blinkered section of sky outside the window.

"Helicopter," agreed Sarr from below, reading his mind. "Forget it. That's the routine search-and-rescue coastal patrol—nothing to do with us. You can set your watch by them."

The helicopter windmilled into sight, flying only a few hundred feet up, following the coastline and heading south. It had a fat, beetle-shaped body with military markings. Gaunt waited at the window until it had vanished behind the cliffs, then climbed down.

"Routine?"

Sarr nodded. "The Spanish have a base over at Pollensa Bay—they used to operate flying boats, now they've helicopters. They work to schedule—you'll hear that one make its return pass in about ten minutes. No more."

"But there will be others?"

"Next is at noon, then the third and last at five. The Spanish military lead a civilized life." Sarr thumbed at the bench still by the window. "Shouldn't we move that back before we have visitors?"

"Wait," said Gaunt.

They did, while the sun continued to rise, the air began to warm, and the flies began to multiply both inside and outside. Then the throbbing beat returned. On his bench again, Gaunt watched the helicopter make its return pass. Then he climbed down and Sarr helped him lift the bench back to where it belonged.

"Always the same timing? You're sure?" Gaunt asked.

"Always." Sarr was curious. "Why?"

"If we could signal—"

"Like wave a shirt out of the window?" A scowl wrinkled up to Sarr's bald scalp. "Or something more exotic—while Darnley's people use us for target practice?"

Another hour passed. It gave Gaunt time to examine the store-house door in fine detail. Short of breaking it down, there was no easy answer to it.

Then he heard noises outside. Moments later, the door was un-locked.

Escorted by Alejandro and the shotgun, Mary Hamilton made a sullen appearance. The tin tray she was carrying held their breakfast —more coarse slices of bread, another lump of cheese, and a jug of lukewarm coffee.

"How are you today, Mrs. Hamilton?" asked Edward Sarr with icy sarcasm. "Well, I hope?"

She looked at him with minimal interest but scowled at Gaunt. "Darnley wants you fed, you get fed."

Then the woman and her escort had gone. Gaunt and Sarr were left the closed door, and the first flies were trying to drown themselves in the coffee jug. They ate the bread and drank the coffee, while the sun coming in at the window-slit struck the metal of the tin tray and reflected up towards the roof. Sitting back, chewing one of the bread-crusts, Gaunt gave a casual glance up then stayed very still for a moment.

Staring now, he got to his feet. Where the reflected light was hit-ting the underside of the roof, he could see cobwebs and grime. But he could also just make out the faint, square outline of a small hatch, a mansized access to the rooftop area. It didn't look as though it had been used for a long time.

"Help me," he told Sarr.

"Uh?" Sarr blinked.

"Just do it." Now that the idea had started, it was shaping fast and growing.

Bewildered but willing, Sarr helped carry the bench over. They used some old but sturdy wooden boxes to form a precarious stairway from the benchtop, then Gaunt climbed up. At the top, he was crouching under the hatch with his shoulders brushing the cobwebs. He could see a pair of rusted hinges. Steadying himself, he pushed at the hatch with his shoulders. Warped wood stirred, some dust fell, then he tried again. This time, he strained every muscle in that upward push while below his feet the old boxes creaked.

It worked. There was a subdued squeal of protest then the hatch had opened and a cascade of old, dried bird droppings and other dirt was coming in around the edges. Straightening, Gaunt pushed the hatch fully back and poked his head through the opening.

He was looking out from roughly the middle of the storehouse's flat roof, and only the tightly shuttered upper windows of the pink stone farmhouse looked down on him. Better still, the storehouse roof had a low dwarf wall, three bricks high, around its edges. A few broken clay pots showed it had once been edged with flowers and plants.

"What have you got?" hissed Sarr urgently from below.

He signalled down to the man to stay quiet. Then he hauled himself up through the hatch and flattened himself on the roof. Some small insects scuttled away from him, and the sun's gathering heat was already soaking into his body as he wriggled forward then risked a look down into the dilapidated courtyard.

He dropped down quickly. The ginger-haired Marran was lounging in an old chair far back in the cool shadows. He was smoking a cigarette, looking bored and half asleep. He had the shotgun across his lap, and he also had a holstered hand-gun hanging by its shoulder harness over the back of the chair.

Very carefully, very quietly, Gaunt eased back and took a long look across to his right, towards the open-sided woodshed. Then he looked behind the storehouse, where those very few stray sheep and goats moved around the low-tumbledown dry-stone walls.

He'd seen enough. He squeezed back in through the hatch, gently closed it again, and climbed back down.

"Well?" Edward Sarr grabbed him by the arm as he arrived. "Now do I get to hear?"

"There might be a way," said Gaunt slowly.

"If you see a way, take it," said the thick-set little man bluntly. "I'll be a 'maybe'—I'm too old to play acrobats."

"It's a 'maybe' idea. You've seen the woodshed outside. We're going to set it on fire next time a helicopter is passing."

"How?" The gnome-like face showed bewilderment.

Gaunt told him and the bewilderment gave way to initial scorn then a doubtful hope.

"It's mad," said Sarr. "But damn, I suppose it might work."

Gaunt nodded. As an idea, part of it came from the Viking way people still celebrated New Year on the Scottish north-east coast. Another part came for the lithe, traditional Balearic figure he had seen in a *Guardia Civil* office in Palma.

"Ever play the stock exchange, son?" asked Sarr unexpectedly.

"A little, small-time," admitted Gaunt.

"Make much at it?"

Gaunt shook his head.

"That figures," sighed Sarr. "All right, what do you want me to do?"

They needed time to prepare. But they had hardly started when familiar noises came from outside. There was barely time to throw a couple of sacks over what they had done, then the door opened. John Darnley came in first, followed by William Hamilton. Each held an automatic pistol, Hilton's moving nervously between the two captives, Darnley content to keep his at his side.

"Goodmorning," said Darnley crisply. He had shaved, he wore a fresh shirt, he seemed pleased with himself. "I think it's going to be a good day, Edward."

"I can do without the weather forecast," said Sarr caustically. "In here, it doesn't make much difference."

"True." Darnley gave a small, appreciative smile. "How about you, Gaunt? Have you been told how that helicopter wasn't exactly the cavalry arriving?"

"I've been told," agreed Gaunt unemotionally. His eyes were on Hamilton. The Englishman was already sweating heavily. But probably not enough to mean there was an immediate crisis situation for them.

"But if anyone should happen to stray this way, Benito or Alejandro will persuade them that Cala Colmena is deserted as usual," murmured Darnley. He switched his attention back to Sarr. "I've good news for you, Edward. It seems that the overnight market reports are showing those first changes we expected. Certain company shares are beginning to shade downward—not panic selling, but as if some surprising people are suddenly unloading stock." He brought up his pistol, and used it to scratch behind one ear. "There's gossip that these people need a lot of cash. Maybe—ah—for some takeover bid, eh?"

"Go to hell." Sarr's eyes glittered dangerously.

Darnley grinned. "If it all continues, then we can all be happy. Including you—and I'll give you Gaunt as a bonus. So far, it looks good. Even Hamilton's wife thinks that way—and she's miserable by nature."

Hamilton gave a gloomy shrug.

"Anyway, we're on schedule." Darnley gestured to Hamilton, and let the man be the first to retreat to the door. The tall lawyer who had come so close to winning The Spanish Maze Game, and could yet have broken it, paused for another sardonic look around. "You've most of the comforts of home. Enjoy them. I'll maybe give you another progress report after lunch—if I survive the Hamilton woman trying to cook something."

He followed Hamilton out through the door, it closed, they waited, and the lock clicked as usual. Immediately, a slow grin began to spread on Edward Sarr's face. He saw Gaunt's surprise.

"I don't care what it costs," Sarr said softly. "I'm still alive—and the only thing I want now is to see that man eat dirt."

Pulling back the sacks, always half listening for any new noises from outside, they returned to work.

They were making a slingshot. It was probably the first slingshot ever constructed from a Gucci leather belt, contributed by Sarr, and a piece of leather from some fragments of mule harness which they'd found.

They were making some very special fireball ammunition. The fireballs swung at Stonehaven were usually about the size of footballs. Theirs were like small tennis balls, made from thin strips of torn sacking tied tightly around some rusty metal bolts from a broken piece of farm machinery, then further secured with thin copper wire they stripped from a piece of electrical flex. By the time they'd finished, their hands were gashed and their fingers bleeding.

But they had ten of the fireballs. They added a short wick to each, made from lengths of teased-out sacking. Gaunt picked up the homemade sling, gripped the ends tightly in his right hand, and gave it a whirling trial over his head. As the whirling accelerated, the sling made a soft whispering sound.

"Tried one of these before?" asked Sarr hopefully as Gaunt stopped.

"A couple of times." Meaning when he was school age, playing David and Goliath. Goliath had been, literally, a barn door. He had hit it a few times. Not always. He gave Sarr a reassuring grin. "The woodshed is big enough to be fairly easy."

Sarr grunted. "Maybe. Do you know how they trained the kids here in the old times? They put their food in a package up a tree. They had to knock the package down with their slings, or go hungry."

"Then I'd have been a thin loser." Gaunt glanced at his watch.

They had half an hour to go before the noon helicopter patrol was due. They checked through the rest of their preparations, Gaunt made sure Edward Sarr understood exactly what he planned—and they swept some sacking over the sling and fireballs as they heard voices and a laugh outside.

When the door opened, they saw the guard had been changed. It was the ginger-haired Marran who came in first, armed with his hand-gun. He was followed by the slightly built Alejandro, who carried the shotgun and had an unlit cigarette dangling from his lips.

It was Marran's first visit to them. Curious, he prowled around then stopped as Sarr ambled towards him. Sarr spoke to him in a hiss of Spanish, Marran looked surprised, glanced round at Alejandro, and the two men grinned. Marran gestured with his pistol, Edward Sarr shrugged and stepped back, and their two visitors took another glance around, then left.

"What was that about?" asked Gaunt.

"Mainly, I called Mary Hamilton a camel. It was to keep their minds off other things." Sarr pointed.

Where Marran had been standing was directly beneath the rooftop hatch—and an outline of dirt on the floor was the debris that had come down when the hatch was first opened.

They had to gamble that there would be no more visitors until after the helicopter pass-overs. With five minutes to go, they built a new, stronger, and slightly higher version of the stairway to the hatch. As they finished, they heard the distant buzz of the machine.

"Son." Impulsively, Edward Sarr stuck out his hand.

Gaunt gripped it, Sarr nodded, and they set to work as the helicopter's noise grew. First, Gaunt went up to open the hatch. He returned, helped Sarr to crawl up and out into the open, then passed out the sling and the fireballs. They also needed the kerosene pressure lamp for its fuel, and what was left of the bottle of firewater brandy.

He followed them out on to the roof, crawling on his stomach, as the helicopter passed across the mouth of the Cala.

"Ten minutes?" he asked Sarr.

Sarr nodded. Ten minutes, and it should be back again. Going to the front of the storehouse, Gaunt risked a quick look over the dwarf wall down into the shadows of the farm courtyard. Hamilton was on duty. He was drinking from a can of beer. Crabbing his way back to Sarr, Gaunt pointed in the other direction, towards the woodshed.

It was time.

Sarr had laid the ten fireballs in a line, his precious box of matches beside them. But the first two were for practice only. Loading the first into the pocket of their Gucci sling, Gaunt paused and listened for a moment. The helicopter's engine noise had faded, there was no sound from the direction of the farmhouse, and he could hear only a faint murmur from the sea and an occasional tinkling from the sheep's bell.

Raised up on one elbow, he set the sling whirling. Unaccustomed muscles took the surprise strain while he increased the whirl's speed, tried to dredge anything out of memory—then released the unlit fireball.

It headed off in the correct direction. He took a quick glance after it, and saw it fall short and to the right in a puff of dust. The second practice shot dropped on the woodshed's roof with a soft thud.

Their next shot was the first for real. They soaked the fireball in kerosene from the lamp, thoroughly moistened the little wick in brandy, used a match to set the wick alight, and fitted the fireball into the sling as the kerosene began to catch.

Immediately, Gaunt began whirling, praying as he did. When he sent the tennis-ball-like missile on its way it was a small, bright glow of fire and sparks.

He saw it curve straight into the shed.

The fourth went to the left. The fifth went into the shed. Number six hit the roof, already extinguished. Number seven went in, so did number eight—and Gaunt stared hard at what could have been a faint curl of smoke coming from the base of sun-dried logs and branches.

Number nine used the last of their kerosene. Gaunt moistened the wick with brandy and held it for Sarr to light with a match. But Sarr was giving him that gnome-like grin and shaking his head.

"You've done it—that's enough!" declared Sarr, and pointed.

Gaunt looked up. His right arm ached, the flat roof felt like an oven, sweat was pouring from his body.

He forgot all that. Smoke and flame were beginning to lick from the woodshed, growing thicker and licking high by the moment. Sarr was slapping him on the back, still crouched down against the roof, the gnome-like grin wider than ever.

"Listen," invited Sarr. "Listen, son!"

For a moment Gaunt could only hear the first crackling of burning wood. Then he heard the other sound, the growing buzz of the returning helicopter. The smoke and flames were growing, becoming a pillar clawing up into the clear sky—and he could see the machine already altering course, beginning to curve in their way.

But then there were shouts of alarm near at hand, a sudden running of feet as people erupted from the farmhouse. He recognized Darnley's voice yelling orders, and answering cries heading for the blazing woodshed.

"Now," he told Sarr.

The older man swallowed but nodded. Together they crawled, beneath the cover of the dwarf wall, to the rear of the roof, the blind side for the farmhouse and around a corner from the storehouse door. Gaunt looked, and the drop to the cracked, dusty ground was less than three times the height of a man.

"Over," he told Sarr.

They had to do it, they couldn't stay trapped on the roof. Whatever else happened, John Darnley wasn't likely to show them any mercy now. Gaunt helped Sarr wriggle over the dwarf wall, took part of the small but thick-set man's weight as he hung poised, then Sarr nodded and Gaunt let him go. He heard the thud and a heavy grunt as Sarr landed, saw him start to limp clear, then swung himself over. He dangled by his fingers then dropped and landed in a perfectly executed paratroop roll.

Up and running, he caught up with the older man, who was limping badly. Seizing him round the middle, ignoring his protests, Gaunt supported him in a rapid limp towards the shelter of the waiting network of crumbling dry-stone boundary walls.

The helicopter was very near now, a descending scream of power. Glancing back, Gaunt saw it hovering, losing height, homing on that pillar of smoke and flame like a beacon.

He heard something else, an almost gobbling shriek of rage—and William Hamilton burst into sight from the direction of the storehouse door. The man started running towards them, the shotgun raised, then the weapon fired as Gaunt started to drag Edward Sarr over the first of the dry-stone field walls. Pellets raked at the rocks, Sarr gave a yelp of surprise and pitched forward to the rough, loose stonework, and Gaunt felt some stray, ricocheting shot claw at his side.

"Damn you—both of you!" screamed Hamilton.

Grabbing Sarr, Gaunt dragged him over into the shelter of the wall as Hamilton, running towards them, stumbled. The shotgun fired again, a wild blast which peppered some rocks. In the background, Mary Hamilton had appeared from the farmhouse and was hurrying to join her husband. Further back, Gaunt had a confused glimpse of more smoke and flames, vaguely realized that the helicopter had landed, and heard some single gunshots then a rasping burst from an automatic weapon.

Still running, Hamilton had been fumbling to reload the shotgun. Now, almost with them, he abandoned the attempt. A blend of fear and anger twisting his unshaven face, the Englishman scrambled over the dry-stone wall and rushed at Gaunt, both hands gripping the shotgun by the barrels, brandishing it like a club.

The butt whistled over Gaunt's head, and the sheer force behind the swing made Hamilton lose his footing on the rocks. For a moment he had to struggle to keep his balance. The moment was enough. Diving forward, Gaunt went in under the suddenly erratic swing of the shotgun. His shoulder took Hamilton hard in the midriff, he heard the man's hoarse rasp of shock and expelled air, then they crashed down together and were rolling. But he had Hamilton's neck in a lock under his left arm, he was pounding at that screaming, cursing mouth with his right fist.

Struggling, they rolled again. He hit Hamilton again, this time hard behind the ear, and heard an odd clicking sound. Then Hamilton had gone limp, his head twisted at a strange angle, his eyes staring blindly up towards the smoke-tinged, cloudless sky.

Shakily, Gaunt started to prise himself loose from Hamilton's lifeless weight, which was trapping his arm. Close beside him, a stone grated then fell, and he glanced up.

Mary Hamilton was standing over them, her unattractive face wiped totally empty of expression, her small chrome-barrelled pistol held in a two-handed grip, the muzzle coming down to point unwaveringly at Gaunt's head. Her lips started to move, her eyes stared at him along that glinting little barrel.

There was a grunt of effort from somewhere very close. Then a boulder flew through the air. Twice the size of a football, it took Mary Hamilton hard and high in her back. She didn't scream. She simply went down under the impact. The automatic fell from her grip, unfired. Where she lay, face down, she was very close to Hamilton. The boulder had landed beside her.

"Don't ever ask me to even lift a thing that weight again," said Edward Sarr in a quiet, almost awed voice. He was sitting on the wall, his face pale beneath its tan, and there was blood oozing from the wound in his leg. "Did I kill her?"

Gaunt had freed himself. He went over to the woman, stooped over, felt for her pulse, then looked up at Sarr. He nodded.

"Her husband. Is he—?"

"Both of them," said Gaunt wearily.

"I never did like her very much," said Sarr. He drew a deep breath and looked past Gaunt, towards the farmhouse, then visibly relaxed. "Looks like it's over, son. Or nearly that way."

The military helicopter had landed close to the farmhouse. Its three-man crew were out of it, two armed with machine-pistols. Two other figures were with them—Jaime Vicente and Dieter Vogt, both armed, already herding their prisoners into line. There were three. A fourth figure lay on the ground near the woodshed.

Jonathan Gaunt helped Sarr limp towards the group. The fair-haired Vicente saw them first and grinned. A moment later, Dieter Vogt hurried to meet them and seized Gaunt in a brief, glad bearhug.

"You're okay?" he asked.

Gaunt nodded. "How's Krissa?"

"On her way here." Vogt stood back and beamed at him. "*Ja*, only dented, Jonny. She won't take long to mend." He took over the task of helping Edward Sarr along, and indicated the fire still blazing in the woodshed. "Yours?"

"Yes."

Vogt nodded appreciatively. "Vicente and I have been flying with these search-and-rescue boys all day. We passed over this place this morning—you know how near you are to Larca?"

"He knows," said Edward Sarr.

"Your bonfire did it—" Vogt's voice trailed off as Edward Sarr physically pushed away from him.

The bald, thick-set little man limped unsteadily but determinedly to where the three prisoners were under guard. Alejandro and Massan were there. The fat, bearded Benito was the figure lying dead not far away. But John Darnley was the third prisoner.

"They didn't run?" asked Gaunt.

"Where's to run?" asked Vogt, and shook his head.

They watched Edward Sarr reach Darnley, who was already hand-cuffed. The two men who had worked together for so long were equally impassive. For a moment, they looked silently at each other. Ice to Ice.

"Nice try, John," said Sarr quietly.

"Edward." Darnley gave a slight nod.

Then Sarr turned away.

Ten minutes later, as the helicopter crew finished using their first-aid kit to fix a temporary bandage to Sarr's pellet-gouged leg and slap a dressing on the shallow slashes on Gaunt's side, they heard vehicles approaching.

A small, mixed convoy of *Policía Nacional* and *Policía Municipal* cars arrived in clouds of dust. The first was driven by Anita Lopez, back in uniform. Her passengers were the *Guardia Civil teniente* who had trav-elled north with them and, shoving him aside as they got out, hurry-ing over, Krissa Vogt. She had her left arm strapped in a sling and some small abrasions on her forehead. But her green eyes were bright with relief. Her good arm went round Gaunt's neck as she hugged him.

"That's a sergeant?" asked Edward Sarr in mild disbelief.

Their prisoners went first. Another helicopter flew in, then more police cars and a mortuary wagon arrived. One of the police cars was detailed to take Gaunt into Pollensa. A third helicopter arrived, to fly Edward Sarr direct to Palma. His leg required treatment. As far as he was concerned, that was secondary.

"I've things to do, things to put into reverse," he said gruffly. He considered Gaunt. "The same with you?"

"Things to do." Gaunt nodded.

They shook hands.

"About the Peter Church shareholding—tell your Remembrancer I'll sort something out," said Sarr. He paused and gave his goblin grin. "Watch out for that female sergeant, son. She could be trouble—real trouble!"

Then he had gone.

Another week and what seemed like several miles of reports and telex messages later, it was Dieter Vogt's turn to leave. Anita driving, Jaime Vicente came to take him to Palma airport and a scheduled flight to Munich. They parted at the foot of the Calvario steps in Pollensa. It was mid-afternoon, the sun was beating down on the long, cypress-lined avenue, but Vogt had insisted on climbing to the church at the top, then back down again.

"So I can say that I did it." Wiping sweat from his face, the young Bavarian looked earnestly at Gaunt. *"Wiedersehen*—till my wedding. Look after—uh—things, Jonny."

"I will," promised Gaunt.

Then, with a wave from Vicente and a wink from Anita, the police car was taking Vogt on his way.

He waited where he was as Krissa Vogt walked along the crowded, narrow street towards him. A week was enough for the abrasions on her face to be almost gone. Her arm had been out of its sling for two days. She was wearing a white cotton dress and her copper hair was tied back by a thin red ribbon. The *Bayers Landes Kriminalamt* had given her an additional week's convalescent leave.

Using a lot of persuasion, Gaunt had persuaded Henry Falconer that the Queen's and Lord Treasurer's Remembrancer owed him the same amount of time off before he had to return to Edinburgh.

"He's gone?" She'd already said goodbye to her brother. She smiled at Gaunt and held out the small, thin parcel she was carrying. "A present for you."

He opened it. Inside was an old, grubby 78 record. He stared. Hardly scratched, it was an original Columbia pressing of a Teddy Wilson classic.

"There's a shop"—she gestured along the street—"that's where I went before I was hit by the truck. They've a box of 78s that someone traded in years ago." She shrugged wryly. "The last time, it got broken."

"This time, it won't," he promised.

He thought of what else might be in the box, then saw the grin shaping on her lips and decided that for once jazz could wait.

"Home?" she asked.

"Bitte," he said solemnly.

She took his arm. That was when Jonathan Gaunt heard someone enthusiastically shouting his name. He turned and swallowed at the sight of the beaming young blonde woman hurrying down the Calvario steps towards him. Some distance behind, a perspiring man was struggling after her carrying an infant and a folded baby buggy.

"Jonny!"

"Someone you know?" asked Krissa politely.

"Patti." He managed a nod. "We used to be married."

Patti, with second husband and second husband's child. The postcard had said they were in Majorca. He hadn't even thought about it.

"Patti." Krissa Vogt kept her hand on his arm and considered the approaching figure carefully. "How interesting."

Gaunt didn't trust himself to say anything.

About the Author

Noah Webster is a pseudonym of the popular, prolific, and prizewin-
ning mystery writer Bill Knox, who is known for the unusual locations of his novels.

The Spanish Maze Game is Noah Webster's eleventh novel for the
Crime Club, and it features ex-paratrooper–turned civil–servant Jonathan Gaunt. Under his pseudonym of Michael Kirk, Mr. Knox writes
of the cases of marine insurance investigator Andrew Laird.

Married and with a grown-up family, the author lives in Scotland
with his wife and their dog. He is an honorary editor of the Royal
National Lifeboat Institution magazine *Scottish Lifeboat.*